GALAXY UNKNOWN

FORGOTTEN GALAXY
BOOK 1

M.R. FORBES

Published by Quirky Algorithms
Seattle, Washington

This novel is a work of fiction and a product of the author's imagination.
Any resemblance to actual persons or events is purely coincidental.

Copyright © 2023 by M.R. Forbes
All rights reserved.

Cover illustration by Geronimo Ribaya
Edited by Merrylee Laneheart

CHAPTER 1

"We're here, Cap!" Ham shouted, his deep voice echoing along the bulkheads stretching from the flight deck throughout the confines of the scout ship Spirit. The rumble pulled Caleb out of his slumber in berthing. Eyes snapping open, his right hand instinctively reached for a sidearm that wasn't there.

Relax. It's only Abraham.

Ishek's alien voice echoed in Caleb's mind, the signal carried by a pair of hair-thin tendrils plugged into his brainstem.

Caleb shed the thin gray blanket covering him and rotated up on his berth to plant his bare feet on the cold metal deck. "You know me, Ish. It's habitual to go right for my gun. And if I'm not relaxed, it's because I'm excited to finally be here," he said out loud, spreading his legs to bend over and open one of the drawers beneath his thin mattress with a tap. The compartment slid open, revealing his magboots and a pair of socks.

"Cap, did you hear me?" Ham shouted. "I said we're here!"

"Everyone heard you, Ham," Corporal Jii Kwon

complained from the berth adjacent to Caleb's. He was still flat on his back, his arms raised overhead as he stretched before sitting up and yawning.

"Everyone?" Ham's voice boomed out. "Last I checked, there were only three of us on this boat!"

"I think everyone on Proxima heard you!" Kwon shouted back. "All the way back home!"

"Maybe all the way back to Earth!" Caleb corrected. "Forty light years! The shout heard across the universe! My ears are still ringing!"

"Mine are bleeding!" Kwon joked.

Grinning, Caleb finished putting on his boots and stood up. He closed the open drawer and tapped the one below it open. It contained a simple wardrobe of black t-shirts and boxer-briefs. Already dressed from the waist down, he plucked a perfectly folded t-shirt, pulling it on over both his lean muscled upper body and the symbiote wrapped around his upper right arm. For anyone getting only a cursory look, Ishek was easy to mistake as a black tribal tattoo, his body two inches wide and lying nearly flat against his skin. The only way to identify him as a living creature, let alone an alien, would be to get close enough to see the sluglike texture of his dark flesh.

"What's our distance from the signal?" Caleb asked Ham as Kwon skillfully hopped off his berth and into his boots, already maglocked to the deck. The fastenings automatically tightened up until they comfortably snugged up to his feet.

Slimmer and shorter than Caleb, he still bore the physique and posture of a Centurion Space Force Marine, though his thick, dark hair had grown out enough during the four-month trip that he had taken to tying it back into a topknot. It was against regulations, but the only rules out here were the ones Caleb enforced. He didn't care how long his men grew their hair as long as it didn't interfere with their ability to get the job done.

"Three point eight AU!" Ham answered.

"Velocity and heading?" Caleb requested.

"Twenty-eight thousand klicks per hour! About the speed of an orbiting satellite! In fact, according to the computer, the source is orbiting Trappist-G!"

"That's right in line with the Astrophysics Lab's projections," Kwon commented, his voice low enough for Caleb's ears only.

"So far, they've been dead on with their calculations," Caleb agreed with Kwon at a normal volume before shouting back at Ham. "Can we get a visual?"

"Negative! We're still too far out!"

"Do you think it's Pathfinder?" Kwon asked Caleb. "After all this time?"

"Orbiting a perfectly good planet?" Caleb answered. "I'd prefer to find it on the surface, surrounded by domes." He raised his voice again. "Any sign of a colony? Comm signals? Radiation?"

"I'm scanning the entire spectrum, but nothing so far!" Ham shouted .

Caleb tensed at the reply. He'd hoped for some sign of human life.

The CSF had spent the last five years working diligently to expand the network of outposts and sensors that allowed scout ships like Spirit to reach further and further beyond Alpha Centauri. It had come as a shock to everyone when they had flipped the switch on the latest and greatest long-range probe and discovered a regular, repeating transmission originating dozens of light years away. It was an even bigger shock when the comms team decrypted the encoded communication.

Two hundred and fifty years ago, a generation ship named Pathfinder had lifted off from a ravaged Earth carrying forty-thousand survivors to a new home in the Trappist-1 system. It had never been heard from again, both the ship and the colonists long considered lost.

Not anymore.

The transmission itself was an automated distress call, repeating every minute for who-knew-how-many years. The location, identifiers, and encryption keys all matched Pathfinder, and the powers-that-be had decided it was in humankind's best interests to track down the signal's origin to find out what had become of the colonists.

Even if he hadn't volunteered, the mission was too important and potentially too volatile for General Haeri to have sent anyone but Caleb. He and his Vultures were the most experienced scout team in the CSF. Caleb had spent the entire transit expecting the worst and hoping for the best, and now that they had arrived, it seemed his expectations were as spot on as AP's fold calculations.

Sometimes, he hated being right.

"What about the enemy?" he asked next.

"Nobody here but us chickens, Cap."

Caleb exhaled. At least he could hold onto the hope they hadn't come all this way for only bad news.

"Coffee, Cap?" Kwon asked Caleb.

"Yeah. Coffee sounds great."

"Ham! Coffee?"

"You know I never say no to caffeine! Although it's dicey when you're the one brewing it! You push the button wrong!"

"How do you push a button wrong?"

"Man, you tell me!"

I hungerrrr.

"Now, Ish?" Caleb asked. "I don't feel anything."

Would you prefer we wait for a less opportune time to feed?

"You heard Ham, it's clear sailing out there."

For now. You of all people should know not to underestimate us.

"So much for hope. I was afraid you might say that."

I only tell it like it is.

Caleb sighed, turning back to his berth as Kwon passed behind him, headed for the galley. Opening the drawer on his left. He shoved aside his spare utilities and went for the cushioned metal tin at the bottom of the compartment. Flipping the cover open, he glanced down at the remaining row of vials inside, sixteen in total. More than enough to get him back to Proxima once this mission was complete. Picking one out, he closed the tin and put it back in the drawer, pushing the compartment closed with his foot while he pinched the vial, cracking it open under his nose.

Electric tingles ran through his body as he breathed in the synthetic pheromones. In addition to the resources Ishek pulled from his body, the alien needed the chemicals to survive. All the members of his parent race, the Relyeh, did. It was what had made them such a blight on the universe. Not only the constant need to feed, but the way they gathered the pheromones to consume. The chemical mixture only occurred naturally through the fear response of organisms evolved enough to be afraid of monsters.

The Relyeh were monsters by nature. And they enjoyed it.

Ishek had been the same once, delighting in the pain and terror of his victims. Their symbiotic connection and the synthetic pheromone had changed that. Unfortunately, the stuff was difficult and incredibly expensive to produce. It would never be a solution to the needs of the Relyeh as a whole. They could never make enough to end the war. And even if they somehow found a way, Caleb doubted Shub'Nigu and the other Ancients of the Relyeh would accept peace. The Relyeh believed it was their destiny to subdue every intelligent life form in the universe. Unlike Ish, they refused to exist any other way.

I am satiated.

Caleb took one more deep breath of the pheromones to completely satisfy the khoron before depositing the empty vial in the enclosed trash bin to the right of the drawers beneath his berth. He moved from the berthing compartment into a narrow, eight-foot-long corridor, pausing where a closed hatch led to the head on the port side and an open hatch exposed the galley to starboard.

Crossing his arms over his chest, he leaned against the bulkhead at the galley entrance, watching Kwon get three thermoses out of the overhead cabinet and set them down on the small metal counter, their magnetic bottoms holding them in place. There was only room for one person in the galley at a time, with nowhere to sit, making it hardly a galley at all. The only thing they could make in it was coffee. All of their nutrition came from MREs.

"I'll have the coffee up in a minute, Cap," Kwon said, noticing him there.

"I'm just making sure you pressed the button right," Caleb replied, grinning. "Can't be too careful you know."

"Hmph. I did my best." Kwon looked drolly at Caleb. "I can't believe Ish was hungry again."

"I know. You'd better not get fat, Ish. I don't want to carry any extra weight around."

Fear is zero calorie.

Caleb paused, surprised by the statement. "Was that a feeble attempt at a joke?"

You are amused. I can feel it.

Still grinning, Caleb continued to the end of the corridor where the bulkhead curved as the corridor split in two. He took the starboard fork, stepping through the open hatch on his left.

The largest, most open space in the ship, the flight deck

was just barely large enough for a raised command station in the rear, and a pilot station and a co-pilot station sitting side-by-side just behind the forward viewscreen. Ham occupied the pilot seat, hands hovering over touch surfaces located at the end of each padded armrest. A thin column rose from behind the seat, curving forward at the top and culminating in a crown-like extension that wrapped around his forehead. Additional extensions secured him in the seat, holding him down as if he were in the clutches of a praying mantis.

Built like a raging bull, with a thick beard, a shaved head, and an intimidating stare, he looked like he should have been a professional wrestler or an MMA fighter, not a starship pilot. And certainly not a pilot for Spirit, since its neural-controlled primary interface required a more delicate approach than a typical Centurion starhopper.

The ship itself was the latest and greatest out of R&D, barely a step beyond experimental. She was currently the only vessel in the fleet outfitted with a fold drive utilizing the Stacker Equation, an upgraded jump algorithm that was the only reason they had the range to venture this far out into space.

"Trappist-1," Ham announced without turning his head. "Looks sweeeeet." He whistled emphatically.

Caleb turned his attention from the pilot to the forward viewscreen, a semi-circular, high-resolution projection stitched together from a composite of the dozens of cameras on Spirit's forward hull. A portion of the Trappist-1 system spread out before them. Still only the size of a baseball in the magnified surround, Trappist G was at least visible, unlike the other three planets within the system's potential habitable zone.

"It is impressive," Caleb agreed, taking the three steps up to the command station and dropping into the seat. Sensing his presence, the column behind him slid forward, the security ribs locking around his upper torso while the crown adjusted snugly to his head. Immediately, the area between his position and the forward viewscreen turned into a heads up display. What he saw there was injected into his brain's interpretation by the ship's computer.

I hate this.

"I know, Ish. Can't be helped."

Ish had to mindshare with the system's neural interface, and his senses didn't react well to the electrical signals altering reality. There wasn't any way around it. They had a job to do. Of course, that didn't prevent the symbiote from voicing his displeasure.

You should have told them to install a normal control system.

"You know I don't get to make those kinds of calls."

I don't know why you insist on being subservient. Together, we're superior to any of them.

"Now you're just being grumpy."

Ishek fell silent as Caleb watched Trappist-G grow steadily bigger until it nearly filled up the viewscreen. Even though it was habitable, it was obvious the planet was anything but hospitable. A small, brown ball of mud with no evidence of an atmosphere. Pulling the sensor readout of the planet up onto his HUD confirmed his visual impression. Still, that didn't necessarily mean the settlers on Pathfinder hadn't established a foothold there. The generation ship was loaded with equipment to survive on a planet like Trappist-G. All they needed was a water supply, and Caleb couldn't discount the possibility that there was plenty of it stored beneath the surface.

"Caffeine delivery," Kwon announced, stepping onto the flight deck with the three thermoses cradled in his arms. "I can't believe we're this close to learning what happened to Pathfinder. Here you go, Captain." He handed Caleb his coffee first.

"Thanks, Jii." Caleb stuck it to the arm of his chair, where it held fast to a powerful magnetic grip.

"No problem. Ham?"

The big pilot reached out to take his thermos just as the neural interface sounded an alarm in Caleb's mind, quickly joined by Ishek's painful scream. Wincing at the instant, dizzying agony he shared with Ishek, Caleb barely made out the sudden appearance of a pair of dark, roughly almond shaped objects.

"Shit!" Anyone with less experience than Ham could have easily mistaken them for asteroids. Until they made an impossible, high velocity turn to vector straight toward them.

Ishek overcame the pain of the unexpected wail from Spirit's sensors long enough to state the obvious in response to the unexpected appearance of the Relyeh attack ships.

I told you not to underestimate us.

CHAPTER 2

"Evasive maneuvers!" Caleb cried.

Not that he needed to tell Ham what to do. The milliseconds the pilot saved interacting mentally with the flight control systems was the only reason they survived the first pass of the Relyeh attack ships.

As it was, the sudden hard shift in their vector pulled the remaining two thermoses out of Kwon's grip, sending them hurtling across the flight deck, one of them whipping past Caleb's head with only a few inches to spare. The heavy Gs tried to pull Kwon that way too, and he strained in his magboots, face twisted in pain. Ham straightened Spirit out, but only for a moment, allowing the artificial gravity inside the ship to pull the thermoses down. They landed upright as designed, their magnetic bottoms gripping tightly to the deck.

"They're cutting back toward us," Ham announced, though his play-by-play was unnecessary. Caleb didn't have a visual through the viewscreen surround, but he brought them up on his HUD, which showed the Relyeh ships making impossible course corrections to bring them back around onto Spirit's tail.

"Damn, that was close," Kwon said, throwing himself into his seat. The seat's ribs wrapped around him, his neural interface moving into place.

'I'm killing gravity.' The interface immediately translated Caleb's thought, passing it on to Ham and Kwon at the same time he shut off the artificial gravity. They didn't need the extra pull while they made high-G maneuvers. "Ham, you're on the helm. Kwon, you have the forward guns."

"Of course, you get to take the rear guns," Kwon said. "Since that's where the baddies are."

"Knuckle up, Vultures," Caleb barked. He was fine with the playfulness and banter. Up to a point. And the arrival of the Relyeh attack ships had pushed them over that point.

"Yes, sir," Kwon snapped back attentively.

Caleb dialed the opacity of his HUD to one hundred percent, switching the view in his eyes to the rear. Another thought told the targeting computer to dim the stars in the background and outline the Relyeh ships, which were otherwise nearly invisible against the black backdrop of space. Spirit's systems could automate the firing solution if he wanted, but he already knew it would struggle against the Relyeh ships, which both the computer and his eyes identified as Shales. Since their movements defied accepted laws of physics, the Advanced Tactical Combat System AI tended toward confusion and would lock up completely. He didn't think Ham would appreciate waiting thirty seconds for their offensive capabilities to return.

With another thought, Caleb armed the ship's guns. Armor plating slid aside to allow the eight tucked-in turrets to expand. "Loading tacks," he announced, referring to the thumbtack-sized, explosive rounds that were one of the ship's two ammunition types. The thought accompanying the statement told the computer to close the linkage to the priming super-capacitor and open the belt feed.

'Not the pew-pews?' Kwon asked, surprised by his choice.

'Haven't you completed Shale training in the simulator?' Caleb replied. With the entire conversation unspoken, entire sentences took milliseconds to cross between the crew, allowing them to communicate easily in the midst of the attack.

'I used the pew-pews', Kwon returned.

'And won?'

'It wasn't easy.'

'Watch and learn, Corporal.'

"Here we go," Ham said out loud as he hit the throttle and threw Spirit into another hard turn. Caleb felt the Gs pulling on him, but the seat's ribs held him firmly and somewhat comfortably in place. The neural interface allowed his view to stay locked on the enemy despite the turn. He watched as one of them rotated ahead of Spirit's vector change, aiming to lead them into its attack.

Caleb focused on one Shale at a time, making judicious use of the tacks to conserve ammunition. He fired single rounds as if he were shooting spitballs, taking quick, specific aim that forced the enemy ship to break from its vector and assume its own evasive maneuvers. By the time Spirit reached the spot where Caleb had hoped to blast them, it was way out of line, forcing him to sweep overhead and try again.

'All I see is you missing.' Kwon's sarcasm transmitted across the interface. *'Is that what you want me to learn, Cap?'*

'All right, smartass,' Caleb came back. *'Beam the other one to keep him honest.'*

'Wilco.'

Caleb stuck to his plan, his attention fixed to the Relyeh ship while Ham continued his evasive maneuvers. Spirit's pilot effected constant vector changes and hundreds of throttle adjustments every second. He fired retrorockets, making rapid changes to their velocity that worked to keep the Shales' aim disrupted.

Meanwhile, Kwon belched an inch diameter focused energy beam from one of the forward turrets rotated to face the rear. While the beam was invisible, the computer colored it in a sharp yellow, allowing Caleb to watch it dig into the front of the second Shale, breaking off a few small chunks of its armored hull.

'I'm hitting my target.' Kwon relayed. *'What about you?'*

Caleb didn't answer. All of his attention remained focused on the first Shale. He continued sending single rounds at the ship, watching the enemy ship's responses. Even though it had no thrusters or vectoring nozzles to speak of, it shifted sideways, dropped back, and shot forward, changing its inhumanly impossible angle of attack from thirty to ninety degrees in the blink of an eye. Marines liked to joke that pure evil propelled Relyeh ships. Since he didn't know enough about their systems to think otherwise, he was willing to accept that explanation.

The Shale finally opened fire, though the term didn't really match the enemy's attack. Pieces of its hull broke away suddenly, launched forward by the same ambiguous pure evil, aimed just ahead of Spirit. The pieces spread out in a line that seemed to make evading them all downright impossible.

Impossible for another pilot, maybe.

Ham reacted to the attack seemingly before the Shale launched it. Punching the bow down and pegging the throttle, he sent Spirit into the hardest vector shift so far. The Gs threatened to steal the breath from Caleb's lungs. He tightened his core against the maneuver, gritting his teeth.

Doesn't he know we have shields?

Ishek didn't like the move either, his discomfort reflected in Caleb's sudden nausea. One of the projectile asteroids filled Caleb's view, coming within centimeters of smashing the camera currently tracking the Shale as it changed course to remain on Spirit's six.

Shut it, Ish, I'm working, he snapped back. He fired three more rounds at the Shale. It evaded the tacks easily, while it waited for another solid opening to strike.

Ham did his best not to give it that opening, continuing to duck, juke and spiral through space. The other Shale remained as tightly glued to their tail as the first, and it too offered an attack that sent shards of its hull spearing out toward them. As good as he was, Ham couldn't avoid every projectile forever. One of the slivers smacked into the shields, where a tremendous burst of energy worked to dissipate it before it could break through. It was only partially successful. Spirit shuddered from the hit, and Caleb nearly lost his aim. Fortunately, the shields absorbed enough of the kinetic energy to prevent the shard from piercing the hull.

"School's out, I guess." Kwon snickered out loud, sending a beam into the second Shale, digging out a larger piece of the hull. "Any day now, Cap."

Caleb smirked as three more of his rounds missed the mark. He had used a total of forty tacks so far. Every single one of them had a purpose, all of them designed for a single moment.

Finally, that moment arrived.

He aimed where the Shale wasn't, unleashing a barrage of tacks.

"What are you doing?" Kwon asked. "There's nothing—"

He fell silent as the Shale moved directly into the tacks, each one punching into the hard stone hull and digging in deep before exploding. A dozen detonations rocked the Relyeh ship. It not only lost the chase, it broke apart, revealing organic matter inside that froze nearly instantly in the bitter cold of space.

Like everything made by the Relyeh, the ship was alive. Or rather, had been. Until now.

"Were you paying attention?" Caleb asked, already targeting the second Shale.

"How?" Kwon questioned in disbelief.

"Have you ever played slap-jack?"

"The hand slapping game? No, but I've heard of it."

"It's all about speed and timing. You get your opponent off-balance while you watch for his tells. Eventually, you can win the slap damn close to one hundred percent of the time. I figured out which way he was likely to go next. While you've been pecking, I went right for the kill."

"I admit, I'm impressed."

"Cap, do you think you can slap the other one before he spanks us?" Ham asked.

"Loading tacks," Kwon said.

"I've got this one," Caleb said. "You can practice tacking Shales in the simulator when we get back to Proxima."

"Spoilsport."

Caleb's lips barely twitched before his expression went stone serious. He watched the Shale for a moment, eyes locked on the target while Ham led the Relyeh attack ship in a merry chase. Firing single tacks the way he had before, Caleb figured out the enemy's pattern fairly quickly. Shales were alive, but they weren't intelligent. They operated like they were in a video game, following a prescribed algorithm, or in their case, instinct, that made them react to stimulus in similar ways.

While the enemy did its best to get a bead on Spirit, it lost its chance the moment the surprise attack failed, though it probably didn't realize it. It unleashed another round of shards. Ham dodged them without difficulty, while Caleb lined up his shot. Twenty seconds later, he spewed another handful of rounds into his predicted vector, grinning when the Shale moved right into it and suffered the same fate as the first.

"Scratch two," Caleb said. "We're clear."

"Or so the sensors claim," Ham said. "We thought that the first time."

"That's why we're riding the hot seats the rest of the way to the signal. I hope you two gentlemen relieved yourselves before you sat down."

"I think I relieved myself when that first Shale sprayed those shards at us," Kwon said. "Nice moves getting us through that one, Hamster. So Cap, how'd you know to hit them with the tacks like that? I haven't seen that move in any of the reading materials."

"I got tired of the Shales handing me my rear on a platter," Caleb replied. "I figured there had to be a better way. After that, it's all trial and error."

"And you haven't shared it with the rest of us?" Ham asked.

"I told General Haeri. He should have disseminated it into the training programs by now."

"Always the last to know," Kwon complained. "I thought we were friends."

"I'm your CO, not your friend."

Kwon looked back at him, only managing to keep a straight face for a couple of seconds. "You're a terrible liar."

"Incorrect, Corporal. I'm such a good liar that I can appear to be a terrible liar at will."

Kwon and Caleb were sharing a laugh when Ham interrupted.

"Uh, Cap."

"What is it?" Caleb replied.

"The signal's gone."

CHAPTER 3

"What do you mean, the signal's gone?" Caleb said, opening the sensor feed on his HUD to see for himself. He hadn't even gotten a chance to see the output before the Relyeh had attacked, and now the grid was blank. Nothing out of the ordinary roamed space anywhere near Trappist-G except them.

Or so your sensors believe.

Ishek made the remark with a hint of malice. For as much as Caleb had integrated with the khoron, it was impossible to completely subdue his nature.

"You already saw it for yourself," Ham replied, having intentionally hesitated before responding, knowing Caleb would check the grid.

A thought caused Caleb's version of the grid to rewind back to the last moments before the signal vanished. He paused it there, silently asking the computer to pick out any other nearby anomalies.

Apparently, there were none.

"Nothing to suggest the Relyeh hit it," he said. "No evidence of outside interference at all."

"Then why would it just stop?" Kwon asked. He leaned

sideways in his seat as far as he could, stretching to reach for one of the thermoses on the deck but coming a few inches short. "Cap, permission to—"

"No," Caleb responded before he could finish asking. "You avoided slamming into the bulkhead and breaking your neck by about two seconds. You can live without coffee."

"That's easy for you to say," Ham groaned. "You have yours."

"I won't drink mine until you can drink yours," Caleb replied. "As for why it would stop, maybe it wasn't needed anymore. Because we're here."

"I don't think it works like that," Kwon said.

"Or maybe it ran out of power," Ham added.

"It's solar powered. And the system's star looks intact to me." A cold white dwarf easily outshone by the light of distant stars, it was visible much further in the distance.

"I'm out of ideas," Caleb admitted. "The point is, we know where it was before it vanished, and we didn't come all this way to turn around and go home without doing some recon."

"Yes, sir. What do you think the odds are that those Shales were the only Relyeh out here? Advance scouts or something?"

"You mean like us? That would be quite a coincidence."

Not as much as you might think. Remember, one thing we do not possess is faster than light travel.

"Or not," Caleb corrected. "Ish says that depending on when the transmission reached the nearest Relyeh, it could have taken them that long to get scouts out here."

Or they may have been lying in wait for someone else to come along.

"You mean to see if us pathetic humans ever made it out this far?"

Yes.

"You'd think they would have sent more than two ships. I'm sure they can spare more."

Two is more than enough. We would have been destroyed if not for your awful neural interface.

"That's a strange way to put it, but true. Ham, bring us to the last known location. We'll go from there."

"Yes, sir," Ham replied. "On our way." He updated Spirit's vector and pegged the throttle, sending them hurtling toward Trappist-G's orbit.

All three Marines remained alert as they rocketed across empty space. The Relyeh Shales had shown an ability to skirt their sensors, a fact Caleb was determined to bring up to the development team as soon as they made it back to Proxima. That the stonelike outer shells of the enemy starships could deflect different forms of detection was nothing new. But the only warning they were given was visual, and Ishek was right. If Abraham had been forced to use manual controls to guide the ship, they'd be nothing more than ash scattering across the universe right now.

The transit time passed in silence, each member of the crew keeping a sharp eye on the expanse around them. Caleb concentrated most of his attention astern, keeping the background dimmed to better spot anything trying to again sneak up on them. As they neared Trappist-G, Ham flipped Spirit over nose-to-tail and used their thrust to slow their approach.

It also gave him a better view of the planet. It was less rocky than he had initially observed, with veins of ice creating intricate weblike patterns across much of the muddy terrain. No doubt, the planet was cold, but the printable domes the generation ships had carried meant the colony could have survived there. The planet didn't spin on its axis like Earth, though. If there were humans on Trappist-G, they would be set up on the other side, facing the dying star.

Out of sight for the moment.

Once they reached G's orbit, Ham rotated Spirit back around. Though they approached the signal's last known position at a much higher velocity, they stayed at the same altitude at the edge of the gravity well. By following the orbital path, they were bound to catch up to the source of the signal sooner or later, unless it had either moved out of orbit or been destroyed.

"Cap, I think I've got visual," Ham announced nearly thirty minutes after reaching orbit.

"Kwon, watch our six," Caleb replied, switching from the rear view to the forward surround. Ham had already marked what he believed was the target. Seeing it, Caleb's waning hope that they might find the settlers nearby dimmed even further.

"What is it?" Ham asked.

"A breadcrumb," Caleb replied as Ham maneuvered them closer, using retro thrusters to slow their approach. The target was rectangular in shape, the size of a small car, with a pair of solar foil wings that stretched out nearly one hundred feet in either direction. One of the wings was heavily damaged, the solar-collecting foil torn almost completely away. "Every generation ship came loaded with five emergency beacon satellites," he explained, "intended to be released if a malfunction or other emergency caused the crew to lose navigational control. Given the circumstances at the time, it wasn't expected anyone would help immediately, but that a future ship like us might pick up the signal and trace it all the way back to the source. Since the ship itself is self-sustaining, as long as the life-support components hold up, they could theoretically remain adrift for hundreds of years, waiting for someone to find them. It was a last-ditch option for a desperate situation. That damage to the solar foil explains why it went silent. It's been running on a power deficit for a long time."

"And just happened to go out when we arrived?" Kwon asked.

"Stranger things have happened."

"You don't think the Relyeh hit it?"

Caleb could sense Ishek preparing to reply, but he didn't need the khoron's answer. He already knew what his symbiote was going to say. "Relyeh don't damage things. They destroy them. It was probably random debris."

"Cap, I just gotta say," Ham said. "Outside of the junk field we created smashing those two Shales, this whole area is as clean as any I've flown through. And that collector is a mess. It's not like a pea-sized rock punched through the foil."

"It could have been damaged on launch," Kwon said. "If the ship was already out of control, it's possible it was spinning or something and then clipped the satellite on its way out. It could have knocked it off course, and it got caught in the planet's gravity well."

"I'll give you that," Ham agreed.

"I doubt anyone was out here sabotaging it," Caleb added. "Anyway, the point of my story is that if Pathfinder did lose navigation and helm control, they should have released additional beacons at regular intervals so that their current heading could be calculated. But checking the sensors AP helped design for this mission, we're not picking up another beacon within our range."

"So it's possible they still could have landed on one of the other planets and set up camp," Kwon said optimistically.

"Without a helm?" Ham replied. "If Pathfinder is on one of these planets, she probably crashed into it."

"In which case, the question would be how hard did they crash?" Kwon said. "And were there any survivors?"

"Bottom line, it doesn't look good. Our mission is to either locate Pathfinder or verify its loss. We aren't done here yet. Kwon, see if you can do anything to better attenuate the sensors. If there's another beacon out there, we need to find it."

"Yes, sir."

"Ham, I need you to work out the trajectory from Earth to right here, and project it forward as if Pathfinder shot through the Trappist-1 system without stopping. Assume the nav control kept them on a direct heading with no outside interference."

"You got it, Cap."

"A figure of speech on this boat, but I've got the stick. I'm going to bring us around to the bright side and see if there is anything to see there. For now, we'll need to go door-to-door to look for evidence of the ship. You both know what to do. It's showtime, Marines."

CHAPTER 4

Caleb maintained Spirit's orbit around Trappist-G, allowing the planet's gravity well to pull the ship around to the other side rather than burn the thrusters. The maneuver would hopefully help prevent any other potential Relyeh ships from noticing them, while at the same time, saving a little extra fuel for the reactor. Caleb handled navigation, while Kwon and Ham went to work on the alternate tasks Caleb had assigned them.

The first hour passed quietly and uneventfully even when the bright side of Trappist-G began moving into view and Caleb directed the relevant sensors toward it. He was hunting for radio waves, microwaves, unnatural heat sources, or any other signs that Pathfinder might have landed on the planet. He didn't have high expectations that he might find something tangible. While the planet had more than enough ice to provide water to the colony for thousands of years and the temperature was within a habitable range inside printable domes, he knew from the briefing General Haeri and his team had given before their departure that Trappist-G wasn't the prime candidate for hosting life. That honor fell to Trappist-D or E, which he was already prepared to recon if this sweep didn't bear any fruit.

They were approaching the second hour when Ham finally shifted in his seat, having gone completely still while he used the neural interface to complete both his research and his calculations. He reached down to unlock the swivel on the chair, swinging it to face Caleb before locking it back in place. If he were still piloting the craft, he would have never made the orientation change, but since he wasn't, Caleb appreciated the more personal interaction.

Noticing Ham's movements, Kwon shifted his head. *"Are you done already?"* he asked through the interface.

"What do you mean, already?" Ham replied out loud. "It's been almost two hours."

"It has?" Kwon's voice conveyed his surprise. "It felt like twenty minutes to me."

"Does that mean you haven't finished working with the comm equipment?" Caleb asked.

"I'm close," Kwon said. "I need to make some manual adjustments to the electronics. Which means I need the gravity back and permission to get out of my seat."

"Granted," Caleb said, restoring the artificial gravity through the neural interface.

The ribs released Kwon from their grip and the neural crown slid back, freeing him from the seat. He immediately bent over to pick up Ham's thermos, passing it to him.

"Thanks, K."

"No problem," he replied.

"You can drink now, Cap," Ham said, pleased to finally have his thermos in hand. All three men took a moment to take a few sips of coffee before Kwon locked his thermos down on his seat and left the flight deck.

"I needed this," Ham said, securing the lid on his thermos and locking it to his seat.

"You've been on duty for eighteen hours," Caleb said.

"I'd give you some rack time if I could spare you right now."

"I'm too wound up to sleep anyway," Ham replied. "I need resolution to this. Lady Luck isn't looking down on us, but I've still got my fingers crossed."

"That's a lot of superstition right there."

"You know me, Cap. I'm not one to take chances when black cats or lost starships are involved."

Kwon returned to the flight deck carrying a hard-case toolbox. He put it on the deck just in front of the pilot's station, locking it down and kneeling beside it. Removing one of the tools, he quickly unscrewed four bolts from the decking at the front of the flight deck and lifted it out of the way. Kwon retrieved a couple of tools and ducked into the tiny crawl space beneath the removed decking.

"Good thing I'm not claustrophobic," he said, his voice muffled as he crawled under the deck.

"That crawl space is the only reason we brought you along," Caleb joked, knowing Kwon could hear him where he was working.

"I'm sure not going to fit down there," Ham agreed. "Cap, let me show you what I came up with."

A box popped up on Caleb's HUD, right in front of his eyes. A request from Ham to control his augmented reality. He accepted it, and the view zoomed out to an expanded image of the universe.

"According to the archival records the nerds uploaded prior to our launch, HMS Pathfinder lifted off from Earth exactly two hundred fifty-three years, one hundred ninety-six days ago as one of the first colony ships to make it off-world. They were sent the updated directives to rendezvous with the other generation ships in the Alpha Centauri system, but for whatever reason, they didn't get the memo or couldn't follow the orders. They never arrived at AC, so it's assumed they maintained their predetermined heading to the Trappist-1 system."

Ham zoomed in on Earth. Pathfinder's departure date appeared next to it, an advancing red line showing the ship making a slight course change at Jupiter. From there, it zipped straight across the expanse toward Trappist, forty light years away.

"Pathfinder accelerated to about thirty-five percent of the speed of light before cutting its main thrusters," Ham continued. "A one hundred twenty-five year trip. None of the colonists who stepped onto Pathfinder would ever step off."

"But their Guardians would," Kwon said. "Royal Armed Forces commandos who volunteered to watch over the ship while it was in transit. You know all about them, don't you Cap?"

"I should," Caleb replied, having been a Guardian on a generation ship himself. Unlike Ham and Kwon, he knew what Earth had been like before the Relyeh ruined humanity's home world. Two hundred fifty years had passed, though he'd only aged about twenty in that time, thanks to stasis, and later Ishek. "It wasn't all it was cracked up to be."

"It's still pretty wild to think about. Getting onto a ship, every colonist knew it would be their distant descendants who got off, none of them having ever lived on Earth."

"It wasn't quite like that," Caleb demurred, not in the mood to talk about his past. Besides, Kwon already knew the important parts of the story.

While Kwon had been talking, the red line in Ham's AR view continued all the way to the edge of the Trappist-1 system. "As I was saying," Ham continued, "Astrophysics did their best to calculate the movements of the planets. I asked the computer for the science team's projection versus the real, observable deal outside, and this is what came back." The planets in the system took on a red shift, moving about twenty millimeters to the right.

"They weren't off by much," Caleb said.

"No. They're good at what they do. And I'm glad because if they had been off by more than three percent I would have had to recalibrate everything." A large clang echoed from under the deck, whatever happened drawing a sharp curse from Kwon. "Are you okay down there, buddy?" Ham asked.

"Yeah, I'm fine," Kwon replied. "Dropped the damn wire cutters."

"Wait, what?" Caleb said. "What are you cutting?"

"The computer told me I need to splice two of the comm array antennas to one system to boost the receiver strength. I figured locating Pathfinder was worth the loss."

"Which comms are we losing?"

"Long range. We won't be able to call home."

"What if we get into some deep trouble out here?" Ham asked.

"If it's that bad, we probably won't want our rescuers becoming the next victims," Caleb said. "Do it, Corporal."

"Yes, sir."

"As I was saying..." His voice grew a little louder. "...if my histrionic compadre would let me finish my presentation. I didn't have to recalibrate anything to advance the timeline. Assuming Pathfinder launched a beacon because they lost control of the ship, and assuming they continued on their same heading, at the same velocity, here's the tricky part. And the reason it took me almost two hours instead of forty minutes."

Ham zoomed in again, until only one side of the Trappist-1 system and its white dwarf star could be seen. The red line continued, showing all the planets as they moved in their orbits around the sun, the line slowing as it neared Trappist-G.

"Pathfinder's heading carried her into the same orbit we're in now," he continued. "Her velocity would have allowed her to break free pretty easily, only not without a minor course adjustment. I've run these numbers a dozen times, and also put in some alternate possibilities, but the computer heavily weighs this one as the most likely."

"I hate the way you're prefacing this," Caleb said, looking down at the deck when Kwon dropped another tool.

"I'm fine!" he shouted up.

"I'm just trying to bring you down easy, Cap," Ham said. He advanced the timeline again.

Caleb watched as Pathfinder took a gentle right turn coming off Trappist-G before going in a straight line across the system, cutting between planets on its way to…Caleb's blood ran cold, his jaw tensed, watching with a mix of anger and resignation as Pathfinder dove headfirst into the heart of Trappist-1's star. According to Ham's timeline, the generation ship collided with the white dwarf. And of course, there was no way anyone on board had survived.

"Like I told you," Ham said in response to Caleb's reaction. "This is a best-guess scenario. There's no way for any of us to know what the absolute reality was. It could be that Pathfinder still had some measure of control and was able to steer around the star. I mean, it's in the name of the ship, right? This is just a projection. A guide. It's not written in stone."

Caleb continued staring at the view, the red arrow piercing through the heart of Trappist-1. That damn arrow had punched through his ticker too. It couldn't be possible that after a hundred and twenty years in space, Pathfinder had been erased just like that. He didn't want to accept it.

Except all the evidence pointed in that direction.

"Bad news on top of bad news," Caleb said. Having had better days, he dropped Ham's shared view and looked out into the black through the forward surround. Remaining silent, he considered what to do next.

He hadn't gotten very far before Kwon climbed out of the crawl space and dropped into his seat to neurally adjust the comms.

"Are we going home?" Ham asked.

"At this point, I don't want to make assumptions," Caleb replied. "At the same time, everything we've learned suggests the worst possible outcome. We already know it may not be safe in this system. As much as I hate it, we could go back to Haeri and tell him Pathfinder is definitely gone, but…." He gritted his teeth, shaking his head. "…giving up has never been one of my strong suits."

"Me, neither," Ham agreed.

"Hey, Cap?" Kwon said. "I think you'll want to stay stubborn."

Caleb leaned forward in his seat. "What is it?"

"You wanted a second beacon? You've got one."

"Where?" Caleb asked excitedly.

"The computer's still processing the signal. We never would have picked it up without my hack."

"That's the real reason I brought you along. I knew your engineering background would come in handy."

"I'm always happy to put my knowledge to use beyond hacking drones in my spare time. We've got initial positioning. The signal's too faint to get a lock until we get closer."

With a thought, Caleb pulled up the grid to see where the computer had placed the source of the new beacon signal. He wasn't completely surprised to see it was coming from the vicinity of Trappist-E. "Maybe Pathfinder didn't smash into the star after all. Ham, you have the stick. Get us there."

CHAPTER 5

It took nearly four more hours to transit from Trappist-G to E, the crossing thankfully uneventful. While Caleb didn't lift the emergency alert status altogether, he did reduce it from red to orange, allowing movement throughout the ship so long as magboots remained active. Kwon took the opportunity to refill their thermoses with coffee, and Caleb relieved Ham on the stick, allowing him to hit both the head and the galley to grab an MRE, followed by some rack time.

The beacon signal increased in strength the closer they moved to Trappist-E, and it wasn't long before the computer determined the beacon was in a fixed location. Relative to the planet, it was either in geosynchronous orbit or on the surface itself. The closer they got to the source, the more dialed-in the system's estimate became, until it finally decided with high certainty that the distress call was emanating from the ground.

The prospect raised Caleb's hopes of finding Pathfinder and the descendants of the original colonists, cut off from the rest of humankind but otherwise surviving on their new home world. And from space at least, it seemed as though the settlers could have done a lot worse.

While Trappist-E wasn't a blue marble like Earth, with an atmosphere, a temperate climate, and abundant life, it appeared comparable to Proxima B. Liquid water was visible from space, with rivers running along deep crags in the rocky terrain. A thin atmosphere helped deflect the worst of the solar radiation, and the gravity was eighty percent of Earth's, making it easier for the mass equalization systems to make up the difference. The most impressive thing to Caleb was the planet's distance from the white dwarf star. The white celestial body loomed large over the planet like a giant spotlight.

Rather than bellow across the ship to wake Ham, Caleb sent a signal through to the speaker inside berthing, the shrill tone no doubt suddenly bringing the stout Marine out of his slumber. He entered the flight deck ten minutes later, after having quickly showered, shaved, and changed into a fresh pair of utilities.

"Hopper's almost full, Cap," he announced as he took his seat, referring to the machine that treated their dirty clothes without water.

"Right on schedule," Caleb replied. "We'll run it on the next cycle. That should give us just enough sterilizer to make it back to Proxima, assuming we spend about a week here."

"At the rate we're going, we won't need a week," Ham added. "Is that E?" The neural crown wrapped around his head. "Oh. The signal's planetside. That's a twist."

"I've got another twist," Kwon announced. "With the light atmosphere the sensors are picking up, the solar foil on the beacon isn't getting enough energy to provide a surplus." He stopped there, waiting for them to figure out the conclusion on their own.

"So, what?" Ham asked. "You're suggesting it's hooked

up to an alternate power supply?"

"Good guess, and that would be a strong indicator that Pathfinder is down there with the beacon. But unfortunately, that's not it."

"Someone modified the beacon to use less power," Caleb said. "That's why the signal is so faint."

"Score one for Cap. That's my theory."

"Which means whoever launched the beacon knew it would wind up on the surface, and adjusted it so that it would stand the test of time."

"Exactly."

"Who?" Ham asked.

"That's the question, along with why."

"Why is easy," Caleb said. "One beacon to another. The first would lead us to the system. The second would lead us to Trappist-E."

"Like K-dog mentioned," Ham said. "If Pathfinder was down there, the beacon would have no reason to use less power. The reactors are designed to last a long time. More than long enough for the colony to build the infrastructure needed to generate energy without them."

"Unless that was the emergency," Kwon suggested. "Maybe Pathfinder's reactors were failing."

"All three of them? Incredibly unlikely."

"But still possible."

The second beacon will not lead you to the ship.

It was the first time Ishek had spoken since the Relyeh attack.

"You seem pretty sure about that," Caleb said.

The circumstances of its positioning and modification suggest there was a lot of forethought to its delivery. Whatever fate befell Pathfinder, they saw it coming, but could do very little about it.

"How is that different from crashing on the planet?"

If you were on a ship destined to crash on an alien world and you had the skill set to modify the power draw of a satellite, such that it would continue broadcasting your whereabouts for over two centuries, wouldn't you be more useful spending your time trying to prevent the ship from crashing in the first place? Besides, what would be the point of sending a call for help if you knew you wouldn't survive? Starships either land on planets or impact them like an asteroid.

Caleb considered his symbiote's perspective. "You might be right. We can theorize all we want, but we're almost there. We'll learn the truth soon enough. Ham, you have the stick."

"I have the stick," Ham said, picking up flight control.

"Was Ish giving you his take on the beacon?" Kwon asked.

"Yeah. He thinks this beacon will be another breadcrumb."

"I respectfully disagree with Doctor Worm. If the second beacon was intended to lead us to the third, we should be picking it up by now, especially with the increased sensitivity of the modified array. But I'm not surprised a Relyeh thinks it knows everything."

Ishek sent a jolt of anger through Caleb, which he registered as a hot tingle that made him jump as it spread from his head to his chest.

"Cool it, Corporal," Caleb said calmly, still fighting off the pain. "We all have a beef with the Relyeh as a whole, but Ishek is part of me, for better or worse, and I don't need you pissing him off. We're all on the same side here."

"Sorry, Cap," Kwon replied. "I didn't mean to insult him. I can't imagine what it was like to be captured by the enemy and forced to bond with one of their body snatchers."

"I got away from them. That's the important part. And the bonding is bi-directional, which is why he can't just be removed. Anyway, he's not the wholly evil monster he used to be."

Are you sure about that?

Caleb ignored Ishek's teasing. He turned his attention to the forward surround, using the interface to magnify the area where the computer claimed the fallen satellite was located. With Spirit only a few minutes from the edge of Trappist-E's gravity well, a composite view of the surface built from the sensor data revealed rocky terrain mixed with both ice and liquid water. There weren't many flat surfaces down there, and his first look suggested the beacon rested somewhere at the bottom of a particularly steep, narrow canyon.

"We won't be able to get Spirit into that canyon," he said. "We'll have to drop from overhead."

"You want to go down to the surface?" Ham asked.

"It's not a question of want. I need to know what happened to Pathfinder. The beacon is down there, which means the answers are down there, too. That's what we came for." He released the interface and the ribs with a thought, standing up as soon as he was clear. "Ham, bring us in as tight as you can. With any luck we'll get a visual before we drop, but the way things are going so far, I doubt that'll happen. Kwon and I will jump in, find the beacon, and hop back out."

"Yes, sir," Ham said. "ETA to enter the atmosphere is a little over an hour."

"That leaves us plenty of time to prepare. Kwon, you're with me."

"Captain, wait," Ham said suddenly, drawing Caleb's attention to the forward surround. A new mark appeared on the composite view, nearly adjacent to the estimated source of the signal. "Something just hit us with a sensor lock."

Caleb stared at the second contact while Kwon voiced what they were all thinking.

"Someone's alive down there."

CHAPTER 6

Caleb and Kwon went from the flight deck to the armory at the ship's bow, headed for their respective lockers. Caleb didn't open his right away. He quickly stripped down to his underwear, neatly folding and laying his pants and shirt on the bench behind him, and then he tucked his boots beneath the seat. Kwon was hardly as neat about his discarded utilities, tossing them into the bottom of his locker. It gave him a head start changing into his Self-contained Advanced Combat Suit, SCACS for short.

Designed to be a one-suit-fits-all approach to outfitting a Centurion Marine, it had evolved over the years from the same Advanced Tactical Combat Armor, or a-tac, that Caleb had worn as a U.S. Marine Ranger on pre-Relyeh Earth. Like a diver's wetsuit, it still featured the same skin tight underlay beneath a thicker, more protective overlay. Together, the two layers were designed to provide moderate protection with maximum comfort. The underlay worked to regulate body temperature while offering a twenty percent strength increase. It absorbed both sweat and urine, wicking it to the suit's exterior where it evaporated, allowing the base layer to be worn for days at a time.

While the underlay barely changed over the years, the outer layer had been vastly improved. Long gone were the hard composite plates that covered the most important bits and left the joints and neck too exposed. Today, the overlay was made of a more flexible reactive material that acted like a third layer of skin. It preserved agility and range of motion while also offering another twenty percent in strength enhancement by means of a passive musculature printed to the inside of the overlay. Being self-contained, the armor was rated for land, sea, air, and space, and was versatile enough to cover any need the Centurion Space Force might have.

It was also ridiculously expensive to produce. So much so that only a few dozen had been made. Caleb had successfully managed to snag three of them. It was more a signal of how important this mission was than to any kind of special favor.

While the powers-that-be had tried to keep a lid on news of the signal and the possibility that Pathfinder had been found, it had only taken one pair of loose lips to spread the news across Proxima. The whole thing had taken on a life of its own since then, the streams and feeds stuffed with rumor, gossip, and general interest in the story. Spirit's departure had been met with inordinate notice and fanfare, drawing a crowd of thousands to the CSF launch dome to see them off. It reminded Caleb of videos he had seen of the early days of space exploration on Earth, when the Space Shuttle launches captured the public interest.

The CSF had pulled out all the stops to give them the best chance of success. Then again, they would have done the same if the story hadn't gone viral.

No, they wouldn't.

Ishek's response to the thought snapped Caleb out of it. "You don't know that."

One thing I have learned since bonding to you is that the

higher the position of power you climb among humans, the more you begin to resemble a Relyeh of a similar status.

"I wouldn't go that far."

I would.

Caleb finally stood and opened his locker, reaching to a lower shelf to retrieve his impeccably folded underlay. Opening it, he pressed it flat against his open locker so that the arms and legs were secured by magnets in the locker doors. Using a fingernail, he turned the sealing clasps in the front to open the gear before turning around and backing into the base layer. He slipped his feet in first and then his arms. He had to tug at the material to get it to stretch enough to contain his warrior's body, taking his time to ensure the attached gloves were snug against his fingers and everything was properly aligned. Once he and Ishek were in, he latched the front closed with small hooks that flattened when he turned the sealing clasps, closing up the base before sitting to put on his boots.

It's a good thing I don't need to breathe.

"Forty-five minutes, Cap!" Ham shouted from the flight deck.

"Copy that," Caleb replied. Ignoring Ishek's comment, he stood back up and reached to the rear of his locker to grab the outer layer of the SCACS. The process for putting it on was identical to the underlay, and he repeated the steps a second time, finishing off by locking the armor's larger clasps closed.

He pulled his helmet off the top shelf. A matte gray to match the SCACS, the helmet was small and sleek, with a tinted gold faceplate and a pair of sensor arrays rising from the forehead area like short horns. The small drawing of a buzzard perched on a branch was painted on the left side, the CSF Eagle logo above his name on the right. In many cases, he would have put the helmet on and finished suiting up there. Instead, he put his helmet on the bench and went to the opposite bulkhead to back into his combined primary battery and air pack, magnetically locking it to the rear of his armor.

Kwon was nearly a minute ahead of him, and had already donned his battery and air pack and returned to his locker to retrieve his helmet, reaching back to drop it on the bench. Still facing his open locker, he eyed the weapons mounted on the inside of the doors. "Ordnance?" he asked.

"Thirty minutes, Cap!" Ham shouted.

"Copy," Caleb shot back before turning his attention to Kwon. "Standard configuration. Ballistic."

"You aren't worried we'll spook whoever's down there?"

"They've been waiting years for help to arrive. I don't think humans with guns will spook them, and given we've already encountered Relyeh and can't see well into the deep canyons, we have no idea what might be waiting for *us*." He pulled a standard issue projectile sidearm from its receptacle on the right hand door and magnetically stuck it to his thigh. He turned and grabbed a coilgun from the lineup on the other door, swinging the squarish, medium-sized rifle around to magnetically attach it to the back of his pack.

Kwon did the same before leaning over to look into Caleb's locker. "I half-expected you to have ninja swords in there."

"I grabbed the wrong spacebag," Caleb replied. "Bucket on and power up. I want full diagnostics."

"Copy that," Kwon replied, picking his helmet up off the bench.

Caleb did the same. Custom-made for his head, the fit was perfect, the bucket lighter than it appeared as he pulled it on. A pair of loud clicks indicated the connectors had secured it to the locking ring. Immediately, the visor gained an augmented reality HUD similar to the neurally injected

HUD of the ship's interface. The only difference...the ATCS wasn't neurally connected, so he had to use blinking patterns and eye movements to use the system. He quickly navigated to the diagnostic screen and began running a systems analysis, searching for any potential problems that would indicate the suit wasn't space worthy.

"Fifteen minutes!" Ham announced just before the diagnostic completed. Caleb hadn't expected any problems, and none were indicated.

"Comms check," he said, activating the channel on the network the two suits created during the diagnostic. Kwon's name appeared in the upper left of his HUD, along with a small humanoid outline that was currently all green. He had the same for Caleb on his HUD. If either of them were in trouble, the system would let the other know.

"Check, check," Kwon replied. "Do you copy?"

"I copy. Comms online. Opening relay channel. Ham, do you copy?"

"Papa Buzzard has you loud and clear, Cap," Ham rumbled through the helmet's internal speakers.

"Signed and sealed," Kwon said. "Now we just need to be delivered."

"Ten minutes," Ham replied. "Better head below."

"How do the skies look?" Caleb asked.

"Clear. As long as it stays this way, we're go for drop on your order, Cap."

"Copy. We're ducking under." Rather than leave the armory through the hatch, Caleb stepped to the port side and tapped a button beside the row of three lockers. A part of the deck moved aside, revealing steps beneath. As he and Kwon descended into the belly of the ship, the deck piece slid back into place behind them.

Barely able to stand upright in the tight confines, Caleb and Kwon made their way into the caution-painted rectangle surrounding the drop doors in the hull's belly. He and Kwon stood facing one another, neither man nervous about the imminent drop. Kwon seemed as placid as the calm after a storm, but as anxious as Caleb was to solve the mystery behind Pathfinder's fate, he was practically vibrating with excitement. "We're in position, Ham."

"Copy that. Six minutes to ingress."

With the lack of atmosphere, Spirit's descent toward the surface remained smooth as silk. The only indication they were moving at all was the changing inertia, which shifted forward while they descended and decelerated.

"Two minutes," Ham said, inertia now beginning to build beneath Caleb's feet. "One minute." The G-forces lessened gradually, itself a silent countdown. "Thirty seconds…twenty…ten…"

"Here we go," Caleb said as the doors beneath them slid open, inertia all that held them in place.

"I don't see a spot to land," Kwon mentioned. "Neither does the computer."

"Four…three…"

"We'll find it on the way down."

"Two…one…"

"Cap—" Kwon started to object.

Ham reached zero, and the inertia holding them up disappeared. They fell toward the rough terrain below.

CHAPTER 7

Trappist-E, with less gravity than Earth, kept Caleb and Kwon from accelerating too quickly as they dropped vertically from Spirit. Since Ham had positioned Spirit in an optimal spot, they could freefall for another fifteen seconds, skimming marginally past the largest spire of rock spearing up from the planet's surface. Their only danger was if their compressed air systems failed and they smashed into the sharp terrain below.

Confident their systems would successfully maneuver them around obstacles to the safest landing zone near the target, Caleb's heart rate remained calm as he set his destination mark on the source of the distress beacon. He blinked rapidly four times, triggering the vectoring jets built into his pack. They spat out the expected compressed air, making sure he remained stable and upright while panels slid away from the bottom of the pack and a pair of ion thrusters fired, pulling energy from the battery to slow his descent.

Normally, with the target marked, the ride down didn't require any real skill, but in this case, the system wasn't finding a safe landing spot within its rapidly shrinking field of view. The terrain below was so rough and uneven it believed there was nowhere to land.

"I'm going manual," Caleb said, remaining calm. "Putting you on mirror."

"What?" Kwon hissed, clearly unnerved.

I bet he wet his suit already.

Rather than attempt to navigate the drop by looking down, Caleb activated the computer generated view in his HUD, shifting his view of the terrain ninety degrees so that it was like running around the obstacles rather than falling toward them. Closing his hands into fists, he used touch-sensitive pads in his gloves at the base of his palms to control the descent. Spotting an opening on the left, he squeezed the pad with his left middle finger, the wall passing to his right. Needing to shift forward, he pressed down with his index finger, and it appeared as if he had jumped onto one of the rocks. He went left again, and then a slight right, before quickly pushing down hard with his ring finger. It slowed this descent just before he hit another rise in the terrain.

Slipping to the left again, he noticed he had gone nearly three klicks off from the target. At least he was almost to the surface. Still falling, he guided the suit around the cliffs and crags as if he were playing a video game, finally getting a green mark from the computer when it spotted a long, narrow patch of ground below. Flipping the system back to auto, he rode the last ten seconds to the surface, splashing down relatively gently in ankle-deep water. Kwon's suit brought him down less than a meter away. He didn't land as smoothly, and wound up face down in the water.

Now he definitely wet his suit, Caleb quipped silently for Ishek, drawing a soft hissing laugh from the khoron. "Buzzard, we're here," Caleb announced through the comms.

"You didn't see that," Kwon said, jumping to his feet,

water shedding off the front of his helmet like the back of a duck.

"See what?" Caleb responded.

"Copy," Ham replied. "I've got you on the grid. Visual is out of the question."

Caleb looked up, unable to find Spirit past the high peaks. "Same here. Don't go anywhere."

"Copy that."

"The beacon's that way." Caleb motioned eastward, in the same direction as the flow of the stream, which went around a rock formation and disappeared from sight. He grabbed his coilgun from his back and flipped a switch on the side to turn it on. Kwon did the same. The weapons immediately linked to their ATCS, and a targeting reticle appeared on their HUDs.

"I hope we don't need to use these," Kwon said, shouldering his weapon.

"Me, too."

Caleb barely noticed the difference in gravity between Trappist-E and Earth as he started jogging, following the stream through the steep, narrow canyon. While neither sensors nor visual observation had turned up evidence of Relyeh, the fact that the enemy had obviously visited this sector in space left him unconvinced that they weren't present in force on the ground. Until he could prove otherwise, he refused to discount the possibility that this might be a trap. He knew from experience how insidious the Relyeh could be.

He ran with his rifle at ready, splitting his attention between the view through his visor and the sensor grid displayed by his HUD. It remained clear as they covered the first two kilometers between the landing zone and the target, able to remain with the stream two-thirds of the way.

For a moment, he thought maybe they could follow the

water right to the source, but it disappeared beneath a huge rock formation that blocked their advance. Pausing, Caleb didn't see an easy way around. The cliffs on both sides of the canyon were over a hundred meters high, and the open gaps on the edges beneath the boulder were too small for even Kwon to fit through.

"I guess we're going over," he said, turning to Kwon.

"Do we have power for that?" Kwon replied.

Caleb checked his battery level for his HUD. They had burned nearly thirty percent of their air coming down, and would need at least twice that to get back up to a level where Spirit could reach them for pickup. That left ten percent to navigate the terrain and power them over obstacles. "We're only one klick out. Unless the path ahead turns into an obstacle course or we need to jet away from something in a hurry, we should be good. Besides, it's not like we have a choice. The beacon is that way." He pointed ahead.

"Yes, sir."

Caleb backed up, taking a running start toward the boulder. Activating the ion thrusters, he launched off the ground, arcing up over the edge of the rock and coming down cleanly on top. He turned in time to watch Kwon mimic the maneuver. This time, he landed on his feet next to Caleb, though he hit hard enough to reach down and rub his left knee.

"We only used two percent on that one," Kwon said, checking his battery.

"Less gravity helps," Caleb added, picking the easiest path across the irregular top of the broad boulder. Looking down over the backside, he saw that the canyon continued some ten meters down, minus the stream. "Save your jets. It won't feel great, but the SCACS can handle the height."

"I was afraid you were going to say that," Kwon said.

Caleb jumped off the side of the boulder, dropping to

the canyon floor. The impact rattled up his legs, the augmented muscles of the combat armor absorbing enough of the blow to prevent injury. He immediately shouldered his rifle, scanning down range through the optical sights as Kwon hit the ground behind him.

"Damn," the corporal complained, hissing painfully. "I like my real knees. I really don't want replacements."

Caleb cast a quick look back over his shoulder. "You have to bend your knees to land, numbnuts." He looked forward again, at his grid. "The beacon should be just up ahead, around that turn in the canyon."

"It seems conveniently placed," Kwon replied.

"You mean the beacon?" Caleb asked, confused.

"No, the boulder. It clearly fell from somewhere up there." He jerked his chin upwards, indicating the jagged cliff wall to his right. "Like it was maybe pushed."

"You're thinking someone's trying to keep us away from the beacon?"

Both Marines froze as a deep, loud wail echoed from around the bend, coming directly from the vicinity of the beacon. Kwon's health monitor on Caleb's HUD moved from green to yellow, indicating a jump in his heart rate and rising levels of adrenaline and cortisol.

"Or trying to keep something in," Kwon replied.

CHAPTER 8

Caleb recovered from his initial shock, keeping his rifle trained forward, ready for something—anything—freakish to come barreling around the canyon's bend. The idea that someone had trapped a monster in the canyon seemed ridiculous. Except most Relyeh didn't need an atmosphere to survive. They didn't even need water. What if Pathfinder had been overrun by the enemy and managed to banish them here? What if the distress call wasn't a signal, but a warning?

"We aren't leaving without finding the satellite," Caleb growled, resuming his advance. Kwon moved up beside him, both Marines prepared to open fire when the danger ahead presented itself. Nearing the turn in the canyon, the wail sounded a second time, the sound carrying poorly in the limited atmosphere but loud enough to incite caution. They stopped., putting their backs flat to the canyon wall..

"What is that?" Kwon asked.

Something about the creature's wail was familiar to Caleb, but he couldn't connect it with any Relyeh noise he had ever heard. "Standby," he said, sweeping his arm out to keep Kwon pressed against the cliff face behind him and out of sight of whatever lurked around the corner. He didn't have to wait long until the sharp wail sounded again. Immediately, he navigated to the ATCS' automated mission recording and reversed it back to the first wail, scrubbing forward to each successive cry.

"Son of a bitch," he said, his mouth spreading in an amused grin.

"What is it?" Kwon asked.

"Godzilla," Caleb replied with a laugh.

"Is that a Relyeh?"

"No. Godzilla's an old Earth movie monster. I'd know that roar anywhere." He stepped away from the cliff. "It's repeating every sixty-three seconds on the dot."

Keeping his rifle at the ready despite his revelation, he moved around the corner, freezing again when he finally laid eyes on the beacon. It rested thirty meters away on the canyon floor. A wire ran from it along the ground and up the side of the cliff to a ledge, where one of the solar foils collected energy from the parent star. The other foil was positioned on a ledge on the opposite side. Its wire didn't go to the beacon, but instead to a laser targeting system mounted on a motorized tripod. Its array swept back and forth, searching.

A small transport shuttle, with a short, stubby thruster on each side, sat on a pair of anti-gravity skids just behind the tripod. Beneath the leading edge of the flight deck transparency, it bore the Union Jack followed by an identifier in faded lettering.

HMS Pathfinder

"What the hell?" Kwon said, pulling up beside Caleb. "Oh. Wow." He paused, staring at the apparent camp. "What the hell?" he repeated in confusion.

Caleb lowered his rifle, staring at the scene. "Ham, are you receiving this?" he asked.

"I'm getting it, Cap," the pilot replied. "This has to be the craziest thing I've ever seen."

Another Godzilla roar echoed through the confines of the canyon, coming from speakers that had once belonged to the transport but had been moved outside.

"Whoever lives or lived here, I guess they were trying to scare something away?" Kwon guessed.

Or hoping to warn off the Relyeh.

"Would you really fall for that?" Caleb asked Ishek.

Personally, of course not. You are aware that our kind possesses a wide range of intellect. It may be effective at convincing scouts that this territory is already claimed by one of the Ancients.

"Ish says Godzilla might be effective at scaring off stupid Relyeh," Caleb informed Kwon.

"Let's keep it playing, then," Kwon replied.

Caleb stowed his coilgun and advanced on the camp, pausing at the beacon and leaning over to touch it. Satisfied, he made a straight line to the transport, pausing at the hatch.

"Should we knock?" Kwon asked.

"Whoever was here, it's been over two hundred years. They're either dead or in stasis."

"True. Do you think they ever expected someone might actually find them?"

"Considering they went through all this trouble, it sure seems that way."

"I hope they're in stasis."

"Me, too," Caleb agreed. "They're bound to know what happened to Pathfinder." He pulled open the panel beside the hatch, revealing the manual override. When flipping the switch didn't convince the hatch to open, he tried to turn the small emergency hand crank. The ancient metal broke off in his grip, brittle from the external cold.

"Stymied by a hatch," Kwon said. "I guess I should have brought my tools down."

"I'm not giving up that easily," Caleb replied. "A little help, Ish?"

Certainly.

Caleb's body began tingling as Ishek stimulated his nervous system, forcing it to produce adrenaline. A sudden high washed over him as he put his palms against the hatch and activated his gloves' magnetic grip. Pulling sideways, he grunted as he fought the locking mechanism holding it in place. With the added strength of his combat armor and the surge of adrenaline, he won the battle, forcing the hatch aside and releasing a burst of stale air.

"Damn, Cap," Kwon said, impressed by the feat of strength. "The little slug occasionally comes in handy."

Must your lackeys always demean me?

Caleb ignored Ishtek's complaining and opened the hatch halfway before ducking his head inside. He looked to the front of the transport first, toward the flight deck. The deck of the transport was covered in MRE wrappers leading into the forward compartment, where Caleb spotted a notebook resting on the instrument panel. The sensor array appeared to be active, indicated by a pair of flashing LEDs. He assumed both it and the targeting system were used to trigger the Godzilla recording.

Turning his head the other way, he saw the seats had all been removed from the transport. The dismantled metal frames were stacked in the corner, the cushions haphazardly arranged around the rear of the craft. Most were stacked on one side, creating a comfortable-looking bed. A simple coffee maker that looked like it had come out of someone's apartment sat near the opposite bulkhead, empty bags and a handful of beans littering the deck around it.

He found the traveler last. Or rather, her remains. The

mummified corpse was propped up against the rear bulkhead beside the hatch leading to the engine room. A moldy coffee mug sat next to her left hand, a tablet computer in her right hand, which was folded over her lap. She wore a gray uniform with a name patch over her chest. *C. Benning. Lead Engineer.*

From the look of her remains, it appeared she had starved to death.

"So much for stasis," Kwon said, peeking in past Caleb and seeing the body.

Caleb entered the transport, moving to crouch in the rear in front of Benning. "These tablets were standard issue for the residents of Metro, the city inside the generation starships where the colonists lived during transit. Although, maybe the Brits called it something else besides Metro. Benning's wearing civilian coveralls, which means she was a member of the city's engineering team, not a Guardian or other military."

"So how did she end up here?" Kwon asked. "They say dead men tell no tales. What about dead women?"

The bones of Benning's frozen fingers cracked as Caleb gently unwrapped them from the tablet and picked it up. Would it still turn on? He held down the power button. The tablet didn't respond. "I'd say, let's find out, but her computer is as dead as she is."

"The ship's still trickling power," Kwon noticed, glancing toward the flight deck. "We can charge it up front."

"I can't believe the reactor's still running after all this time," Caleb said, passing him the tablet.

"It isn't," Kwon said, carrying the tablet forward to the flight deck. "The sensors are pulling from the battery. But it's a dense battery." He paused between the pilot and co-pilot seats to swipe MRE wrappers and crumbs off of them before sitting on the co-pilot side. "Benning was a slob."

"She had limited air," Caleb pointed out as he leaned against the arm of the pilot's seat. "Probably only enough to leave the ship once to set up her camp. If she hadn't starved, she would have run out of oxygen long before we got here."

"I didn't see any excrement." Kwon opened a panel on his right, extracting a connection cord and locking it into place on the tablet.

"We haven't opened the access panel to the electronics bay in the floor."

"Let's not, if we can avoid it." Kwon tapped on the tablet's screen, which showed an icon indicating it was charging. "What do you think could have happened that would convince a civilian to take an emergency beacon, launch a transport shuttle from Pathfinder, and land on a planet like this with no chance of survival?"

"I don't know," Caleb said. "Whatever happened, it seems pretty desperate." The screen on the tablet changed, indicating it had started booting. "Hopefully, we're about to find out."

CHAPTER 9

The tablet only needed a few seconds to boot before landing on a login screen. Caleb and Kwon looked at one another before glancing back at the username and password boxes.

"Stymied by credentials," Kwon commented. "We can bring the tablet back up to Spirit with us. It'll take some time but I'm sure we can brute force it."

"The software's designed to lock out for increasing periods of time after a few tries. If it takes us more than ten guesses, we'll be here for the rest of our lives. We don't have the tools onboard to disassemble it and try to work around the security."

"Another dead end?" Kwon coughed lightly after he said it. "No pun intended."

Caleb ignored him, considering the problem. His eyes landed on the notebook resting on the instrument panel. "I don't think so. Miss Benning knew she was going to die here. But the beacon suggests she expected someone to find this place someday. She also knew enough about the Relyeh to set up the Godzilla recording, which is concerning in its own right." He picked up the notebook, opening the cover.

The first page was a handwritten note, addressed to *whoever finds me*. "If she didn't leave her credentials in here, I guarantee she left them somewhere." Caleb didn't read the note, instead flipping through the pages, searching for the info he needed to unlock the tablet. The interior pages were stuffed with a mixture of advanced mathematics, notes, technical drawings, and more creative renders. Even just a cursory look revealed that C. Benning was an incredible artist, in addition to her obvious intelligence. "Not here. Go check the back. She might have written it on an old coffee bag or MRE wrapper, or etched it into the bulkhead so there would be no risk it would wear away."

Kwon stood to return to the rear. "She should have just turned the tablet security off, or at least taped the credentials to the back. Why'd she have to make this so hard?"

"Maybe she was concerned the Relyeh would find this place first and that her makeshift warning wouldn't work. It seems whatever's on the tablet, she didn't want it falling into the wrong hands."

"The plot sickens. She seems to have left copious notes in her log."

"Of limited usefulness, I would imagine. We have six hours of oxygen before we need to leave. Let's not waste any of it."

"Yes, sir." Kwon stepped off of the flight deck, pausing beside the open hatch. "Cap, do you hear that?"

Caleb paused to listen. "I don't hear anything."

"Exactly. I guess the roar stopped because we're inside the ship." He shrugged and then turned to continue to the rear, stopping again. "I really hope Benning didn't hide the credentials in her toilet."

Caleb could hear him rifling through the garbage and moving the cushions while he returned to the letter at the front of the journal and started reading.

Whoever finds me,

My name is Charlotte Benning. I am (soon to be was) the head of Metro Engineering. It was a job I was literally born to do, a descendant of Claire Benning, who was also the head of Metro Engineering, and so on back to Charles Benning, who boarded the HMS Pathfinder one fateful day over a hundred years ago, having survived the invasion and joined the expedition in hopes of a better life for himself and his children. But that's all ancient history you probably already know, assuming you're human.

I'm guessing you followed the beacons here, as I intended. You've probably already gotten a look at my corpse. I hope I still look presentable. Without oxygen, heat or bacteria, I imagine I should be mummified. Yes, I'm going to starve to death. I figured I would run out of food, water, or air. I just didn't know which one would go first. I'm sure you're wondering why a person would sacrifice themselves in this way. Perhaps you're wondering if it was some grand gesture for the good of the colony and the ship. I wish that were the case. Maybe then I wouldn't have to die so bitter and angry. The truth of the matter is, I left because I had to leave. The only other option for me was the brig.

My crime?

Knowing the truth.

Not about the Hunger, or the Relyeh as they prefer to name themselves. Though you may or may not know that I had to do some very illegal things to come across mention of the alien race who laid waste to our home world. If I hadn't already been wanted for murder, perhaps that indiscretion would have landed me in prison instead. No matter. Knowing what the military knew allowed me to prepare as best I could. I always loved the idea of Godzilla. A monster who seemed to be an enemy to humankind, but was actually a friend of man, trying to save us from ourselves. I'm laughing as I write this. You probably don't even know who Godzilla is. In that case, it might as well be me.

I escaped custody to get here. I had help on the inside, but I won't say who. I doubt that it matters now. I had to leave, even though it meant my death. I had to believe that one day, someone would read this letter and flip through this notebook. I had to believe that even if I couldn't save the people I loved the most, even if I couldn't save myself, I could communicate across time and space to warn you of the dangers this system holds.

I dare not say more. Not in the open like this. I don't know who was involved, or how, or why. All I dare say is that Trappist-1 wasn't chosen for our ship at random, and the fate of Pathfinder was no accident. They knew, and they had an agenda.

If you'll excuse me, my coffee is ready (and yes, I know. I'm British, so I should drink tea. I much prefer coffee).

See you in the afterlife,

Charlotte Benning

She signed the letter with a flourish that guided the C and B halfway across the handwritten text. Caleb stared at the note, his gaze catching on a few choice words.

Bitter and angry. Crime. Murder. They had an agenda.

He had hoped coming here would provide answers. Instead, there were only more questions. Foremost was that Charlotte was a loose cannon who went to great lengths for whatever she believed in, possibly to the extent that she had murdered someone. Could anything she said be trusted?

Caleb leaned back in his seat. It was too bad Sheriff Duke wasn't here. He would know what to do with a mystery like this. Caleb was a warrior and explorer. A scout. Solving riddles wasn't his forte. Even growing up, he never had patience for them.

He paged through the notebook again, much more slowly this time. The mathematics scribbled onto nearly every page was meaningless to him. The diagrams were only slightly more comprehensible. He understood the creative artwork better. One was a self-portrait of Charlotte as she saw herself in the reflection of the forward transparency. She had been at least forty pounds heavier when she did the drawing, her face more round, her eyes full of life, her determination clear in her expression. She certainly didn't look like she couldn't be trusted.

Turning more pages, he smiled at the whimsical drawings of unicorns and fairies that speckled the paper amidst the algorithms and diagrams, his eyes glossing over whenever he tried to make heads or tails of the math. His best guess, based on the drawings, was that it had something to do with Trappist-1's star, but he couldn't begin to guess what.

There was more information on the tablet. He was sure of it. Charlotte herself had said she couldn't say more in the open. From her other veiled suggestions, Caleb wondered if she thought Pathfinder might circle back for her. Of course, if that were the case, then it would mean the generation ship never lost helm control and could be somewhere nearby. Or maybe she'd believed a second ship might come, trailing Pathfinder. A human ship. But that couldn't be possible. Could it?

"Kwon, sitrep," he said, leaning sideways to look into the rear of the transport. He found Kwon leaning over Benning, checking the cuffs of her coveralls as well as her wrists, still searching for the logic credentials for the tablet. "Kwon?"

Possibly feeling Caleb's eyes on him, Kwon stopped what he was doing and looked back. "Still looking, Cap. Nothing so far, and I've turned most of this place over while you've been leafing through the notebook. There's really only one other place left, and I do not want to go there."

"You can't smell it. It's got to be pretty dry by now."

"I still don't want to stick my gloves in it. No thank you. Not until it's the absolute last resort." He turned back to Charlotte, checking the collar of her coveralls before moving on to her boots. He took them off one at a time, reaching into them to feel for a piece of paper before peering in, making sure she hadn't written the information inside. Finally, he sighed. "I guess that's it, then."

He turned away from the body, crawling across the deck to the center, where the latch for the subdeck access was located. He paused to look at Caleb, eyes likely pleading for a reprieve behind his tinted faceplate. Caleb didn't plan to give him one, but one more idea hit him before Kwon could remove the cover.

"Jii, move the body away from the bulkhead," he said.

Kwon looked back at Charlotte. "You don't think?"

"The woman was starving to death. She would have been incredibly weak. Yet, instead of lying down, she died sitting up."

Kwon returned to the corpse, easily shifting it out of the way. "Cap, you're a genius," he said, shifting her enough to reveal the credentials scratched into the bulkhead. "Username, *Charles*. Password, *Coffeeismycupoft3a*. The first letter is capitalized, and the e in tea is a three. No spaces."

Caleb picked up the tablet from the co-pilot seat, entering the credentials in the box. "Yes!" Caleb cried when the screen gave way to the tablet's primary interface. "We're in."

CHAPTER 10

Successfully logging into the tablet and knowing what to look for on it were two very different things. It left Caleb staring at the screen, uncertain how to proceed. Kwon returned to the shuttle's flight deck and sat down in the co-pilot's seat, leaning toward Caleb so he could see the tablet too.

"Check the video files," he suggested. "She might have kept a mission log, same as you."

"I should have thought of that," Caleb said.

"That's why you picked Ham and me. You can't think of everything yourself. Besides, at least you know how to work that thing," he added as Caleb navigated through the screens to the video recordings. "Talk about antiques."

"I grew up with more primitive tech than this," Caleb replied. "But you're right." He scrolled through the list of files. "You're right about the video logs, too. This thing's packed with them. I don't know where to start."

"Close your eyes and point?" Kwon suggested. "Or start at the end and work backward?"

"Both methods could take awhile to find what we're looking for."

"Maybe we should head back to Spirit now. We'll have plenty of time to figure it out where we don't need to worry as much about oxygen."

Caleb glanced up at Kwon. "Yeah, you're probably right. This could take hours to sift through."

"Give me some time, and I can link this thing's data storage to the ship's computer. It can build a summary for us."

"It can?" Caleb asked.

Kwon grinned. "I know you don't pay much attention to technology. Yes, it can."

"You should have said so in the first place." Caleb was ready to stand when he caught a glimpse of one of the video files. It sat about a third of the way from the most recent log, the still frame filled with Charlotte Benning's clearly thinning face. A subtitle at the bottom of the frame read *Summary*. "Hold up. I think Charlotte may have done the computer's work for us already." He showed Kwon the thumbnail.

"She thought of everything, I guess," he replied.

Caleb tapped on the image, opening the recording. It appeared to have been taken with the tablet propped up by something on the deck, with Charlotte sitting cross-legged in front of it. Her coveralls hung loosely on her shrinking frame, her face sunken and sallow, skin jaundiced. She didn't look good at all.

"Day one hundred and twelve," she said softly, looking down at the tablet. She had a light, raspy voice like a chain-smoking chipmunk, though the composure of the thin atmosphere also played a role in altering the sound. A caption with the date appeared at the bottom of the recording as well. "Congratulations to whoever's watching this. You must have found my login. I'm probably not as clever as I think I am and it wasn't all that hard." She chuckled lightly. "I ran out of food twenty-one days ago.

My water supply is getting low, too. I don't know how much time I have left. It certainly wouldn't do to force you to sit through all my ramblings to understand what happened to Pathfinder, or why I did what I did. To speak about torturous circumstances. Ugh." She rolled her eyes and smiled. Immediately, Caleb felt an affinity to her. She had surely been a spitfire during her life. "Consider this the cheat sheet version of everything you can watch in painful detail on the rest of the vids, and an overview of the data stored on this device to back up my claims. Everything I'm about to say can be proven, though I imagine some of it will come across as too fantastical to believe, which is what got me into this entire mess in the first place. Not because my cold, hard, irrefutable proof would never be enough to convince a mind unwilling to bend. Rather it's because that unbending mind had solved the equation long before I did."

"That sounds ominous," Kwon commented.

"And a little too familiar," Caleb added, thinking back to his experience on the generation ship Deliverance.

"Since this is a summary, I won't bore you with all of the gory details, but I will provide some basic background. As you've already learned, I was the top engineer in the Metro Engineering Department. As such, I had full access to all of the systems needed to keep Metro humming during my lifetime of transit, which excitedly for me, was due to culminate with our arrival and settlement in the Trappist-1 system. As you know, we did arrive. But my excitement was short-lived. Two months before we neared the outer reaches of the system, nearly seven months ago now, a malfunction in one of the containment door servos led me to run full diagnostics on them. With our journey nearly over, the military contingent was newly out of stasis and the ship's Guardians were preparing to reassume control prior to establishing an atmospherically sound settlement.

Mayor Pine tried to convince me not to bother. Normally a bland procedure, this diagnostic sent me down the proverbial rabbit hole. I discovered that the malfunctioning containment hatch had been installed with a controller that didn't match any of the others. It lacked the hardware needed to trigger usage warnings within Systems Control."

Benning paused there, as if waiting for a shocked reaction from whoever was watching. Kwon wouldn't understand what that revelation meant for the generation ship, but Caleb did. He just wasn't as surprised as she might have expected.

"The separation between the military and civilian population had clearly not been maintained in accordance with the bylaws of the colony," Benning continued. "Someone, or perhaps multiple someones, had been entering and exiting Metro at will for almost the entire duration of the trip. I considered approaching the mayor with my findings, but after he had attempted to dissuade me from examining the door controls more closely I didn't believe I could rule him out as the potential rule-breaker." She paused, her intensely focused expression fading to a more defeated frown. "And perhaps I should have let sleeping dogs lie. If I had, I wouldn't be in this situation today. My Charlie would still have his mother." She fell silent for a few seconds before regaining her stiff upper lip. "But when evil is afoot, someone needs to show the courage to fight back against it."

"Didn't she say she wasn't going to bore us with all the details?" Kwon asked, growing impatient. "How long is this recording, anyway?"

Caleb checked the time on the tablet. "Nearly an hour."

"Maybe we can scrub forward a little?"

"I don't want to miss anything."

"We can review it all in full later, can't we? Right now, we just need to know where the heck Pathfinder is."

Caleb nodded after brief consideration. He dragged the time forward, advancing through the recording until Charlotte held up one of the pages of her notebook. It contained a heavy dose of math and a diagram of what he had taken to be a funnel. He backed the recording up a little to catch her at the beginning of the section pertaining to it.

"...been very good with using my finger to draw, which is the main reason why I brought the notebook." She lifted it up. "This is the mathematical proof that the anomaly exists. If you go back to the first page of equations, you'll see that's where I plugged in the initial data as relayed by the navigation computer's scans. I've already explained how I came about the discovery of a secret government faction known only as the Organization and how they were implanted within the RSF. It turned out that they had already mapped the anomaly. Even more damning, their work predated not only the launch of Pathfinder, but also the invasion of Earth. If you look here, the anomaly manifests as an expanding spiral within the fabric of time and space. A reverse funnel, if you will."

Caleb made a face at that. He had read the diagram backwards.

"What isn't in this drawing is that the spiral has a mirror image on the other side. I know what you're thinking. The other side of what?" She smiled. "That's the perfect question, and the answer is simple. The universe."

"There's nothing simple about that," Kwon said.

Caleb didn't reply, engrossed by the recording.

"This diagram and accompanying math are irrefutable proof of the existence of wormholes. But this, ladies and gentlemen, is not your typical Einstein-Rosen bridge." She laughed lightly, perhaps expecting Caleb and Kwon to do the same. "This is a variation nobody had theorized before, at least not publicly. The only way this form of passage can be algorithmically resolved is through the assumption of interuniversal travel. In other words, this wormhole crosses into a parallel universe, or perhaps between two parallel universes, and then returns to the original universe." She turned the notebook to look at her drawing. "Perhaps I should have drawn a Slinky instead. Charlotte Benning's Slinky Equation of Much-faster-than-light Travel." She laughed again. Caleb wondered if she might have been getting a little punch drunk due to her lack of food. Regardless, the revelation sent a chill down his spine.

"Did she just suggest that Pathfinder is on the other end of the universe?" Kwon whispered in disbelief.

"It sure seems that way."

"At least, this is what it should have looked like," Benning continued. "The diagram the Organization created was correct. The mathematical equation was not. What they believed they were getting was a Slinky. What they calculated instead was a one-way trip to a fiery demise. I tried to warn them. I tried to tell them it was a mistake, and they were putting the lives of every man, woman, and child on Pathfinder at risk. I told them I didn't care about their plans to drag Pathfinder across the universe. Trappist had already proven to be less hospitable than hoped, and what was one pimple on the ass of existence versus another, anyway? But they only cared that I had figured them out. They only cared about their stupid little secrets. They believed I'd fabricated my equations to convince them to remain on this side of the galaxy, closer to home. Damn Colonel Haji and his arrogance for damning me. And damn him double for damning every civilian on Pathfinder, including my boy." Tears welled and streamed down her cheeks, and she lowered her head into her hands to sob while still recording.

"That doesn't sound good," Kwon said.

Caleb nodded. "Let's see how this ends." He scrubbed

forward again, bypassing the rest of her tears and stopping the video only a minute from the end.

"...watching this, I implore you to heed my warning. They tried to navigate Pathfinder into the wormhole and failed. The ship and all souls on board were lost. I came here, I gave my life not only so you might know the truth, but also so that you won't make the same mistake they did. So that you won't throw your lives needlessly away. Even with my Slinky equation, the wormhole is too unstable to traverse. There's no telling where or when you'll emerge, and even if you do survive, it's impossible to come back. Whatever thoughts you might have had of benefiting from the anomaly, forget about them. If you don't know of the Organization, be careful. They know more than they'll ever let on. They know the invasion of Earth was no accident. I have no proof, but I suspect they may have even caused it. If you're part of the Organization, to hell with you for your reckless stupidity. For your arrogant superiority, and for the murder of over forty-thousand souls. Their blood is on your hands. Was the risk worth the reward?"

The recording ended abruptly there, with Benning's furious visage haunting the final frame. Caleb and Kwon remained silent, mentally trying to sew together the different pieces of the narrative they had listened to and come to grips with the warning Charlotte Benning had delivered. Caleb might have remained in that thoughtful frame of mind for longer, but a different sound at the edge of his consciousness dragged him alert.

"Kwon!" he snapped. The other Marine flinched, breaking out of his own thoughts and immediately catching on.

"Is that?" Kwon started to ask.

"Godzilla," Caleb finished, pivoting toward the half-open entrance hatch.

He came face-to-face with a monster.

CHAPTER 11

Large and humanoid in shape—with dark, chitinous flesh, big hands terminating in curved, serrated claws, and a small frog-like face with no obvious eyes—the creature moved fast.

Caleb moved faster.

He began unloading his sidearm into the creature, firing round after round into its face and chest as it stretched an arm toward him through the open hatch. The bullets failed to penetrate the hard skin of its chest, the slugs either bouncing off or embedding superficially. He had better luck blasting its face, some of the rounds exiting out through the back of its skull. It took one final swing at Caleb as it fell, the claws nearly stabbing through his boot as it fell dead at his feet.

Too close.

As another roar echoed through the canyon, Caleb snagged a fresh magazine from his belt and quickly swapped out the empty, holstering the pistol. He was too slow bringing up his rifle.

"Duck!" Kwon shouted as another frog charged toward

the open hatch. Caleb was barely able to jerk back as Kwon's well-placed rifle burst took it down.

More roars reverberated off the canyon walls as Caleb nodded this thanks to Kwon. He knew there were probably a dozen more of these creatures closing in on the shuttle. Maybe more.

They were Relyeh. Caleb was sure of it. They had all the tell-tale markings. Demonic appearance, dark flesh, sharp claws, no fear. He'd just never seen ones quite like them.

Rezca. Similar to your trife, but better suited for environments like this one. Diggers. They must have a nest nearby. Their skin is tough, but their heads are vulnerable.

"Thank you, Captain Obvious," Caleb told Ishek as he poked his head out of the hatch, his next target presenting itself as a claw came at him from above. He twisted away from it, swinging his rifle straight up and firing point-blank into the face of a creature crouched on the ledge just above the shuttle. He jumped back inside before the heavy body could land on top of him. He glanced at his HUD to get a count of the enemy the ATCS had captured. Thirty-eight. The overwhelming numbers was also a Relyeh specialty.

"Cap, what the hell is going on down there?" Ham cried, the ATCS syncing with Spirit's systems. "My sensors are clear, and I can't see a damn thing in that canyon."

"Some uninvited guests stopped by for dinner," Caleb replied. "We're making a break for the LZ. Be ready for a quick pickup."

"Copy that. I'll be there. Don't get dead."

Caleb fired on a few more of the frogs as they closed on the shuttle, moving back and reloading while Kwon took his place to pick off the incoming demons like fish in a barrel. It didn't matter if they killed all thirty-eight. Caleb knew from experience there would be more.

They just hadn't arrived yet.

"Why aren't they afraid of the big G anymore?" Kwon complained, picking off another Relyeh.

"You don't want to know," Caleb growled in reply. He didn't take his eyes off the incoming creatures, firing between Kwon and the doorway to bring down another two.

"I kind of do," Kwon countered, killing three more.

You should tell him. We will enjoy the taste of his fear.

"Later," Caleb promised, sweeping the oncoming assault for an opening to punch through.

You are no fun.

"Cap, we can't stay here much longer," Kwon said, downing two more. "They're multiplying."

Caleb checked his HUD again. Despite nearly a dozen kills, the thirty-eight had grown closer to fifty, as he had guessed it would. "I'll take the tablet," he said. Kwon didn't hand it to him, but rather stuck it to the side of Caleb's magnetized battery pack. "On my mark, take off and run up to the ledge with the solar foil. You'll have a good angle to lay down cover fire. I'll come out shooting and create a line up the middle. Once it's open, you join me there."

"Seriously? How are you going to cut through the center of that?"

"Watch and learn," Caleb replied with a smirk. He wasn't trying to sound arrogant. He just had enough experience to know what he could handle. And as frightening and overwhelming as a slick of Relyeh could be, they were dumb as as a bucket of nails. They needed large numbers to stand a chance against a smarter, more agile opponent. "Step aside and get ready." He swapped places at the hatch with Kwon, opening fire and concentrating his attack to the right side of the oncoming slick. He ripped through the rezca with consistent headshots, one after another, until he opened the barest path for Kwon. "Now!"

Kwon didn't hesitate. He burst from the transport,

leaping the dead rezca's sprawled leg and sprinting toward the ledge with armor-enhanced speed. A handful of the Relyeh changed course to follow him. He sprayed them with gunfire, the roughness of his run ruining his aim, his slugs smacking the creatures in their protected chests until he zeroed in on their heads. Nearing the ledge, he engaged his jump thrusters, launching up to the ledge where the solar foil sat. Landing cleanly, thanks to the ATCS, he poured bullets into the chasing creatures, solidifying his position.

"Help me out here, Ish," Caleb said. "Kwon, I'm marking targets for you."

"Copy," Kwon replied.

Beast mode activated.

Ishek used his connection to Caleb's nervous system to force his body into immediately producing a massive amount of adrenaline. At the same time, he injected some additional chemicals to add a little more help. Within seconds, Caleb started tingling from his shoulders down into his feet. His senses heightened, the universe around him seeming to slow down. He had been a top tier Marine before he and Ish bonded. With Ish, his abilities surged to virtually superhuman.

"Kwon, take them out," he ordered. Right away, the Relyeh he had marked for the other man began to fall, hit with perfectly aimed single round headshots that told him Kwon had found his sweet spot.

Caleb exploded out of the transport, his rifle wreaking carnage, two rounds punching into each of his targets, just in case his first shot missed its mark. None of them did.

The battlefield around him moved as if it were drenched in knee deep molasses, the frog-like aliens unable to zero in on him as he charged up the middle like a hall of fame full-back, the creatures around him dropping like flies. His peripheral vision caught sight of claws coming at his head, but they were moving so slowly he felt like he could have painted the creature's nails before they could contact his helmet. Easily ducking aside, he buried the butt of his rifle in the creature's abdomen and lifted the demon up, throwing it into the one next to it. The two of them pitched over like bowling pins.

Caleb dived, tucking his head down and rolling between two more creatures to come up shooting point-blank into the side of one's skull and then the other. Another Relyeh came up behind him, but Kwon dropped it before Caleb could swing his rifle around to nail it himself.

He sidestepped another swipe and grabbed the offending arm in his free hand. With a sharp pull, he lifted the creature and knocked it down long enough to shove his rifle against its head and squeeze the trigger. Quickly reaching for his sidearm, he smashed one of the demons in the head with his rifle and put a bullet through its mouth with his pistol. The slug came out of the back of its head, and it dropped like a rock.

Leaving a trail of dead Relyeh in his wake, he turned to find himself in the clear. "Let's go, Kwon!" he shouted.

The Corporal immediately fired his jump thrusters, leaping the twenty-meter gap between himself and Caleb while dropping six more creatures before he landed. He smirked at Caleb. "Talk about jealous. I'm good, but hot damn, you're a superhero, Cap!"

Doesn't he know it's all me?

"Now's our chance," Caleb replied, ignoring both Kwon's and Ishek's remarks. "We can outrun them to the LZ."

"I'm right behind you," Kwon answered, sprinting behind him.

Caleb's HUD still showed twenty-seven Relyeh on his threat display, the count quickly increasing as they raced back toward the large boulder he now assumed Benning had somehow managed to place there. The rezca trailed behind them, unwilling to let their quarry escape.

Caleb and Kwon triggered their jump thrusters, arcing up to the top of the boulder and maintaining momentum as they darted across it. Reaching the far end, what they saw awaiting them on the other side was enough to send nauseating spurts of adrenaline coursing through their veins. They both fell to their knees, friction helping them slide to a stop before they went over the edge and fell into the many jaws of death.

"A xaxkluth?" Kwon said, as surprised as Caleb to see one of the creatures here.

Large enough to scale the boulder with ease, it was one of the most common support units in the Relyeh's arsenal. This one was only a medium-sized version compared to others he had encountered, but it was still plenty big enough to cause them all kinds of trouble.

Numerous thick, ten-meter length tentacles stretched out from its large, round center mass. In the middle of that center mass, a huge gaping mouth was stuffed with multiple layers of grinding teeth. Dark and foreboding, a multitude of eyes ran along the top of the bulging mass over its maw. Dozens of its oozing suckers slapped sloppily against the rock. One of its long limbs stretched out toward them, revealing a smaller but equally disgusting mouth mounted at its end.

We can't defeat this one and the rezca with the firepower we have.

Once again, Ishek had stated the obvious. "Fall back," Caleb grunted.

"Fall back to where?" Kwon asked, the pair jumping up and backpedaling away from the xaxkluth only to skid to a stop, the rezca behind them and the xaxkluth in front of them.

Despite the seemingly impossible situation, Caleb's

experience helped him remain calm despite the seemingly impossible situation. Nobody could work their way out of anything if they lost their head. "How much power do you think is left in the transport's batteries?"

"Cap, you can't seriously—"

"Do you have a better idea?"

"I wish to hell I did."

"Ham, the LZ's out of reach," Caleb announced. "Stick tight overhead; this is going to get dicey."

CHAPTER 12

"*Get* dicey?" Kwon said in response to Caleb's statement. "I think we're already well past dicey and approaching pureed."

"Damn, Cap," Ham declared, "I wish I could get a clear view down there so I could help you out."

"Just keep your eyes peeled for incoming Relyeh ships."

"Copy that. Skies are still clear."

"Kwon, we need to get back to the transport. Stay close behind me."

"Yes, sir," Kwon replied.

"Ish, keep me juiced."

Our physiology can only handle so much.

"We're both dead otherwise. Keep me juiced."

One of the xaxkluth's tentacles slapped down on the rock just in front of Caleb, forcing him to hop back to avoid its barbed tip and the sharp mouth behind it. Rather than shoot the appendage, he dashed back toward the transport, body tingling as a fresh round of stimulants coursed through him. Pausing at the boulder's back edge, he kicked the rezca in the head that was about to crest the top, knocking it to the ground. Several more, with at least two dozen right behind them, scrambled over the fallen rezca, advancing on the boulder. Caleb wasn't sure he could get himself and Kwon back to the transport through such a huge pack of aliens.

He had to try.

Checking his HUD, he saw his pack had thirty-eight percent of its energy stores remaining. Kwon's pack would be virtually the same. If they were to have any chance of reaching the transport, they would need to burn most of that energy on their jump thrusters. If the transport didn't have the power needed to get off the surface, they would be completely out of options. Double down, or come up with Plan C? He didn't have much time to decide.

"Kwon, we're bouncing off the canyon walls," he said, making his decision. "Burn all your thrust if you need to. It's do or die time."

"Copy that," Kwon replied, an edge of fear in his voice.

I can taste it. I hunger.

"You just ate," Caleb grunted to Ishek as he took two steps to the edge of the boulder and pushed off, jumping at an angle that carried him toward the side of the canyon. Kwon stuck tight behind him, following the trail the ATCS painted for him on his faceplate. Caleb triggered his thrusters at the halfway point, drawing his legs up and turning nearly sideways as he neared the opposite rock wall. When he landed, his armor absorbed the majority of the impact instead of his legs, allowing him to push off the wall. In this way, he ping-ponged from one side of the canyon to the other. Only a few seconds behind him, Kwon matched his maneuver, managing to duplicate Caleb's rebounds with nearly equal precision.

The constant burn of their thrusters kept them well above the heads of the rezca, but depleted their packs in a hurry. By Caleb's calculations, the number of hops they would need to make it back to Benning's shuttle would leave them nearly out of power.

Nearing the transport, he risked a glance back at the boulder to see the xaxkluth pull its central mass over the top edge of it. The huge monster was still about twenty seconds behind Kwon. Not a lot, but he would take what they could get.

Caleb checked his HUD. The system counted nearly a hundred of the frog-faced creatures churning in the canyon below. More were still bubbling up from the presumed underground caverns through the pair of small holes in the base of the rock near the turn in the canyon. Glancing up, he noticed the tallest spire was relatively thin. He blinked twice to mark the upper portion of the pinnacle before looking back at the canyon wall to time his next leap.

Bouncing off it, he was halfway back across the canyon when Kwon suddenly cried out, jerking his attention back the other way. Caleb spotted the other Marine spinning out of control and plummeting toward the ground. He watched Kwon open fire on the rezca just below him, temporarily clearing a landing spot for himself. Caleb looked up, marking the coordinates he needed and immediately cut his own thrust, altering course to head for Kwon.

"Ham, I need two EWs, asap," he barked, quickly adding the coordinates.

"Bombs away," Ham replied almost before Caleb had finished giving the order.

Not bothering to take aim, Caleb opened fire on the rezca scrambling to get to Kwon. His rounds chewed into the creatures, but Caleb feared his firepower combined with Kwon's wasn't going to be enough to keep the creatures at bay until help arrived from above.

Landing next to Kwon, Caleb heard the missiles hit, the reverberations rolling through the canyon, but he was too busy clubbing the two rezca immediately in front of him with his empty rifle to look up. With a crunching groan, the rock column lost integrity and began to give way.

Pulling his sidearm, he shot two more creatures in the face as Kwon backed up closer to him, blasting another demon point-blank. "Reloading," Caleb announced, needing four seconds to holster his pistol, drop the spent magazine and replace it with a fresh one to continue shooting. "We need to move!" he shouted, the falling rock column heading straight for them, so close now that it blotted out the light of the star.

Small rocks began raining down on them as Caleb lunged forward, shooting one Relyeh and elbowing another aside. Swiping claws scraped his armor, but he forced his way through the creatures toward the transport. Kwon backpedaled right behind him, his rifle spewing bullets.

They were only ten meters away now. Anyone could cover ten meters through a slick. At least, that's what Caleb told himself.

Larger pieces of rock came down behind them, taking down the nearest of the pursuing rezca and allowing Caleb and Kwon to smash through the enemy line in front of them. They covered half the last ten meters to the shuttle as the major portion of the rock spire hit the canyon floor, shaking the ground and crushing dozens of Relyeh beneath it. The spire crumpled in a billowing cloud of dust and debris, the resulting rock pile closing off their entrance tunnel from the caverns below.

The cloud of dust and debris quickly enveloped Caleb and Kwon, robbing them of visibility. Caleb's ATCS immediately outlined the surrounding enemy. Apparently lacking eyes, the rezca had no problem with the cloud. If anything, their attack intensified.

A burst of pain stung Caleb as one of the rezca broke through his armor and sliced into his forearm. Immediately, his skin began to burn from the caustic atmosphere, calming a moment later as the underlay self-healed the puncture. He grabbed the arm of his attacker and pulled it toward him, coming face to face with it before Kwon shot it in the side of the head. The creature dropped to the ground, and Caleb pushed through the final stretch to the transport's entrance. It was only then that he noticed Kwon's health meter had gone orange, indicating he was injured.

At the entrance to the transport, he turned to see that Kwon's armor was torn open across his side, raked by a demon's claws. The underlay had already healed to protect his skin from the atmosphere, and the pressure it would put on the wounds would help stem the blood flow, but Caleb knew it had to be a much worse wound than his own. Although, with the adrenaline that had to be flowing through him, he doubted his fellow Marine felt much pain. At least not yet.

"I'll keep the bastards honest. See if you can get this thing started," Caleb ordered as Kwon passed in front of him, slipping inside the shuttle. Rather than rush to the flight deck, he went immediately to the rear, opening the hatch to the engines. "What are you doing?" Caleb asked, as he fired on the rezca rushing their position.

"The battery has a reserve management feature to ensure there's always enough juice left to start the reactor. I'm checking to see if Benning manually overrode it."

"Why not just use the key and see if she turns over?"

"Not sure what that means, but this is what they teach at the Academy."

Caleb blasted another incoming creature. With the debris cloud beginning to clear, he could see the thick pile of rubble a short distance away, along with the dead creatures it had left behind. The attack had thinned out considerably, enough so that he was certain that as long as the transport had power, they could get away.

"Bad news, Cap. She overrode the reserve power."

The five words stole Caleb's confidence in an instant. All of that effort, and they had wound up right back where they'd started, except injured and running low on both battery power and ammunition. At least they were still alive. "Options?" he asked, refusing to panic.

"If I'm getting the gist, use the key and see if she turns over."

"Go for it," Caleb answered, shooting two more rezca as Kwon bolted for the flight deck.

Our fate comes down to pure chance. I am greatly amused.

"That makes one of us." Caleb hissed, aiming and firing at another demon. A flash of red on his HUD informed him his rifle was again empty. He quickly dropped the magazine out and replaced it. The few seconds it took gave one of the Relyeh time to lunge at him. He caught its mouth with the muzzle of his rifle and fired as he moved aside, the force of the blast nearly blowing its head off as it crashed into the transport.

"She isn't turning over!" Kwon shouted, growing panicked in his voice now that they appeared to be stranded.

Mmmmm. Delicious.

Caleb cursed under his breath. The only good news was that between his gunfire and the collapsed rock formation, he'd whittled the remaining rezca down to under two dozen. He would have considered it much more of a victory, except a large tentacle exploded out of the haze, slapping to the ground only a few meters short of the transport.

For the first time, Caleb was tempted to panic right along with Kwon. He fought against the urge, keeping his eyes on the enemy. "How much power do we have?"

"Not enough to reach orbit. Not even close," Kwon replied, his voice breathy, shaking. Caleb knew he was starting to feel his wound, but right now, there was nothing he could do about it.

"Keep trying to engage the engines!" He knew they at least needed to get off the ground, and they needed to do it sooner than later.

The xaxkluth's appendage and huge central mass with its gaping maw appeared out of the dust. It hadn't escaped the collapse unscathed. Two of its limbs had been severed, and it wasn't happy about it.

"Do we have enough power to get us out of this frecking canyon?" Caleb asked.

"Well...maybe!" Kwon said, suddenly excited by the prospect of escape. "The only thing we can do is try."

"Then do it," Caleb snapped. "One punch of thrust, and throw the rest into the anti-gravity plates."

"Copy that. Hold onto your butt. On three."

"Forget three, just go!" Caleb shouted as the xaxkluth shifted forward, swinging its limb, mouth snapping, at the transport. He maglocked his boots to the deck and his free hand to the ceiling just ahead of a sudden loud hiss and ion burn from the thrusters. A thrumming vibration started beneath his feet, and the shuttle began to ascend. When Caleb glanced forward, nothing but a solid wall of rock filled the forward surround and then a sliver of sky.

"Come on, baby. You can do it!" Kwon screamed. Caleb could picture him with his hands locked to the controls, knuckles white, trying to will the shuttle up and over the wall of rock right in front of it.

Caleb's stomach clenched when it appeared a collision was unavoidable. He barely noticed the xaxkluth's long tentacle, streaking upward toward the transport, trying to pluck it from the atmosphere. Swinging his rifle one-handed back in its direction, he opened fire, bullets ripping into the end of the limb. It writhed and turned away from the assault, giving up on its quest just as the shuttle's skids scraped over the top of the rock wall.

Looking down, Caleb let out a relieved breath the moment he saw the edge of the canyon pass beneath them. Battery spent, the anti-gravity plates shut off and the shuttle began dropping back toward the surface. Within feet of setting down, he heard another scraping sound before the ship flipped violently, stern over nose, leaving Caleb swinging by his feet as the ship slammed upside down into the ground. The impact crushed the domed top inward as the craft came to rest. Before he even stopped swinging, he exhaled in relief, only for the ship to begin slowly tilting forward.

"Off!" Kwon shouted, running awkwardly past him, hand clutching at the three rips in his overlay. The shift in weight as he stumbled toward the still open hatch, stabilized the ship's critical balance long enough for Caleb to release his maglock, tuck his shoulder, and flip in midair to land on the shuttle's crushed dome. The little ship teetered with his weight change and then started sliding forward. He broke into a run, leaping through the hatch right behind Kwon, his back foot still leaving the hatch as the ship pitched over the edge. Dropping thirty meters, it crashed into the rocky gully below with an echoing crunch.

"Too close," Kwon wheezed, peering down over the edge at the wrecked shuttle.

"Cap, I've got visual," Ham announced as Spirit swung over the top of a nearby formation. "Can you get to me?"

"We're damn well going to try," Caleb replied, checking his HUD. He still had eight percent in his battery. It would have to be enough.

Caleb's stomach dropped as Kwon's orange status circle on Caleb's HUD suddenly flashed red. He turned just as Kwon dropped to his knees. Even though his underlay had sealed, keeping out the elements, what had to be deep wounds, with probable internal damage, to his side were still there, still bleeding his life away..

"Cap...go," Kwon said, beginning to fall forward.

Caleb caught him, hefting him up in a fireman's carry. "Not gonna happen, buddy." He shifted Kwon's weight, getting him in a better position as he took a step, breaking into a run toward the edge of the gully, aiming for the other side and its rocky incline.

"You don't...have battery... for the...weight," Kwon managed to grunt out.

"Then I'll climb us up by hand," Caleb grunted back. Hanging onto Kwon with one hand, he fired his jump thrusters as he leaped. Needing double the power for nearly double the weight, he burned half his power to land just ten percent of the way up the slope.

He would have to climb the rest of the way.

He didn't hesitate or complain, dropping his rifle to pick his way up the sharp incline. It took every bit of his natural strength in conjunction with that of his armor to make his way up to where the slope became more severe. And more rugged. He stopped to gather his breath.

"Come on, Cap," Ham encouraged. "You can do it."

Caleb gritted his teeth, refusing to look at the orange status circle on his HUD as it turned to solid red. He doubled his efforts and began to pull himself and Kwon up the side of the formation.

Caleb?

Ishek's voice prodded gently at his mind. He ignored it, completely focused on reaching the summit.

You're wasting your energy. He's dead.

The last two words hit Caleb like a sledgehammer. He froze mid-climb, forcing his eyes to shift to Kwon's status symbol on his HUD. The solid red circle had gone dark gray.

"Son of a..." Ham growled, trailing off before he lost his

composure.

Numb shock settled over Caleb. He had lost Marines before. Too many to count. Many of them, like Jii, he'd known long enough to consider friends. After the invasion, his line of work had been the most dangerous on Earth. Squeezing his eyes tight, he exhaled slowly, forcing himself to let go of his immediate fury and grief. Looking down, he saw the rezca had scaled the side of the canyon and would soon be on his heels again.

And he had pitched his rifle.

"Semper Fidelis, Corporal. Godspeed, Jii," Caleb said softly, the pain of the loss crushing his chest. He had only one way to make it out of here alive, and he knew Kwon would want him to survive. With as much reverence as possible, he shifted his weight, sliding Jii off the back of his shoulder until his lifeless body tumbled down the slope.

Caleb didn't look down. He fired his jump thrusters and pushed off, shooting up the last fifteen meters. Grabbing the edge of the rock, he pulled himself up to the ledge as Spirit dropped down to land in front of him, the rear hatch lowering. He stumbled to it with his head bowed, tears threatening at the corners of his eyes. One last look down at Kwon, and he hopped inside.

"Ham, get us out of here," he said flatly.

"Yes, sir. Your wish is my command," Ham replied, though the reply lacked its typical enthusiasm.

Caleb's gratitude for making it back onboard alive was tempered by Kwon's death. His knees gave out, and he sat down hard on the deck. As the hatch closed, he draped his hands over his raised knees and hung his head.

Spirit lifted away from the planet's surface, ready to climb into orbit.

"Uhh, Cap?" Ham said, fresh urgency in his voice. "Better get up here, asap. This party isn't over yet. We've got incoming."

CHAPTER 13

"What do we have?" Caleb asked, his eyes lingering on Kwon's empty co-pilot seat for a moment before he finished making his way to his command seat. There would be time to finish processing his loss later. Right now, he and Ham still had work to do.

"Three Relyeh Monoliths. Damn battle cruisers," Ham replied. "They just appeared from the backside of Trappist-C"

"Hiding out there," Caleb said. "Waiting for someone to show up. It was a damn trap after all. Bastards." He had shed his spent power pack in the hold, but still wore the rest of his armor, minus the helmet. Carrying both the headgear and Benning's tablet under his arm, he magnetically attached both to the side of his seat before falling into it. The ribs enveloped his chest, while the neural crown moved into place around his head. "But I don't think it was meant for us."

"You mean they were waiting for the Axon to show?"

"Either that, or they're incredibly disappointed by the size of our expeditionary force." Caleb brought up the ships on his HUD. Long and wide, but not very deep, the Monoliths, unlike the Shales, were actually composed of the same material as a more typical asteroid. Or maybe they had been collected as asteroids, chosen for their size and shape, hollowed out, and put into service. Even Ishek didn't know their origins for certain, only that many were hundreds of thousands of years old.

They were rare enough that Caleb had only seen one other before, though it had been much larger than the three approaching now. Each ship could carry dozens of Shales and hundreds of the smaller, rounder ships the CSF called Pebbles. One of the warships was more than enough to obliterate a Spacer scout ship with minimal effort. Three was maximum overkill.

For humans, anyway. Not so much for the other intergalactic race humankind had been exposed to. Where the Relyeh were masters of genetics and organic manipulation, the Axon balanced them with their advanced mastery of technology. An ancient, highly evolved and nearly extinct race, their artificially intelligent machines explored the universe with a complete indifference to humankind. Even their mutual enemy, the Relyeh, hadn't borne any fruit toward an alliance with the Axon, or even a tenuous acceptance. Humans were a primitive nuisance to the Axon at best.

An Axon Star would give the three Relyeh Monoliths nearing Trappist-E a run for their money. And it seemed to Caleb that was what this Relyeh fleet was here to ambush.

They'll take what they can get.

They already took Kwon, Caleb mentally growled back at Ishek. *They can't have anything more.*

We shall see.

Sometimes, he hated how Ishek seemed to root for his old masters.

"We need to get out of here," Caleb said, noting the position of the warships. They were closing in quickly enough that they would begin launching their fighters any moment now.

Ham responded by punching the thrust to max, shoving Caleb back in his seat as Spirit shot away from the planet's surface, leaving Kwon's body farther behind. They rocketed upward toward orbit, and toward the enemy. The Relyeh ships had spread out enough to cover a wide swath of space overhead. They could attempt to circumvent it, but in doing so, Caleb knew there was no guarantee of escape, and it had the potential to allow the warships a better intercept position. No, it was better to take the direct route and try to blast through their formation.

"They're throwing Pebbles," Ham said out loud. Of course, Caleb could already see the smaller ships on his HUD's sensor grid, pouring out of craters in the sides of the Monoliths. Within minutes, hundreds of them would litter an orbital path, each with the same goal. To intercept and collide with Spirit. Of course, the hit would destroy the lucky Pebble too, but the organic mind in the center of the hard shell was incapable of caring. And the force driving it couldn't be denied.

"I'm on the guns," Caleb replied, though he held off activating the fire control system. Trappist-E's atmosphere was minimal, but he didn't want additional friction from the turrets to slow them down. *"Ish, do you know which is the command ship?"*

No. The Korath could be on any of them. Or all of them. Or none of them.

Caleb's mind tingled in response to Ishek's amusement. Kwon had asked him why the rezca had attacked despite the continuing Godzilla roar. He hadn't gotten the chance to tell the other Marine about the Korath, the Relyeh commanders who steered the wills and minds of their foot soldiers, seizing mental control and forcing them to overcome their natural fear of fighting. Their orders weren't limited by distance. The Relyeh had an information network unlike any other, an organic means to pass communications across the universe in real time.

The rezca hadn't stopped fearing the roar. They had simply lost their autonomy to a more powerful Relyeh. A much greater threat. And he had known as much from the moment he realized that the Relyeh were in the Trappist-1 system in force. But of course, it had already been way too late to do anything about it. He had taken the risk of dropping onto Trappist-E because the CSF brass had deemed the mission top priority, and this was the job he was assigned to do.

Spirit barely shuddered as it broke through the planet's atmosphere into the troposphere, velocity increasing more rapidly as they moved further out of the gravity well. Ahead, through the forward surround, the burns of a growing number of Relyeh fighters made the stars sparkle.

Reaching the vacuum of space, Caleb activated the fire control system. Once more, the collection of turrets slid out from Spirit's hull. He would need to be judicious in his use of the guns. They had only so many ballistic rounds remaining before they would be forced to switch to the inferior but much more plentiful energy beams.

The ships' computer signaled its warning as the Pebbles began converging on Spirit, closing the gap as the Korath onboard each enemy ship became more confident in their course, the margin of error decreasing for both sides.

"Here we go," Ham said, turning off Spirit's internal gravity plates. The incoming Pebbles were painted red in Caleb's HUD, allowing him to target the dark objects against the black backdrop of space. He didn't try to hit them himself, but rather marked the most worrisome kamikaze ships for the fire control system to develop a solution. The guns opened fire, short bursts of titanium slugs spilling out into the black and smashing into the

Pebbles' hard shells. Enough of the rounds pierced the protection of the ships, destroying the organic minds inside and turning the stricken craft into unguided munitions.

Spirit slowed slightly, retro thrusters firing, avoiding one of the Pebbles as it zipped past. Cutting the reverse thrust, the ship jumped forward while dropping, another Pebble crossing just overhead. A hard corkscrew turn, another dive, and a sharp hook carried Spirit through the enemy attack. The Pebbles often zoomed by inside a few hundred meters, amounting to less than a second from impact at their current relative velocities.

The guns continued spewing slugs, rapidly burning through ammunition as Caleb targeted the enemy fighters most likely to succeed in their collision course with Spirit. With no time to watch the guns swivel and shoot in nearly every direction, his eyes flicked rapidly back and forth, selecting bogies with nothing more than a spontaneous thought.

Ham maneuvered the ship through the maelstrom at full-throttle, ripping hard to break through the swarm. But with Shales closing in behind the Pebbles, the fighting intensified. The less agile, but smarter and more heavily armed craft vectored toward Spirit, launching shards from hundreds of kilometers away. From farther away, the larger warships joined in, firing high-velocity projectiles of their own.

"Cap!" Ham cried, unnerved by the massive attack.

"Keep going," Caleb shouted back. "We'll get through them." He switched the fire control system from bullets to beams. They still had nearly thirty seconds of rounds remaining, but it would be hard enough to hit the incoming projectiles with energy, nevermind slugs.

His HUD showed the barrage of rounds coming at them, but it couldn't automatically target any but the largest of the shots fired from the warships. Caleb handled the task mentally. Rather than trying to hit individual targets, he fired beams in a cone along their forward path, like a snow plow, vaporizing shards in their path. Without oxygen igniting, he couldn't see most of the explosions, but he knew the beams were protecting Spirit from amidships forward because their shields were only triggering on the back half of the ship.

At least for the moment, the shields were able to absorb the energy, but with each passing second, the Shales grew in numbers, making it harder for Ham to maneuver through the enemy hell. The forward shields started flaring in swelling numbers. The computer beeped shrilly inside Caleb's brain, a warning flashing in his eyes that the guns were overheating.

'Cap, we need to get out of here!' Ham shouted in his mind.

'We can't fold unless we come to a full stop,' Caleb replied, but of course Ham already knew that.

'If we stop, we're dead.' They both knew that too. *'But if we stay here much longer, we're also dead.'*

'Where are we supposed to go?' Caleb asked. *'We can't outrun them. We can't out—wait a second.'* He snagged Benning's tablet from its position on his armrest and turned on the screen. *'Ham, do you know how to link this thing to the computer to extract its contents?'*

'You want to do that now*?'*

'Want. No. Need. Yes. Benning went on and on about Pathfinder entering a wormhole. That might be the only ticket out of here that doesn't lead straight to the afterlife.'

'I was listening in, remember? Benning said Pathfinder was destroyed inside the wormhole. That it's unstable. And even if you make it through, you can come out anytime, anywhere, with no way back.'

'That has to be better than this, doesn't it?'

Ham's hesitation seemed to last forever in the quick

pace of their mental conversation. *'Yeah, you're right. You'll have to take the stick.'*

'I have the stick. You have the tablet.'

Caleb seized control of Spirit at the same time he frisbee-tossed the tablet to Ham. The Marine caught the device, turning it over to examine the back.

'What are you doing?' Caleb asked, spinning Spirit away from an incoming Pebble. It missed them by meters, torn to shreds by friendly fire a moment later.

'I need to remove the data chip from the tablet and hope we have a compatible reader.'

'R and D knew the mission; they better have provided the right tools.'

'I need to get up to grab my screwdriver. Fly straight for a few seconds.'

'Are you kidding?'

'I wish I was.'

'You have ten seconds.'

Ham practically ripped the ribs away to get out of his seat. He vanished from the flight deck as the computer again shrilled in Caleb's head. The turrets' internal heat was critical. They would at best shut down, and at worst, blow up at any moment.

Caleb deactivated them before that could happen, shutting down the energy cone and retracting the weapons to cool down. Left without the protection, Spirit began taking additional hits, putting more strain on all the shields.

"Time's up!" Caleb shouted, reaching the ten second mark. Ham burst through the doorway and threw himself into Kwon's co-pilot seat. Each seat was coded to the Marine who sat there, and when the ribs wrapped around him, they practically squeezed the air out of his much larger frame.

'Damn, that's tight,' Ham complained, the neural crown

dropping into position as he went to work, opening the back of the tablet with the small screwdriver.

Caleb refocused on his flying by watching the sensor grid instead of focusing on the forward surround. Mentally, he turned the raging storm of Relyeh ships around them into a four dimensional image, putting his vantage point outside Spirit, looking down on the whole thing as if he were playing a video game. He swung left, dropped, spun, and climbed, keeping the throttle pegged, their velocity continually increasing.

Ham managed to get the cover off the tablet, grinning as he used the screwdriver to leverage out a small card the size of his thumbnail. He froze for a moment before feeding the card into the proper port on his instrument panel.

'It's processing, Cap.'

'Process faster,' Caleb replied as a new warning appeared on his HUD. The constant energy flare from the shields was overheating the circuits, putting their last line of defense into the same position as the guns.

'This isn't magic, Cap.' After all, they were working with a two hundred-year-old data chip, one with less than a hundredth of a percent of the capacity of a modern, tinier data storage unit. *'There's a lot of work going on behind the—oh, done.'*

With a thought, Caleb requested the position of the wormhole according to Charlotte Benning's research and calculations. He asked the computer to paint it yellow on his HUD.

He was sure something had gone wrong when the entire face of Trappist-1's white dwarf star suddenly gained a yellow hue.

CHAPTER 14

'This can't be right,' Caleb said, staring at the yellow fill covering the face of the star. *'Ham, you must have input the data wrong.'*

'There's only one way to do it, Cap,' Ham replied. *'What's the problem?'*

'According to the computer, the wormhole is either sitting on top of Trappist-1's star, or it is *Trappist-1's star.'*

'What?' Ham replied out loud, taking a moment to see the output for himself. *'This is crazy. But there's no way the system can get it wrong. There's only one input, and it extrapolates the data based on that input. It's using the algorithms it found on the data chip.'*

'You're sure?' Caleb asked as the computer sent another shrill tone through his ears to upgrade its warning of imminent shield failure.

'As sure as I can be.' He turned his head to look back at Caleb. "You can't seriously be thinking about flying us into a star.'

"It has to be better than this death by a thousand rocks," Caleb replied. 'The only question is whether we can get there." He checked his HUD for the ETA. At their still increasing velocity, and assuming they didn't make any adjustments to their speed or general heading, they would arrive in just over an hour. It might as well have been a lifetime considering their predicament.

He had to try.

"Pass me back the stick," Ham said, his tone as tight and focused as Caleb had ever heard. "Do what you can to keep them honest. I'll get us there."

"You have the stick," Caleb replied without hesitation. Immediately, he was pulled in what felt like every direction at once as Ham swept through the enemy assault, his every maneuver and adjustment to their vector so much more efficient than Caleb had managed, the number of hits to the shields dropping by nearly half almost instantly.

Reactivating the fire control system, Caleb noted the guns had cooled back to within their tolerances, though he would need to be judicious in his defense to keep them from overheating again. With Ham's improved flying, the temperature of the shield conduits quickly stabilized as well, though it would only take a couple of good hits to burn them out completely. A successful hit by a kamikaze Pebble would surely be the end of them.

Rather than target incoming enemy fire again, Caleb focused on the potential sources of those good hits. He fired beams from three turrets at a pair of Shales tailing them and four other guns to launch the last of their remaining ballistic ammunition at the Pebbles he decided presented the greatest threat.

With the same focus shooting as Ham had flying, he tore the enemy ships apart, disabling one after another and leaving them to drift into the line of fire from the warships and the Shales. They made good shields, catching enough projectiles to give Spirit's systems a short breather, the temperatures dropping enough to stop the incessant shrilling in his ears. Even so, the energy use had raised the temperature on the flight deck considerably, leaving both he and Ham soaked in sweat.

The minutes passed like hours, the unceasing need to stay perfectly focused becoming more challenging as time progressed. They ran out of rounds after eight minutes, no longer able to easily disable the Pebbles still trying to reach them. By twelve, Caleb had to stop shooting again altogether to again give the guns time to cool. At sixteen, the shields were in danger of giving out as well.

They were twenty-three minutes into the hour-long escape when the shields finally failed. A single shard from a Shale overloaded the power delivery system with a series of sparks resulting in an isolated fire inside the central cabin. The automated safety systems quickly extinguished the fire, but the loss of external shields also triggered the sealing of the flight deck hatch. A backup battery came online to power a secondary shield that protected only the small compartment. The second level of protection would buy them more time.

Would it buy them enough?

And where the hell were they going, anyway? Into a wormhole they had no idea how to traverse that would dump them out who-knew-where, with no chance of rescue and probably only slightly higher odds of survival.

We've been in worse situations before.

Caleb smiled. "You aren't wrong, Ish."

It was nearly another five minutes before the first Relyeh projectile made it through Spirit's armored hull, punching through the cabin and hitting the opposite bulkhead. The trick now was to keep the thrusters running for as long as possible, though thankfully Spirit had one more trick up her sleeve. One Caleb was ready to play if it came down to it.

By the thirty-five minute mark, the last of the Pebbles had fallen behind, unable to match the velocity Spirit had achieved. The larger Monoliths and the Shales weren't quite as underpowered, but had also begun struggling to keep up. That didn't prevent them from sending a steady stream of projectiles toward Spirit, forcing Ham to maintain his evasive maneuvers and the guns to keep firing an occasional energy beam. Less than two percent of the enemy rounds impacted Spirit, but two percent of hundreds was still a lot. The larger shards made bigger holes in the armor, a few of them hitting the secondary shields. Caleb watched the backup battery drain in his HUD, dropping a little over one percent with each hit.

At forty-one minutes, the reactor took a fatal blow to the coolant line. The computer announced the damage with yet another shrill beep and a flashing red symbol on Caleb's HUD. The text underneath warned of critical reactor overheating if they didn't switch to the emergency generator and effect repairs as soon as possible.

Ham saw the warning too and immediately killed the thrust.

'*What are you doing?*' Caleb asked through the neural interface.

'*What do you mean? Thirty seconds and the reactor will blow.*'

'*We need as much velocity as we can get. They're already gaining.*'

'*What good is more speed if we explode?*'

'*What good is not exploding if we get shot down instead? That wormhole is our only hope. Keep burning, Ham. That's an order.*'

'*Yes, sir.*' Ham stopped arguing, bringing the throttle back up to max. They started accelerating again, but the damage had already been done, costing them thousands of kilometers in only a few seconds.

And the wormhole was still twenty minutes away.

Caleb watched the reactor temperature rising as the

seconds ticked by. Ham was right that they would need to jettison the reactor before it exploded, but they had to gain as much speed as they could before jettisoning it or the pursuing Relyeh would again get close enough to pound them with projectiles.

I have an idea.

The smug tone in Ishek's voice told Caleb the khoron believed it was a good idea. "What have you got?"

What have you got, Caleb?

"This isn't the time for riddles, Ish. What's your big idea?"

What have you got, Caleb? One overheating primary reactor. Also known as a very powerful explosive device.

Caleb smiled. "Damn, that *is* a good idea. Ham, I'm going to jettison the reactor when it reaches six seconds to overheat."

"Isn't that cutting it a little close?"

"Yup," Caleb replied. "Get ready."

Somehow, the seconds found a way to pass even more slowly than before. Each one seemed like an eternity as Caleb watched the temperature of the reactor continue to climb while he counted down from twenty toward six.

When he reached the magic number, a simple, deliberate thought ordered the ship's computer to release the clamps holding the reactor in place. Controlled detonations pushed it out through the bent tail end of the superstructure. Debris spilled out around the reactor, which began spinning wildly the moment it was clear, thanks to the still-attached thrusters.

With the emergency generator automatically coming online, the ship never came close to losing power. They continued along their way, covering thousands of kilometers in the three seconds it took for the system they had dumped to reach critical mass. The Shales leading the charge, lacking the intelligence to understand what was happening, continued chasing without regard to the reactor. Only five seconds behind Spirit when Caleb dumped the reactor, they were almost in line with it when it exploded.

The ball of energy from the destabilized fuel source powering the reactor quickly expanded in a sphere nearly two hundred kilometers in diameter, incinerating every ship caught in the blast. While the larger Monoliths were too far back to be hit by the explosion, the entire leading group of Shales that had fallen in directly behind Spirit were vaporized, as were any nearby Shales. Nearly forty Relyeh ships were wiped out in the explosion, but more importantly, the rest were forced to take evasive maneuvers, slowing them down and ruining the angle of attack for many.

"Woooo!" Ham shouted in response to the mayhem. "Nice work, Ishy."

I hate it when he calls me that.

Caleb ginned. "Regardless, thanks for saving our butts, Ish."

I don't actually want us to lose if it means I die.

"Thanks for caring about me."

I'm only being honest.

"We're not out of this yet," Caleb said, loudly enough that Ham could hear. "That should buy us some time, but they'll catch up again now that we don't have thrusters."

"We're in better shape than we were ten seconds ago," Ham replied. "I'll take it."

They continued toward the star in tense silence, closing to within five minutes of the star before the Relyeh had regrouped enough to resume their attack. Maneuvering became a much bigger challenge with the mains gone, leaving Ham making lesser adjustments that led to absorbing more firepower.

The secondary shields flared again and again, the

battery power draining fast. Visible on his HUD, the yellow overlay on top of the sun still promised salvation, but peering through the forward surround, there was no visible sign of a wormhole in front of the star. No indication they weren't flying to their death either. It was a leap of faith. An act of desperation.

The only chance they had.

With a thought, Caleb asked the computer to plot a course through the wormhole, based on the data Charlotte Benning had provided. The result appeared on the sensor grid, a three-dimensional spiral that started wide and became narrower and narrower the deeper it traveled.

"Looks like it's getting too hot for those cruisers to handle," Ham said, drawing Caleb's attention to the Relyeh ships on his HUD. The Monoliths had apparently given up the chase, falling back while the Shales continued the chase. Their shards punched through the open rear, caught by the secondary shields. Yet another warning triggered when the battery's charge dropped below twenty percent.

They were only two minutes out. So close he could feel the temperature on the flight deck rising again, the heat slowly becoming more and more unbearable. Ham did his best to evade the Shales, but there was little left he could do. More shards hit the shields. The battery dropped from eighteen percent to eight. Six. Four. Two.

The secondary shields went out. The temperature on the flight deck spiked to over a hundred and twenty degrees. They were only thirty seconds away, so close Caleb could see the chemical reaction at the core of the star violently churning plasma directly ahead.

There was still no evidence of a wormhole.

"Sorry, Cap," Ham said. "That engineer was full of it."

"It was an honor serving with you, Ham," Caleb replied.

"The honor was mine, sir."

A shard from one of the Shales must have punched into the armor surrounding the flight deck, because the power flashed off then, leaving Caleb and Ham blind in the darkness. It only lasted for a few seconds, but when the power rerouted, the ship's computer, along with the neural interface, was dead.

"Switching to manual," Ham said, grabbing the joystick. With the computer offline, there was no countdown to their destination. There was nothing except the big pilot at the controls, left to thread the needle at half a million kilometers per hour. "Might as well die trying."

"Oorah," Caleb replied.

They approached the surface of the star, both Marines certain they were going to die. The Shales behind them pulled back and away, also convinced their death was imminent. Except Caleb noticed that the temperature on the flight deck had stabilized, even though they were so much closer to the star now that their gooses should have already been cooked. He stared straight ahead, a fresh sense of calm overcoming him as the furious solar storm approached.

Before he could take another breath, Spirit dove into it.

CHAPTER 15

The blinding white light of Trappist-1's star gave way to total darkness, much like space itself, only darker.

This doesn't make any sense.

Ishek was right. How anything could be darker than space didn't add up. But somehow, this place had achieved it. At the same time, there was an obvious depth to the blackness. A sense of location within the absence of time or place. Charlotte Benning had called it a place outside of the universe. Being in the midst of it, Caleb found the description apt.

Most importantly, Spirit remained intact. He and Ham were still alive. And the Relyeh had given up the chase.

"Ham!" Caleb shouted. The big Marine had frozen in a state of shock moments before they should have collided with the star. "Don't fall out of the Spiral!" Without the neural interface, he couldn't reclaim control of the ship without transferring to the pilot's seat.

"Damn, we're not dead!" he exclaimed, snapping out of his daze. He reached back to release the ribs holding him in Kwon's co-pilot seat and leaped out of it, sliding into his own seat, the ribs quickly closing him comfortably in.

Caleb released the breath he was holding as Ham visibly steadied once he was in his own familiar niche, his shaking hand stilling an instant before he wrapped it around the stick. He didn't have the sensor grid between his eyes or the forward surround, the way he would have if the Shale hadn't gotten lucky and killed the computer. He had to navigate the spiral manually even though it was impossible to see, but he was once again in his element, even if it wasn't exactly a comfort zone at the moment.

Fortunately, either the beginning of the twisting path through spacetime was quite large or entering it had inexplicably slowed Spirit to a manageable speed, though of course even that was impossible to judge without a point of reference. Regardless, Ham fired the retro thrusters, likely hoping to bring the ship to a full stop.

Caleb wasn't idle. He tapped on the control pads at the end of his seat's armrests, quickly activating the backup computer and a projection system that would cast data to the forward surround like a secondary HUD. The backup systems were a massively trimmed down version of the primary, covering only the most rudimentary and critical functions. No neural interface. No fire control. No data from Benning's tablet. At least it provided their velocity, which remained unchanged during their entry. They were traveling at over a hundred kilometers per second. They had already covered nearly a thousand klicks.

"How am I supposed to fly like this?" Ham complained. "I can't see a damn thing."

"I don't know," Caleb replied, staring into the black. "Just do your best."

You're not looking correctly.

"What the hell does that mean, Ish?" Caleb snapped, short on patience.

I know you can sense the depth. Focus on the negative space.

Caleb stared out through the forward surround, trying

to follow Ishek's advice. Rather than looking for shape in the blackness, he did his best to search for the absence of shape. Impossibly, he realized that different shades of nothing composed the inside of the wormhole. "This is incredible. Ham, look at the negative space. The wormhole has a defined shape after all."

"Are you kidding?" Ham asked, gasping a few seconds later when he saw the same thing Caleb did. "What the hell is going on here?"

"We're inside a wormhole," Caleb replied, as if that answered all the questions about the impossible physics. And maybe it did.

"I've got the spiral," Ham said, leveling Spirit and following the vague outline of the shape. "How far do I go?"

"To the end, if we can."

"Do you think Pathfinder made it that far?"

"Seeing as how they came here for the wormhole, I see two possibilities. Either they changed their math in response to Benning's corrections and made it to the end of the line, or they remained stubborn and flew out of the spiral pretty quickly after entering. The latter means they could have fallen out anywhere, and Benning wasn't clear if that meant returning to the universe at a random place and time or instant annihilation."

"So even if they didn't make it to the end, we should."

"Unless you have an argument against it."

"No, sir. I can't believe we got away from the Relyeh. I can't believe the wormhole is real."

"We're living proof that it's real."

"Yeah, I suppose we are." He paused, his next words coming more quietly. "There's no way back from this, is there? My wife. My little girl…" He trailed off, the sentiment wringing Caleb's heart like a wet towel.

"I tried to talk you out of volunteering for this mission," Caleb said. "I feel bad I couldn't change your mind."

"You needed me," Ham replied. "And Maria insisted you needed me, too. She was a Spacer like us before Callie was born. She knows what the job requires. And what it means for me to do it." He paused, regaining his composure. "And it's obvious she was right. You wouldn't be able to fly us through this. Although it begs the question. How can black be blacker?"

"Again, I don't know. Ish?"

There's no light here.

"Is that the best you can do? If there's zero percent light, then there must be one hundred percent dark. But the darkness has shadows. Explain that."

The shadows you see are unrelated to light. Perhaps this place has no concept of light and dark. Perhaps the shadows are echoes of entire universes—past, present, and future.

"Okay, don't explain that," Caleb decided.

"What did Ish say?" Ham asked.

"You don't want to know. It makes no freaking sense."

Benning suggested there were no guarantees of where or when we would be when we emerged from the wormhole. That in turn suggests that the wormhole's passage through the sediment outside the universe winds through the fabric of spacetime that composes said universe. What if the shadows are artifacts of every possible time and place, stacked infinitely atop one another at chaotically organized intervals?

"Didn't I just say, *don't* explain that?" Caleb replied.

Too big of an idea for your puny human mind?

"Your brain is literally the size of a pea," Caleb retorted.

It's all in how you use it.

Caleb groaned in dismay. "Ham, just don't let us fall out of the spiral."

"Copy that, Cap." He paused again. "Jii was—"

"Later," Caleb interrupted. "When we're safe."

"That could be a while."

"Let's hope not."

Ham kept his attention on the forward surround, making minor adjustments with the vectoring thrusters to keep them within the confines of the spiral. They traversed it in focused silence, Caleb keeping a sharp eye out for any miscues from his pilot. Not because he didn't believe Ham was up to the task, but because the task was so difficult he would have wanted a second pair of eyes if he were the one steering the ship.

He did his best not to think about Kwon. He had lost more than his fair share of team members over the years. Sometimes he would have liked to be more callous and cold, the kind of man who saw his subordinates as a means to an end, rather than as people. And friends. It would have made it all so much easier.

Instead, he remembered the name of every Marine who had fallen under his watch. More than that, he remembered the names of their loved ones. The people who would miss them more than he did. The people who had waited for them to come home, only to learn that they never would. The Relyeh invasion had only made it harder, because those loved ones were also on the run, fighting for survival in a rapidly changing universe, and missing the one person in their life who had the strength and training to protect them.

Perhaps something to ease your mind.

Caleb shook his head, rejecting Ishek's offer. The last thing he needed right now was to be sedated. The last thing he wanted was to forget. *You should know me better than that, Ish.*

I offer. You reject. That is how we coexist.

"The spiral's getting tighter," Ham commented, giving Caleb an out from his thoughts. "We should reach the other end soon." He paused. "And then what?"

"We survive," Caleb replied. "We find a way back."

"What if there isn't one?"

"We still survive."

The looping turns of the spiral shortened, the leading edges closing in on them. Ham's minor adjustments turned into constant course corrections to keep them away from the sides, where the dark shadows of infinite possibilities appeared to grow deeper and more dense, convincing Caleb that falling out of the wormhole meant destruction. After all, if only portions of the ship occupied any single thread of reality, then the whole would be scattered across hundreds, if not thousands, of universes. It was a chilling thought he had trouble wrapping his mind around. A few hours ago, he wouldn't have believed anything like this could even exist.

The sudden shrill of the backup computer's warning echoed across the flight deck as the system projected the sensor grid in front of the forward surround.

"What the hell?" Ham complained, nearly overcorrecting out of pure surprise.

A yellow mark stood out on the grid, appearing almost directly behind them. Hoping to see what the sensors had just picked up behind them, Caleb reached for his controls so he could bring the rear view up in the corner of the forward surround. From the way it was closing on them and the path it was on, he had a feeling he already knew what it was. His instinct was to try to arm and use the fire control system through the neural interface, his thoughts turning to the turrets mounted on the hull. But the fire control system was gone, the guns inaccessible. Without the reactor, without the primary computer, they were maneuvering through space and time in what was essentially a lifeboat about to be broadsided by a great white.

"Ham!" Caleb shouted, trying to warn the pilot of the imminent collision. Of course, he had already picked up on it, too. His need to balance navigating the shape of the spiral with the immediate desire to get out of the way left him momentarily paralyzed. For whatever reason, the sensors had failed for too long to detect the incoming object. Even if Ham had reacted instantly, it would've already been too late.

Caleb activated the camera on the upper half of the starboard stern just in time to get a glimpse of the Pebble before it slammed into Spirit's side. It ripped through the unshielded armored hull, sending them into a sudden, uncontrollable spin.

The impact wrenched Caleb against his seat as Spirit spun through the wormhole like an overturned top. The view through the forward surround was a blur of shifting shadows and debris as the Relyeh ship shattered from the hit, the rear of Spirit completely sheared away. If the flight deck hadn't already been sealed, the suddenness of the crash would have vented all the atmosphere in an instant. As it was, they tumbled end-over-end toward the side of the wormhole.

Toward their death.

"Ham!" Caleb again cried through gritted teeth. Ham's knuckles were white on the stick, working hard to make the adjustments to stabilize their path, with no time to spare.

"Cap, blow the shell on my mark!" Ham shouted, maintaining his composure despite the predicament. Or perhaps because of it.

The constantly shifting inertia made it harder for Caleb to use the command pads, and it took him nearly five seconds to reach the emergency command that would jettison the encapsulated flight deck from the rest of Spirit.

"Now!" Ham cried, Caleb reaching the executable function on his pad milliseconds later.

A simple finger press was all it took. Formed explosives surrounding the flight deck blew the remainder of Spirit apart from the inside out. Emergency thrusters beneath the deck fired at full blast to ensure they cleared the area without being hit by any potential debris.

"Come on, come on, come on!" Ham growled as the forward surround's view shifted to a new set of cameras mounted to the flight deck's armored exterior, the stitched composite aiming to give them a full three hundred and sixty-degree view. The Shale had destroyed a few rear cameras earlier, leaving a blank spot in the coverage, but what Caleb could see was more than enough. The wormhole remained a blur as they rotated like a centrifuge, the inertial pressure intense.

The push from the bottom and Ham's expert steering had erased the capsule's topspin and given the pilot back some control, which he used to maneuver them away from the edge of the wormhole. He guided them around the last sweeping bend in the spiral.

Caleb saw the rest of Spirit impact the shadows. The hit created a strobe effect in the spinning capsule, the absolute black flashing with white light, giving the appearance of stars that blossomed into existence before fading away almost as quickly.

I feel sick.

Ishek wasn't the only one. Caleb could sense himself losing consciousness, his vision losing clarity, his mind beginning to feel as if it had left his body completely. In his mind's eye, he was looking down on the flight deck as though he were a fly on the ceiling. Ham had slumped in the pilot's seat, having already succumbed to the constant high-Gs of their spin.

A moment later, he did too.

CHAPTER 16

Caleb. Get up.

Ishek's harsh mental order and a jolt of adrenaline jerked Caleb awake. He remained motionless while his eyes danced across the flight deck. Across all that remained of the scout ship Spirit. His perspective muddied, it took him a few seconds to realize he was hanging upside down from his seat, the capsule resting at a forty-five degree angle.

Inert but not weightless. Not floating. Wherever they were, they had gravity.

The next thing he noticed was Ham dangling from the co-pilot's seat, still out cold. He didn't have a symbiote to pump him full of hormones and scream in his brain to wake up.

"Ham!" Caleb hoarsely called out. He tried to pull moisture from his mouth to wet his throat, but there wasn't much there. "Ham!" he repeated, with only slightly less rasp. "Ish, how long was I out?"

I'm unsure. I was also unconscious.

"I didn't think that was possible."

We exited the wormhole at high velocity and out of control. With you unconscious, I was not able to see. I believe the emer-

gency systems identified a nearby planet and brought us down. Roughly. The turbulence ultimately caused my blackout.

Caleb reached back for the rib controls and released himself from his seat. His legs were weak as he balanced on the tilted decking, forcing him to grab hold of his seat to remain stationary. "I need a little more juice."

You need a moment to recover your equilibrium.

"Ham!" Caleb again called out. The pilot remained unresponsive. He looked past Ham to the forward surround. The impact with the ground had left a web of shattered substrate and dead pixels across the screen, but the lack of warnings was at least somewhat comforting. No hull breach. No loss of oxygen. Nothing about the situation was ideal, so every bit of good news was a plus.

His strength and balance returned as his mind and body came back into sync. He called out to Ham one more time before moving forward to grab the Marine by the shoulder, trying to shake him awake. "Ham!"

When Ham still didn't respond, Caleb pressed his fingers against his thick neck, feeling for a pulse. Rewarded with a steady beat, he exhaled his relief. At least Ham was still alive. He had an idea how to wake him, too. Reaching across the aisle, he slid Ham's coffee thermos forward to release its magnetic grip. Twisting open the sealed top, he held it like smelling salts beneath his fellow Marine's nose.

Ham came to with a start, breathing in deep before bolting upright, hands out to brace himself for impact.

"Ham!" Caleb said. "Relax. It's okay. We're on the ground."

Ham looked over at him, his tight, fearful expression relaxing, a big grin sliding across his face. "Cap?" He laughed sharply. "Damn. We're still alive." He seemed to reconsider his initial reaction. "We are still alive, right? This isn't purgatory, is it?"

Caleb had to laugh. "Your heart's still beating. So's

mine. And we're breathing. I think that means we're still alive."

"Maybe that's not such a good thing. Do you know where we crashed?"

"Crash landed," Caleb corrected. "We're going to walk away from this one. Where to? I don't know yet. I was worried about you. How do you feel?"

"I'm good, all things considered. You?"

"I'm fine."

He nodded. "That's right, you have Ish to speed your recovery. No sore muscles for you, I imagine."

"No, but I do have an ugly alien worm living in my armpit."

I'm not ugly.

"That's debatable. I'm glad you're okay, Ham." He squeezed the other Marine's shoulder and returned to the command seat to tap on the armrest controls. "Computer's still online," he said as he swapped the useless external camera view for a composite view built by the sensor data after they emerged from the wormhole.

The planet they had apparently crashed on had been less than an hour away, and the only celestial body within range of Spirit's few remaining sensors. Those same sensors were too primitive to provide detail about the planet, so he traded the sensor data for a recording of the approach. Starting out as a mostly green marble in the distance, the planet grew quickly when Caleb scrubbed the recording forward. There were no ships in orbit around the world. No apparent settlements or other signs of human occupation. There was life, though. The greenery visible from space was an endless sea of vegetation broken up by veins of water, mountain ranges, and an occasional lake. Watching the descent through a thick upper atmosphere, Caleb was sure he spotted a large *something* pass beneath the capsule, skimming the dense tops of the high trees. They had crashed through the upper branches, snapping off thick limbs and denting the capsule's armor until finally slamming into red dirt.

"Ouch," Ham commented in response to the impact. "No wonder my neck hurts."

"Let's check the environmental sensors," Caleb said, tapping on the touchpad to change views. "Gravity is one hundred twenty percent of Earth's. That should be fun."

"A quick and easy way to pack on fifty pounds in a hurry," Ham agreed.

"Twenty-three percent oxygen, six percent argon, one percent helium, seventy percent nitrogen. Not too much different from Earth." He glanced at Ham. "This place is actually pretty nice."

"Do you think Pathfinder is here?"

"The camera didn't catch sight of any settlements on the way down, but it's possible the ship landed on the other side. A rotation is twenty-seven hours, according to the computer."

"I can live with an extra three hours per day. Getting to the other side of the world won't be easy without a ride, though."

"Let's not get ahead of ourselves. Ambient temperature is thirty-two point four degrees celsius. Humidity is ninety-six percent."

"Hot and humid? I've never felt that before."

"You won't be excited about it for long, believe me."

Ham chuckled. "It's not like we have a choice."

Caleb grabbed his helmet from where it remained magnetically stuck to the side of his seat, sliding it over his head. It latched automatically. It would get hot inside the sealed armor pretty quickly without a power pack to move the coolant gel around, but he didn't trust this place anywhere near enough to go outside the ship unprotected.

"I'm going to crack us open."

"Yes, sir," Ham replied.

Caleb crossed to the hatch and tapped his code into the door control. The armored blast door struggled to move aside, only making it halfway before it jammed. When he tried to coax it open, a shower of sparks from its motor ended the argument.

"So this is what humidity feels like," Ham said as the thick air began pouring into the capsule. "It's not bad."

"Give it ten minutes," Caleb replied before squeezing his way outside through the smaller than expected opening. He had left his rifle in the hold with his power pack, but he still had his sidearm. He drew it as he stepped sideways through the opening, his eyes quickly scanning the lush greenery that surrounded them.

Some of it had been burned or torn away by the capsule's vectoring thrusters, but there were still plenty remaining. Thick, dark trees with stout trunks covered in heavy bark stretched upward, spreading into strong limbs capable of fighting the increased gravity. Equally chunky leaves dangled from the limbs, which intertwined in such a way that it was hard for Caleb to tell where one ended and another began.

Thorny red and green vines with darker red leaves ran amok around the tree trunks, satisfied to stay near the ground, which itself was covered in red moss and patches of dark green that reminded him of moldy Jell-o. Different kinds of colorful insects avoided the goop to crawl across the moss, passing into and out of the web of vines oblivious to the alien visitor standing over them.

"Okay," Ham said, appearing at the threshold of the capsule. "I'm hot."

"It hasn't even been three minutes, nevermind ten," Caleb replied, glancing back at him.

"What do you want from me? I grew up in a climate

controlled dome," Ham answered. "So, we didn't die. What do we do now?"

Caleb continued scanning the immediate area. He had learned from experience not to lower his guard too quickly. "I'll keep watch out here. Collect the crash mule from under the command chair, activate the emergency beacon, and see if you can recover Benning's tablet and data chip. I don't know if she knew anything about the far side of the spiral, but it could come in handy."

"Copy that." He paused. "Cap, about Kwon..." He trailed off.

"He was a good Marine," Caleb replied. "He gave his life for this mission. We have a duty to him, that no matter what happens from this point forward, we never give up. We never stop fighting."

"That's always been my MO, sir."

Caleb smiled. "Mine, too."

"You don't think the Relyeh followed us through the wormhole, do you, Cap? That Pebble probably just forgot to turn away."

Caleb could tell by his tone that Ham desperately wanted him to confirm the statement. He refused to sugar-coat anything. Looking up through the hole the capsule had made in the canopy when it crashed, he noticed the sky had a slightly purple hue. He also didn't see any starships up there. He shook his head. "I sure as hell hope they didn't." His gaze rested on the sky before he looked back at Ham, standing just behind him, peering out at the forest around them. "But if they did, that's all the more reason not to linger here."

"Copy that. I'll be back in two shakes." Ham disappeared inside the capsule. A moment later, Caleb could hear him open the compartment beneath the command seat to retrieve the mule. A few more pops and bangs echoed inside the capsule before the mule appeared behind the half-open blast hatch, unable to fit through.

The robot more closely resembled a spider than it did a donkey, with a short, square face and flat body supported by six long, segmented metal legs. A large, square pack rested on its back, creating a bulbous abdomen like that of a Black Widow. The pack contained food, shelter, water, and various other tools and sundries. The mule also carried an oxygen tank with a week's supply of air for both of them. Glad the planet's atmosphere was breathable, Caleb found that detail amusing.. He had a feeling they were going to be here for much longer than a week.

Maybe even the rest of their lives.

CHAPTER 17

"Hold on," Caleb said, talking to the mule as if it could understand him. Powered by a simple AI, it was programmed to each member of the crew in rank order and knew to follow him wherever he went, or to fall back to Ham if it lost sight of him, but it didn't speak and couldn't fight. It was meant to carry a pack. Nothing more.

He returned to the hatch. Planting his foot against the side, he wrapped his hands around the stuck door, leaned into it, and pushed. At first it didn't budge, leading him to wonder if they would have to abandon the mule too. Then Ishek fed him a jolt of adrenaline, extra energy pouring into his limbs. The door shifted slowly at first, still fighting against the immense pressure he put on it. The locking mechanism snapped with a loud crack, and Caleb fell forward to his knees as the hatch rolled the rest of the way open.

The mule didn't move until he returned to his feet and stepped back out into the jungle. It moved outside with a soft whirring of the servos directing its limbs. It paused nearby.

Caleb again scanned their surroundings, taking note of

something small and brightly colored moving through the branches a short distance away. It was there one second and gone the next, disappearing before he could make out any details. If nothing else, its presence had proven there was life on the planet beyond the assortment of insects wandering the moss beneath his feet. He hadn't been looking forward to the prospect of eating insects. Animal meat would be a definite upgrade.

"I assume you don't want your envirosuit," Ham said, returning to the capsule doorway holding one of the environmental suits packaged in clear vinyl wrap. Bright yellow, the rubbery suit was designed to be used in conjunction with the oxygen tank on the mule. With it, he could survive for up to ten days in a hostile atmosphere while waiting for rescue.

"Thankfully, no," Caleb answered.

"I'm going to pass on mine too, with your permission."

"I don't see any reason to put it on. I'll probably abandon my outerlay once it gets too hot to wear. Do you have the tablet?"

"I have the data chip. The tablet came free of the magnetic hold at some point. It's a total loss."

"Damn. Well, that's the least of our concerns right now. I spotted something in the canopy out that way." He pointed. "It didn't stick around, but I'm hoping that means we can find edible meat here."

"There's a box of MREs on the mule, too. Sixty count, I think."

Caleb laughed. "A week of oxygen, a month of food if we only eat one meal a day. Somehow that math doesn't add up."

"You got that right. I need more than one meal a day," Ham said, patting his stout barrel-chested torso. "The emergency beacon is active." he went on. "I know there's a chance the Relyeh may have tailed us through the wormhole, but I think the bigger possibility is that they believe we died on impact. That or they don't care about coming after us. Do you think we should wait here a day or two, to see if they come for us? Speaking of which, do you think the CSF will come looking for us?"

Caleb shook his head. "Negative on both counts. I agree that the Relyeh will probably wash their hands of us. As for the CSF, even if they could retrace our steps, it's nearly a four-month transit, and without Benning's tablet, they aren't going to even know about the wormhole, much less be able to navigate it. They'll probably just declare us lost and go home."

"Yeah, makes sense. Do you think we can find our own way home?"

"Who knows. We can survive here, assuming the rainwater is drinkable, and we still have a mission to finish. If Pathfinder's on this planet, I'm going to find it."

"Yes, sir," Ham replied, morale improving with Caleb's confident demeanor. "I'm with you. Which direction do we go?"

"We need a better vantage point," he replied, looking to the thickest nearby tree trunk and following it upward. "I'm going to climb to the top of the canopy. See what there is to see." He held his sidearm out to Ham. "Keep a lookout."

"Yes, sir," Ham said again, accepting the weapon. He checked the pistol before pointing it toward the ground. "Are you expecting trouble?"

"Given a choice, I'd prefer to expect trouble," Caleb replied, "rather than having no idea what to expect."

"Copy that."

Caleb approached the tree he'd chosen, putting out his gloved hand to touch the bark. It was denser than any he had seen before and like sandpaper to the touch. As he pressed on it, a handful of tiny, multicolored insects scattered from beneath, their home in the crevices of the tree's skin momentarily disturbed. As soon as he pulled his hand back, they rushed back into hiding.

The lowest limb was at eye level. Caleb tried to give it a light shake, testing it for more insects or other wildlife. When nothing emerged from the wood or moved on the branch, he grabbed on with his other hand and smoothly pulled himself up, swinging a leg over and straddling it. He bounced on it a few times, testing the general strength of the limb to ensure it, and the subsequent higher branches, would hold his weight. It barely moved despite his efforts, proving its sturdiness.

"Here we go," Caleb announced to Ham, reaching up for the next branch and pulling himself up to stand on it. Balancing there, he leaped up to the next branch, catching hold of it and doing a pull-up to swing a leg over it and climb higher. Halfway to the top, he paused to look around.

With the limbs growing more dense and intertwining further up from tree to tree, Caleb wasn't sure he was still on the branches of the original tree, or if he had transferred to another one. He saw small mites on the branches now, their color shifting to camouflage them as they moved along from one thick, droopy leaf to another. They didn't pay him any mind as he brushed the leaves aside, reaching up to continue his climb.

Advancing upward, he paused again when he caught another glimpse of something bright yellow moving briskly through the canopy. It vaguely resembled an octopus, its thick body ending in a number of tentacles wrapped around the branches, swinging from one tree to the next like a monkey.

Freezing suddenly when it seemed to spot him in the trees, it immediately changed color, blending in with the surrounding vegetation so well that Caleb completely lost sight of it. He stared at the spot where he believed it to be, remaining still for nearly a minute before deciding the weird octopus would outlast his patience. Resuming his climb, he glanced back toward the creature when he reached the next branch. It still hadn't moved, leading Caleb to wonder if it had frozen because of him or something else.

Caleb looked down, spotting Ham and the mule waiting below. Ham's head moved constantly as he kept an eye out for trouble. Bringing his attention back to the dense leaves and branches surrounding him, he wondered if trouble may lie up here with him. It was impossible not to consider that predators on this planet might have the same evolutionary trait of camouflage as the octopus and mites. If so, something deadly could be hunting him and he would never know until it was too late.

"You okay up there, Cap?" Ham shouted.

"Yeah, I'm having the time of my life," Caleb shouted back, resolving to focus on what he could control instead of what he couldn't. There was only so much he could do about the unexpected. He resumed his climb, quickly reaching the uppermost limbs. They were thinner at the top, but so thickly intertwined he could sometimes get one foot on two branches, allowing him to punch through the top layer of leaves and finally get a good look at where they had landed.

The jungle canopy stretched into the distance around him, the landscape relatively flat save for an occasional gentle hill. From his perspective, there were no breaks in the foliage or any other indication there was any civilized, intelligent life nearby. Thankfully, the air was clear, and he was able to make out the hint of mountains further away.

Shifting his footing on the branches, he turned around, pausing at the sight of a break in the greenery, where a large lake took up a good portion of the horizon. More distant than the mountain range, it was so big, he could barely see the other side of it.

Looking up at the system's sun, it was smaller than the white dwarf of Trappist-1, and much closer. He imagined their way home was there, hidden within the glow. Or maybe it wasn't. Benning claimed entering the wormhole was a one-way trip. They might have come out near the star. That didn't mean they could do the reverse.

He wondered if Pathfinder had made it this far? Despite his determination to find the ship, he wasn't convinced he would. If a colony had been settled here, there should have at least been satellites, if not starships. Scouts, if not transports. Some signs of life. As it appeared, he and Ham were all alone.

A cry from below, followed by gunshots, challenged that opinion almost before he'd finished forming it.

CHAPTER 18

Six rapid-fire gunshots nearly drowned out Ham's shout. Unable to see his pilot through the thick growth beneath him, Caleb quickly descended, leaping and swinging recklessly from one branch to the next, his heart racing as the faint echoes of the discharges rippled through the air.

He was almost to the ground when his fingernails scraped off the rough bark of a thick branch, sending him tumbling down through the foliage. He broke through smaller branches before slamming into a thicker limb with enough force to knock the air out of him, despite his armor. He tried wrapping his arms around the limb but couldn't get a good enough grip on it to break his fall. Breathless, he hit his shoulders on another branch before falling the rest of the way like a pinball, ricocheting off one limb after another until finally landing on the ground, flat on his back and just in time for a dark blur to shoot past him, moving too quickly for him to tell if it was a Relyeh or something else native to the planet.

At least the moss broke our fall.

"Shut up, smartass," Caleb hissed, still getting his air back as he slowly pushed himself to his feet. The pain in his chest and back quickly subsided, eased by the chemicals Ishek pumped into his system. He quickly took stock of his surroundings, Ham and the mule nowhere to be seen. "Ham! Where are you?" he shouted.

Nothing. No answer. No sound that even suggested Ham was still in the vicinity. Or even alive.

With Spirit's flight deck only a dozen meters away, he hoped maybe the Marine had retreated back inside. Rushing over to it, he poked his head through the capsule's jammed hatch, his hopes of finding Ham there were dashed when he found nothing but empty silence.

Suddenly, he regretted he hadn't ordered Ham to wear the environmental suit. At least the helmet had comms inside. Of course, he hadn't expected the man to disappear into thin air.

He turned back to face the jungle, hands on his hips as he scanned his surroundings. Throwing caution to the wind, he took off his helmet, knowing his voice would carry further without it. "Ham!" he shouted, unable to believe everything had gone sideways in such a hurry. "Where are you?"

Caleb cursed when he spotted Ham's sidearm abandoned in a patch of the dark goop surrounded by the jungle's prevalent moss. Dropping into a defensive crouch, he moved purposely toward the flight deck capsule, stopping to pick up Ham's pistol. The goop it was lying in was thick and sticky, and it clung to the grip like glue. Rather than take the time to wipe it off, he held the weapon as is, the goop oozing out between his fingers. Gross, but harmless. A quick check showed the gun had four rounds remaining.

He dropped to a knee, examining the jungle floor more closely, hoping for footprints. As spongy as the moss was, it did a great job covering any potential tracks, and it appeared that Ham's assailant had avoided the dark green goop, for obvious reasons. Only the barbed vines snaking around the base of the trees helped him narrow down which direction Ham and his attacker had gone. So thick they blocked most of the jungle floor to anything larger than the weird yellow octopus he had seen, he knew Ham hadn't run through the forest and nothing had dragged him through the vines.

"Ham!" he shouted, louder this time, his voice echoing off the trees. Now that he was armed, he wanted the attacker to come back for him, to give him a chance to disable it. "Ham, can you hear me?"

"Cap?"

Ham's voice was hoarse and weak, making it difficult to pinpoint. "Ham! I hear you. Where are you?"

"Over here," he replied. "Behind the capsule."

Caleb ran to the rear of the capsule to find Ham sitting against the side of the downed pod, the mule beside him. He had one hand on his chest, putting pressure on the bloodstain beneath his palm. "What the hell happened?"

"Something thought I was lunch," he replied. "Came out of nowhere. It swatted my gun away and then laid into me. Got me pretty good." He lifted his hand so Caleb could see his torn shirt. Blood oozed out from the wound beneath. Ham stared, laughing.

"What's so funny?" Caleb asked.

"I backpedaled to get away from it. The mule moved to follow. The thing that got me didn't know what to make of it and got spooked." He laughed harder before wincing in pain. "Saved by a dumb robot."

The fact that he was laughing was a good sign. Caleb smiled back as he approached the mule, opening a drawer on the bottom of the pack. "The dumb robot's going to save your life again," he said as he withdrew a first aid kit. "Get your shirt off."

"Maybe we should go back into the capsule and shut the door for a little privacy."

"I'm not flirting with you, Ham," Caleb joked.

His halfhearted grin was filled with pain. "That thing could come back, you know." He pulled his bloody shirt off over his head, revealing three deep lacerations. "Or there could be more of them out there. We'd be safer inside."

"The door is shot. It won't close. I think I got a glimpse of your attacker when I hit the ground. Dark skin. Long and lean."

"Definitely long and lean, it was like somebody combined a crocodile with a chameleon."

"I'm surprised you know what either of those things are."

"I've watched the Life on Earth documentaries. Do you think if we make it back, General Haeri will accept a request for Earth deployment?"

"What about your family?"

"Earth can't be more dangerous than this place."

"Let's hope it is, we only have four bullets left." Caleb put the gun on the moss beside Ham, using his foot to hold it while he pulled his glove away. A line of the ichor stretched from the gun grip to the glove, finally breaking away from the gun and snapping into his palm.

"That's disgusting," Ham commented.

"I don't know what this green goop is, but it's all over the place." He carefully removed the snot-covered glove with his other hand, placing it on the ground beside the gun before removing his other glove and taking a roll of tape out of the kit. Biting off several strips, he stuck them to Ham's chest, pulling the edges of the cuts together and attaching them to his abdomen to hold them closed.

Ham didn't react to the effort, though Caleb knew it had

to hurt. He put the tape away and lifted out a small spray can, quickly washing down the wound.

"Shouldn't you have sprayed first? That's how they taught us in training."

"The tape doesn't stick if you spray first."

"That's not what they taught us," Ham insisted.

"They taught you wrong. Every CSF Marine who does a field dressing finds that out pretty fast." He dropped the spray back into the kit and removed a square of thin paper, which he tore away to get at the patch inside. Removing the backing, he placed it over the tape, its separate adhesive holding in place. "Three days or so, and you should be good as new."

"Thanks, Cap," Ham said, shaking his head. "I can't believe I needed healing after only five minutes out here. I'm embarrassed right now."

"I'm tempted to make you wear the envirosuit so you'll have comms."

"Aww, c'mon. It's too hot for that suit."

"Lucky for you, I made it to the top of the canopy and took a quick look around. There's a lake that way." He pointed away from the capsule. "And a mountain range that way." He spun around and pointed toward it.

"Which direction are we going?"

"If I had seen any breaks in the treetops, I would have said to the lake, hoping we could follow it to Pathfinder. It's smart to set up the colony next to a water source. Since I didn't see any openings in the vegetation, I think the mountains are the better bet. We'll have a better vantage point once we start climbing, and maybe when we get to the top, we'll find Pathfinder there too."

"That makes sense. I don't suppose there's a change of clothes in that pack?" He motioned to his crumpled, bloody shirt.

"Envirosuit," Caleb answered, grinning.

"Smartass," Ham replied. "Is that a no?"

Caleb opened the top of the pack. Of course, the envirosuits were on top. He pushed them aside. Everything else was stored in individual, marked boxes, with the oxygen tank on the bottom. He didn't want to take everything out in a hostile environment, and there were no clothes on top.

"Sorry, Ham. Apparently, the logistics team who filled this thing didn't plan for us to get clawed by a crocochameleon. You've got three choices. The envirosuit, wear your bloody shirt or go bare-chested."

"I don't like any of them."

"Knuckle up. At least you're still alive."

"Only time will tell if that's a good thing."

"Don't start getting all down on me already."

Ham smiled. "Nah. I'm good, Cap. I'm going to get back to my family come Hell or high water."

"That's the spirit." Caleb returned the first aid kit to the pack and held out his hand. Ham took it and let Caleb help him to his feet.

"Shall we try this again?" Ham asked.

Caleb looked down at his gloves and the gun. He wasn't sure it was worth it to keep the gun with only four rounds for it. Remembering the size and speed of the crocochameleon, he decided to keep the gun. But what to do about the goop?

He was able to scrape most of the goop from his glove and gun grip with his knife, but it had left a sticky residue on both. Coating the palm of his glove with dirt worked to offset the residue on it. Likewise, tearing a length of fabric from Ham's shirttail and wrapping it around the weapon's grip had negated that stickiness before returning the gun to his hip.

"Stick close to me. Considering the lizard that attacked you waited until I was high in the trees and ran when it saw the mule, they probably won't bother us if they're outnumbered."

"Just call me goop," Ham joked, tying the sleeves of his shirt around his waist. "Let's hope those things are the most dangerous creatures in this miserable jungle."

"Or on the planet," Caleb added.

"If I had a beer, I'd drink to that."

"You and me both." Caleb pantomimed throwing back a cold one.

I don't think either of you are dumb enough to believe a big lizard is our worst problem.

No, Caleb silently replied. *But give us a few minutes to pretend.*

CHAPTER 19

"We'll camp here for the night," Caleb said, appreciating the rare sight of open ground amidst the jungle's heavy vegetation. Not that it was a large patch of open space. A few meters in diameter. Big enough for the portable shelter.

He looked up at the persistent heavy canopy. Hardly any sunlight pierced the treetops, having left them shrouded in semi-darkness during their six hours of hiking through the wilderness. With the sun now going down, it was getting too dark to see at all. While they had lamps in the pack and the mule had lights mounted above the sensors that served as its eyes, it made more sense to settle in, get some rest, and resume the trek in the morning.

"Seems as good a spot as any," Ham agreed, slumping onto the moss next to the mule. Bugs scurried out from beneath his body, eager to escape his weight.

Fortunately, none of the insects had turned out to be dangerous, and they had seen plenty beyond the iridescent bugs that lived on the jungle floor. A multitude of flying creatures of all shapes and sizes had zipped, flitted, and buzzed past over the last few hours, in such numbers that Caleb had at first worried about Ham's shirtless state. He had been ready to order the Marine into the envirosuit the moment anything landed on him, but nothing did. Either none of the insects were bloodsuckers like mosquitos, or their evolutionary process had left them unable to identify humans as a food source. Whichever the reason, it worked out in their favor.

They had also seen a wide variety of other wildlife along the way. The yellow octopuses seemed to be the most common jungle dwellers. They usually moved through the trees in small groups though they had paused to watch nearly twenty pass overhead, freeze for a few seconds and change color when Ham coughed. Numerous smaller lizards occupied the jungle floor. They hid among the thorny vines and the roots of the trees, darting out to snap up insects with long, frog-like tongues before disappearing back into the brush.

There had also been a few flying creatures that had swooped by from overhead, but they were nothing like the birds on Earth. They reminded Caleb of cuttlefish, with tentacles on their faces and wide, thin membranes that vibrated rapidly to provide lift. He had counted at least a dozen general variations in size and shape. Of course, they didn't see another croco-chameleon the entire time, but they both agreed they had been followed at different points during their march. Every so often, Caleb caught a glimpse of *something* nearby. A weird shadow. A wayward reflection. But nothing openly challenged them.

Even so, he couldn't shake the sense that they had yet to experience anywhere near the worst the planet had to offer.

The mule bowed its legs, lowering its compartment as he approached, allowing him easier access to the top of the pack. The envirosuits were already pressed against the side to provide easier access to the more important equipment and sundries inside. He removed a pair of water pouches, their innards still moist from earlier use, and slid open a small door on the side of the pack, revealing a spigot. Quickly filling the pouches, he handed one to Ham before drinking from his own.

The heat and humidity had taken nearly three hours to penetrate the protection of his combat armor. At this point, the overlay had become a sauna, forcing the underlay to work overtime to draw moisture away from Caleb's body to keep him cool and dry. His relative physical comfort was an illusion, his hydration just as much at risk as Ham's, perhaps even worse. Sweat dripped off the pilot's chin and ran down over his muscled chest, his bare torso so wet he looked as if he had just stepped out of the shower.

Each of them guzzled an entire pouch. Caleb immediately refilled them, and both men finished off another half pouch. The mule carried fifty liters of water that was supposed to last a week or more in an average climate. Using only the water they had on hand, they would run out in less than four days. Fortunately, the pack had a built-in condenser, and in a climate like this could capture plenty of water vapor from the air, making hydration one less thing they had to worry about.

Reaching back into the pack, he retrieved the box of MREs and placed it aside before claiming the largest item in the pack. He placed it near the center of the small clearing and connected a wire from the mule to it before pressing a button on the pack. The box unfolded on its own, and a polygonal structure expanded out from the center on telescoping arms. Opaque gossamer fabric strung to the connectors covered the shelter. At first, it resembled a limp tent, but as it completed its automated expansion, an electrical charge to the fabric changed its properties, turning it into a hard shell. While the atmosphere was breathable, Caleb connected a hose from the mule to the shelter, providing air conditioning to remove moisture from the air while storing it to drink. At least they could control the climate inside the shelter while they rested.

"Ham, go on inside while I finish setting up the perimeter," Caleb said.

"Gladly," Ham replied. He moved to the shelter and opened the now-rigid door, crouching low to squeeze through before sealing it from the inside.

Caleb reached back into the pack, retrieving another box and opening the lid. Inside were eight narrow cylinders and an equivalent number of small tripod mounts, plus a small handheld screen. He quickly attached each cylinder to a mount, placing them around the shelter. Finally, he flipped a switch on the mule to activate its sentry mode before collecting his water pouch and the MREs and entering the shelter.

Ham was splayed out on the fabric floor, already looking refreshed from the much cooler air. He lifted his head to look at Caleb. "I didn't realize how exhausted and overheated I was until now. I'm starting to reconsider what I said earlier about deployment on Earth."

"Not everywhere on Earth is this hot," Caleb replied.

"I'm just saying, a natural climate isn't as great as the documentaries made it seem."

Caleb opened the box of MREs. "What flavor do you want?"

"It doesn't matter. They all taste like dog food."

Caleb picked out one labeled *Salisbury steak* and tossed it onto Ham's chest. He dug through the box until he found a *Thanksgiving Dinner*. His favorite. He figured he had earned it.

Removing his helmet, he breathed the conditioned air deeply into his lungs before sitting cross-legged on the floor. Ham sat up across from him, and they tore into their MREs.

"The gravity here doesn't help with the fatigue either,"

Caleb commented as he ate. "It's like constantly walking uphill."

"At least I'll be able to skip leg days for a while. I think we *were* walking uphill for a stretch there."

"Topography does trend upward in the direction of mountains," Caleb agreed, "though I think we've only covered about ten klicks so far."

"The geniuses in logistics should have included a machete," Ham said. "Those vines are a real pain in the ass. For me, anyway. You can just stomp right through them with your big-assed feet and Ishek power."

"Jii joked with me about having a sword in my weapons locker before we dropped onto the planet. It would have come in handy." He frowned, sighing dejectedly. "I really wish I hadn't had to leave his body behind." The comment instantly soured the mood, and Caleb regretted voicing it.

"You didn't have a choice, Cap. Jii would have understood."

"I know, but still…"

Ham raised his water pouch. "Here's to Corporal Jii Kwon," he said. "A good Marine. A better friend. May he rest in peace."

Caleb tapped his pouch to Ham's, and they both drank, falling silent afterwards, each lost in their own thoughts. Caleb just couldn't get past Jii's death. Unlike anything he'd ever carried away from a battle before, it was sitting in his gut like a dead weight.

"How far do you think it is to the foothills?" Ham asked a few minutes later, as the tension eased.

"Fifty klicks, give or take. I think we can make it in three days once we can start moving at the first crack of light."

"Not too bad. In my mind, I see us getting up to the summit, looking over the edge, and spotting a city in the bottom of a valley with Pathfinder as the centerpiece." He paused. "Not very likely, but you never know, right?"

"You never know," Caleb agreed.

"You should get some shuteye, Cap," Ham said after finishing his water. "We've got a long, hot day ahead of us tomorrow."

"The perimeter's set," Caleb replied. "We should both get some rest." He put the handheld on the floor between them and laid down. "Goodnight, Ham."

"Night, Cap," Ham answered.

Goodnight, Caleb.

Wake me up if there's trouble, Caleb replied, knowing the khoron didn't sleep.

He closed his eyes, almost certain Ishek would give him a solid jolt to wake him up before the night was over.

CHAPTER 20

Ishek didn't wake him that night, or the next night, or the night after that. Caleb and Ham continued their trek, making slow but steady progress toward their goal of reaching the mountains. Having covered ten kilometers in the first day, they managed over twice that each of the next two days.

They spent most of the time telling stories about their lives before the Centurion Space Force, reminiscing over their friendship with Jii, and pointing out the different plants and animals they passed along the way. By the third day, they had compiled a mental list of names they had bestowed on the different creatures. Beyond the croco-chameleon, they had given identities to the cuttle-shuttle, the octo-monkey, and the shimmerbug, among others. In the hot, humid drudgery of traipsing through the seemingly endless jungle, it was an entertaining way to pass the time.

"I'm going up," Caleb decided, pulling to a stop beside the short, wide trunk of one of the stout trees they had named barrel-bellies. The mule came to a quick stop behind him, while Ham paused and glanced his way.

"Are you sure that's a good idea? It didn't go so well for me last time."

"I want to see how much farther we have to go. We must be getting close."

"Won't we know when we get there?"

"Sure. But will that be an hour from now or two more days? It's easier to set the pace with some idea of where we are in relation to our destination." He detached his sidearm from his armor and held it out to Ham.

"It's deja vu all over again," Ham said, accepting the weapon. "How do you know a croco won't jump me the minute you're out of sight?"

"Keep moving so the mule follows you. That'll keep it outnumbered."

"The mule is useless in a fight."

"Good thing the croco doesn't know that."

"I have an idea," Ham said. "Why don't I go up, and you stay down? I can tell you how close we are. And I bet the croco's claws can't get through your armor."

"Have you ever climbed a tree before?" Caleb asked.

"No. How hard can it be?"

"You're built like a bull. Or an ox. A powerful ground dweller."

"After one of the Life On Earth documentaries, my wife called me Abe-Ape for a while. She thought I looked like one of the monkeys on the show."

"The one with the bare ass?" Caleb asked, grinning.

Ham's eyebrows crinkled. "Damn, how did you know that?" Caleb couldn't hold back his laughter. "I watched you climb," Ham continued. "It's no harder than the CSF obstacle course."

"I can't argue with that," Caleb replied. "I wiped out on that course the first time."

"Everyone wipes out on that course the first time. It

doesn't matter how much prior training or experience you have."

Caleb motioned to the barrel-belly. "Okay, Sergeant. But if you fall and break your neck, I'm leaving you for dead right where you land."

"No you aren't," Ham countered knowingly. He approached the trunk, glancing up at the lowest hanging branches. Grinning, he grabbed one of them and pulled himself up, swinging his legs onto the branch and slowly standing. "See, it's not that hard."

"Get to the top and then tell me that," Caleb replied.

"On my way, sir." He reached for the next branch, balancing on it more quickly than the first. Within a couple of minutes, he had climbed nearly halfway, moving through the canopy like one of the octo-monkeys. Or an Abe-ape.

Caleb stopped watching him at that point, instead remaining in motion while scanning their surroundings for evidence of croco-chameleons or anything else that might be a threat. He kept his gun in hand, ready to use if anything managed to sneak up on both him and Ishek. Ham was right in that regard. He was much more equipped to handle trouble.

Not that he expected trouble anymore. After three days without incident, without even a scratch or a bug bite, save for their rookie mistake with the croco-chameleon, he felt relatively confident that his initial impressions of the planet were wrong. While the place still appeared uninhabited by intelligent life, it thankfully wasn't as much of a proverbial jungle as it was a literal one. It was nowhere near as dangerous as he had first believed.

Glancing up every twenty seconds or so, he watched Ham disappear into the upper canopy, where it was impossible to see past the branches and thick foliage. The rustling of the leaves signaled Ham was still climbing. Off to his right, Caleb caught a glimpse of a vine shifting slightly and swung his gun toward it. A nauty-dog burst from the protection of the vines, pouncing on a bit of moss. A dozen tentacles on its face snapped down, collecting shimmerbugs and feeding them into its shovel-shaped mouth. A snap-dragon leaped from another group of vines, catching the nauty-dog off guard. It clamped down on the other animal's hard shell, only to fail in breaking through it. The nauty-dog whipped its head around and wrapped its tentacles around the snap-dragon's throat. The two creatures wrestled in the underbrush for a few seconds before the snap-dragon managed to break free and take off running. The nauty-dog turned back toward the moss, thought better of continuing to eat out in the open and vanished into the vines.

Caleb smiled, glad both animals had escaped unscathed. He didn't need to watch the food chain in action up close.

"Cap, can you hear me?" Ham shouted from above.

"I hear you!" Caleb yelled back.

"I'm here. I can see over the treetops. We're about fifteen klicks from the foothills. If we haul ass, we can probably be there before nightfall."

Caleb was happy to hear they were closer than he'd thought. "Do you see anything else noteworthy?"

"There's a huge flying creature circling about five clicks north of here. It has to be twenty feet long. It looks kind of like an upright squid, with skin between its tentacles that it's somehow using to stay in the air."

"It figures there would be something interesting when I send *you* up there," Caleb joked. "Can you tell why it's circling?"

"No. All I can see are trees, trees, and more trees. It just looks to me like it picked a random spot to hang out. Though I guess it could have babies down there. Or it might be like a vulture, circling something dead."

"Either one of those scenarios makes sense. Come on down. We've got some hauling ass to do."

"Yes, sir. On my way."

Caleb waited while Ham made his descent, continuing to move around the area near the tree to keep the mule following him. He turned to retrace his steps back to the tree when Ishek screamed.

The cry split Caleb's head like an axe, sending an intense wave of pain, dizziness, and nausea through him. He cried out and fell to his knees, dropping his gun and reaching up to grip his head. "Ish, what the hell?" he whispered.

Ishek didn't answer. Caleb gritted his teeth as the agony continued. He did his best to fight through it, but with everything spinning around him, he toppled forward, catching himself on his outstretched hands, his ears ringing. He wasn't sure how long the ringing pain lasted, but it vanished just as quickly as it had come. It took longer for the dizziness to subside.

"Ish, what was that?" he asked as his head began to clear.

I am unsure. I have never experienced anything like it. A sense like my soul was being ripped out of my body, if I had a soul. A piercing dagger from within.

"Through the Collective?" Caleb asked. "Did you drop your guard?"

No. It came from an external source. I am sure of it.

"The Relyeh battle cruiser? The Korath?"

Caleb, I do not know.

"Why did it stop?"

I do not know. I am grateful that it did.

"So am I." Caleb lifted his head, looking up into the tree limbs, expecting to find Ham almost all the way down from the heights. When he didn't spot him, he looked around, afraid the Marine had fallen after all, but he wasn't lying on the ground either. "Ham?" he called out, confused. "Ham!" He tried to stand up, settling for his knees when the world began to spin again. "Ham!" he screamed even louder, voice echoing through the trees.

The Marine didn't answer.

As impossible as it seemed, he was gone.

Again.

CHAPTER 21

Caleb fought his way to his feet despite his lingering dizziness. "Ish, can you clear my head?"

I cannot clear mine.

With pure determination, Caleb managed to stagger to his feet and toward the tree Ham had climbed. He braced one hand against the trunk to keep his balance as he looked up, searching for anything that might indicate a fight had taken place. He found no broken branches. No scuffs in the bark. Nothing.

He shifted his attention to the ground, searching for any indication of a struggle. The spongy, springy moss was no help. It bounced back into its original shape within seconds of being trod upon, leaving no tracks, traces, or clues behind. And while the dark green goop had covered so much of the jungle floor when they had first arrived, it had become decreasingly less abundant as they'd moved toward the mountains. There was no sign of it here.

The only way Ham would go quietly was if he never saw the attack coming. "Do you have any idea how long our seizure lasted?"

I do not.

"It had to be an attack," Caleb decided. "It can't be a coincidence we were disabled when Ham disappeared."

I agree. But who would know how to attack us in such a way? And why would they use the opportunity to seize him and leave?

"Both great questions. We need to find him to learn the answer."

He walked the area around the barrel-belly, still hopeful of finding something, anything, that might give him a lead. Failing that, he turned to the mule, which had continued trailing dutifully behind him while he stumbled around the site. "Where did Ham go? Who took him? How?"

Why are you talking to that machine like it understands you?

"Because I can," Caleb replied. "I'm angry and frustrated." Of course, the mule hadn't responded. It continued standing behind him, waiting for him to move.

Knuckle up, Caleb.

The words froze him in place. He often used the phrase to focus his troops. To remind them to control the situation, rather than let the situation control them. Running chaotically across the surrounding area in a panic wouldn't help him find Ham.

Closing his eyes, he concentrated on his breathing. The carefully crafted calm not only allowed him to think more clearly, it drove out the residual pain and dizziness from the attack. As an added bonus, closing his eyes turned his mental attention to his other senses. While he hadn't seen any evidence of Ham's abduction, he heard something now, a light hum that stood out over the rattle of branches in the breeze, the clicking of insects, and the weird whistle-slaps and other noises of the jungle's wild inhabitants.

"Ish, correct me if I'm wrong, but that sounds like the hum of anti-gravity plates."

I find that difficult to believe, but I also cannot be certain you're wrong. Regardless, it isn't close.

Caleb's eyes snapped open, and he looked toward the

jungle behind the tree trunk, the direction from which the noise emanated. "If it's close enough to hear, it's close enough to catch."

I don't believe it works that w—

Caleb took off through the thorny vines before Ishek finished making his point. The barbs on the vines bit at his gloves as he tore at them vines, pulling them aside until they snapped. Clearing a path, he picked up speed, charging recklessly through the dense vegetation, his only thought to find Ham. The mule kept up with him, its spindly legs able to navigate the creepers with relative ease, stepping between the strands, its metal body impervious to the thorns.

Within a few minutes, he reached the largest clearing he had seen in the jungle thus far. Nearly twenty meters in diameter, it was too perfectly shaped and too perfectly barren of tree trunks and vines to be naturally made. Moving to the center of the clearing, he closed his eyes, using a few precious seconds to listen. He just barely made out the echo of whirring from anti-grav plates, moving perpendicular to the mountain. The familiar, rhythmic hum had become more faint, the machine clearly outrunning him.

I told you it doesn't work that way.

Caleb gritted his teeth, turning in the direction of the sound. He wasn't giving up that easily. Damn it, he wasn't giving up at all.

A different sound, coming from a different direction, stole his attention before he could take another step. He reached for his gun as a dark blur faded into existence at the edge of the clearing. He pointed the weapon at the croco-chameleon as it exploded from the brush faster than any croc or gator on Earth could move.

Rather than wasting his last four rounds on an uncertain shot, he dove to the side just before it jumped him. The creature's sharp, curved claws grated along his overlay as it shot past. Caleb rolled to his feet, his eyes once again on the croc as it planted its hind quarters to slow its momentum and spun smoothly around, rushing back toward him.

Again, he didn't shoot, unable to get a bead. The creature had already learned from its first mistake, and rather than leap up at him, it came in low, shifting its weight. Too slow this time, Caleb wasn't able to dodge the croc's claws. The sharp talons yanked his leg out from under him, but fortunately, didn't penetrate his overlay even though the attack sent him tumbling.

Managing to come to a stop on his hands and knees, he wasn't quick enough to avoid the creature's jaws. His faceplate fogged up from the creature's breath as its jaws clamped down around his helmet. All Caleb could see was the croc's dark tongue and fleshy throat as it shook its head, dragging him back and forth with ridiculous ease. Cracks spread across his faceplate, the integrity of the headgear failing.

Caleb reached back over his head and punched his fist into the soft orb of the croc's eye. Single-mindedly intent on killing its prey, it refused to release him, the pressure of its bite twisting and collapsing Caleb's helmet.

He knew he had seconds before he was going to die.

Caleb wrapped his arm around the creature's head and jammed the muzzle of his pistol against the croc's throat. He fired all four bullets into its gullet. Just as he'd hoped, the slugs penetrated its skull and lodged in its brain. It let out a final huff of fetid air Caleb could smell through his cracked faceplate and slumped to the ground, dead.

Caleb holstered his pistol and forced his way free of the croc's jaws, but he wasn't yet free of his predicament. The damage to his helmet had changed its shape just enough to jam the mechanism locking it to the overlay of his armor. Gritting his teeth, he growled as he strained to twist it free.

Finally, it snapped loose, and he yanked it off, throwing it into the tree line in a fit of rage.

Breathing heavily, he remained slumped in the dirt until fresh motion in the vegetation forced him back to his feet. He discarded his empty gun, useless now that he had no more ammo for it, and balled his hands into fists.

Waiting.

The mule emerged from the brush, finally catching up to him. He expelled the breath he hadn't realized he was holding, his shoulders slumping. In his desperation to catch up to the anti-grav noise, he had inadvertently given the croco-chameleon an opening it might have been waiting days for.

He had lost Ham and nearly his life.

"Stupid," Caleb chided himself. Turning back to the dead creature, "You almost had me, you bastard." He hauled off and kicked the thing's head hard enough to lift it off the foot it rested on, blood flying from its wounds. Ironically, Caleb's attention settled on its clawed foot. "But maybe…" His mouth slowly stretched into a smile. "Just maybe some good will come of it." He kneeled in front of the croco's frying pan-sized foot. He had seen grizzly bears during hikes in the woods, way back before he had enlisted. He remembered being awed by their size and power, but had wondered if a croc came to blows with a grizz, which one would win.

A croc. Definitely.

There was no hesitation in Ishek's reply.

"Yeah, I think so, too." He paused. "I also think there are humans here, Ish."

You have no proof of that.

"Someone grabbed Ham. I'm sure of it. If they have anti-gravity tech, they probably took off on a hovercraft of some kind."

That doesn't automatically make them human.

"Another species, then. Either way, they knew how to

disable us. That at least makes them intelligent. And it probably means they've encountered Relyeh before. You don't think…"

…they believed Abraham was in trouble and were trying to protect him from us? It would be an interesting twist.

"At least if we're right, it would mean he's safe. Maybe he can even convince them to come back for us."

And if we're wrong?

Caleb picked up the croc's foot to study its three-inch claws. "That's why we aren't chasing after them unarmed."

CHAPTER 22

Caleb remained in the clearing for the next two hours, fashioning new weapons and ostensibly waiting to see if Ham's abductor would return to apologize for attacking them. In his most wishful thinking, they would lead him back to where Pathfinder had landed so long ago that the vegetation had covered the ship, the colony alive and well in Metro.

He wasn't surprised when no one showed, but he was disappointed, leaving him even more concerned for Ham's safety. At least he hadn't wasted his time ripping the claws out of the croco-chameleon's carcass. He'd used them to cut a pair of stout, roughly straight branches about a yard long from the nearest barrel-belly, trimming away all the offshoots and leaves. Retrieving adhesive from the mule's pack, he had attached four claws to the end of each stick, creating two primitive, nasty-looking, and hopefully effective clubs. He'd sliced off strips from one of the envirosuits to create relatively comfortable hand grips.

Armed, he considered setting up camp for the night before rejecting the idea. The sun was sinking low on the horizon, the trees casting long shadows into the clearing. It would be dark in an hour or two, but with Ham possibly in trouble, every minute counted. Careful to keep better track of the mule, he started off through the forest in the direction of the sounds he had heard, which he was still convinced had come from a hovercraft of some kind.

As he thrashed his way through the jungle, the same questions swirled through his thoughts like a CD on repeat. Who had taken Ham, to what ends and where was he? Why was there no sign of them on the recording of their descent to the planet's surface? Were they on their way to investigate the capsule's crash when they'd come across him and Ham? Were they human? Did they come from Pathfinder? Did they really have experience with the Relyeh, and more specifically khoron like Ishek? Could they be reasoned with? Did they even exist at all, or did something snatch Ham to eat him? Was he simply convincing himself that he heard the sound of gravity plates and that Ham might still be alive?

Although Ishek could read his thoughts, the symbiote remained silent while Caleb stewed. One of the most unfair parts of the relationship was that the mind-reading wasn't bi-directional. It didn't go both ways. Caleb didn't know what Ishek was thinking, even though Ishek knew his every cognitive thought. In fact, that was the reason the enemy had bonded the khoron to him against his will. They had never suspected how he would turn the tables on the symbiote and convert Ishek into an ally.

You would not like the way a khoron's mind functions.

"Oh, now you have something to say?" Caleb asked.

I refuse to dignify our obsessiveness with a response. There's no value in being consumed by questions that cannot be answered. You should know better.

"I'm worried about Ham."

Understandable, and ultimately pointless. You will either find him alive, or you will find him dead. Or perhaps you won't find him at all. That outcome doesn't change our predicament.

"Don't you care about anything at all?"

Survival. Both yours and mine.

"You only care about my survival because you die if I die."

I believe we established that early in our bonding.

"I really don't like you sometimes, Ish."

A natural reaction. I don't like you sometimes, either. But I've accepted my fate. We will resolve Ham's disappearance, one way or another. Be careful not to let your personal feelings cloud your objectivity. You are a Marine above all else. And you still have a mission.

"And right now, that mission is leading me in the same direction as Ham's disappearance," Caleb agreed. "There's a chance whoever took him is from Pathfinder. A slim chance, maybe. But it isn't zero."

According to Charlotte Benning, some level of the military or government of Pathfinder knew about the wormhole, and the ship entered intentionally. I do not believe it was to land on the first planet they discovered. Perhaps not zero, but I wouldn't put the odds much higher than that.

"Then who are they? Where did they come from?"

I know what you're trying to do.

"What's that?"

Caleb smirked when Ishek didn't answer. He'd tried to drag the symbiote into his rumination and failed. Maybe he was obsessing, after all. He forced himself to drop it, clearing his thoughts as best he could and concentrating on picking up his pace. Darkness was falling, and he would need to stop soon.

I have a question.

"And you don't already know the answer?"

If Abraham was taken, then whoever took him has the means

to disable us from a distance. Even assuming we can catch up to them, how do you intend to defeat that ability?

"You didn't catch me thinking about that already?"

I must not have been paying attention.

"The fact that they grabbed Ham and ran suggests they weren't confident whatever they did would work. Which means it can probably be defeated. We just need to figure out how. And before you ask how we figure out how, I haven't solved that one yet. But if you describe your experience, maybe we can come up with some ideas."

It hurt.

"Always starting with the obvious. What did it feel like, besides painful."

Ishek remained silent for a few moments, a good sign that the symbiote was assembling a serious answer.

As you know, the Collective operates via an organ we call a collar, *which phases between this universe and the pocket universe where communication between Relyeh entities can occur in real time. I'm able to wall off my link to that universe by pushing a constant flow of garbage energy mentally out through it. Like singing loudly to drown out someone else speaking. I've become so accustomed to it that it takes no effort at all anymore. The weapon put my collar out of phase. Confused it, creating a feedback loop so powerful it spread from me to you.*

"Someone would need to have pretty intimate knowledge of Relyeh anatomy to build a weapon like that."

Yes. It is very concerning.

"Can you do anything to prevent the phase change?"

There is one thing. And this may be why they were uncertain the weapon would function. But I am not enamored with the idea.

"Don't keep me in suspense, Ish."

I can strengthen my connection to the Collective by communicating directly with another Relyeh, one that is powerful enough to hold the link despite their efforts to destroy it.

Caleb groaned under his breath. "If you stop singing to

link with another Relyeh, that Relyeh will know where you are. And once one Relyeh knows where you are, they all do."

I told you that I'm not enamored with the idea.

"Who would you try to contact?"

A lesser Relyeh. A Korath. Perhaps the one that was chasing us?

"Are you sure that's a good idea? If they came through the wormhole, they'll be able to find us pretty easily."

I can locate another, but as you said, once one of my kind knows where we are, any with enough interest will also know, including the Korath.

Caleb pulled to a stop, no longer able to see well enough in the increasing darkness to make out much of anything in front of him. For as much as he wanted to help Ham, he couldn't find him if he wound up with a broken leg, even though Ishek could help it heal faster than normal.

"I guess we'll have to cross that bridge when we come to it," he said. "Is there another way we can defend against that kind of attack?"

Short of removing my collux, I do not believe so.

"Can we remove it?"

Only if you'd like us both to die.

"Scratch that idea."

He smirked despite himself as the mule moved in behind him. If anyone had been around to hear him, they would likely think him insane for talking to himself, especially in such a one-sided fashion. He was used to it. While he did occasionally speak to Ishek in silence, he preferred speaking out loud when Ham and Jii were around. It was so they knew he was talking to his symbiote and could include them in the conversation. Now, he just supposed he liked to hear himself talk.

Caleb quickly set up the shelter and placed the sentry devices around the perimeter before ducking into the hardened tent. Sitting inside without Ham for the first time, he became angry at the sense of loneliness that began creeping in. With Ishek, he was never alone. But Ishek wasn't human. The symbiote didn't always understand.

I don't always want to understand.

"In some ways, having you always here makes it worse," Caleb said, in no mood to try to explain what he meant. "Wake me if you hear anything."

As usual.

Caleb laid down on the floor of the shelter and closed his eyes. He barely had a chance to doze off before Ishek sent chemicals surging through him, shocking him back awake.

Caleb, we aren't—

The sentries around the perimeter started wailing, and an instant later, the shelter was violently lifted and thrown aside.

CHAPTER 23

The flash of light, its underlying heat, and loud boom told Caleb the tent had been hit with an explosive like a rocket or grenade, tossing him around inside it like a ragdoll.

The hardened shelter rolled over vines and slammed into a tree, leaving him on his head and shoulders in the back corner when it came to rest. Made of a similar material to his overlay, the tent's protective properties had absorbed everything from the blast except the kinetic force. It was the only reason he was still alive.

Smaller weapons fire peppered the tent. Instead of the more conventional chemical firearms or coilgun, each thwipping sound and the dents in the shelter told him a railgun had targeted him.

We need to get out of here.

Caleb didn't need Ishek to tell him as much. The shelter would only hold for a few more seconds at the current rate of fire. Fortunately, he had fallen asleep with a grip on each of his makeshift weapons, and experience had kept him holding onto them during the attack. He shifted to his knees now, aiming his attention on the shelter's exit. He would need to rip open the internal clasps holding the exit closed just before he punched through it.

"Here goes nothing," Caleb growled as he sprang forward, swinging one of the croc-clawed clubs at the clasps. The talons sliced through all three, and he kept going, blasting through the front flap and tumbling out of the shelter like a cannonball. He landed flat on his stomach in a thicket of thorny bushes behind the tent and stayed there, the shelter still providing cover.

His luck was holding.

His belly flat against the above-ground roots, he leopard-crawled around the barrel-belly that had stopped the shelter's headlong tumble and stopped there. His attackers, having punctured the tent with at least fifty rounds, suddenly stopped firing. He crawled to the tent and peered around it. With the initial explosion having left the jungle on fire at the point of impact, he had enough light to see movement in the brush. A soldier moved out of the darkness and into the light of the flames. Quickly, as more soldiers emerged from cover, he recognized the echelon formation. Whoever they were, he felt fairly certain they were military trained.

He was also fairly certain they were human.

Nearly two meters tall, they wore green camo patterned armor with hard plates attached to a thick overlay, reminding him of the earlier models of advanced tactical combat armor he wore on Earth. A bulky helmet covered their heads, their nearly opaque faceplates reflecting the small fire. The long railgun the lead soldier cradled in his arms was similar to kit he had seen in the Centurion Space Force armory.

He had no lingering doubt they were human. But it was more than that. They were equipped like he might have expected Pathfinder's Guardians to be outfitted. Had he inadvertently found the descendants of the ship's survivors? Or rather, had they found him?

If that was the case, why the hell were they trying so hard to kill him?

I don't know whether we should surrender or attack, he said silently to Ishek.

Our mission is to find Pathfinder. If these soldiers are from the ship, then your mission is complete. However, based on the violence with which they hit the shelter, I do not believe they will accept your surrender. It may be because of me they believe you are a threat and not someone they should negotiate with.

I can't prove they're from Pathfinder. It just seems that way based on their gear. But you're probably right about negotiation. They could have surrounded us and forced us out of the shelter. They probably thought the bomb would be enough to kill us in our sleep.

Which wasn't very nice.

No, it definitely wasn't.

Caleb...I—

Don't even think about it.

But I hunnggerrrr.

Forget it, Ish. I'm going to disable them and get them to talk.

Injury creates more fear than death. Especially when the vulture is circling.

I hate when you say that.

I know.

Ishek's chuckle lingered in his mind as he shifted forward, bringing himself to a crouch beside the tent as the lead soldier reached the battered shelter, his rifle trained on it. Two others pushed into the vines on the other side of it, the other two remaining further back in defensive positions. They would be the most challenging part of what came next.

Ish, power me up.

You've asked for that a lot lately. You risk burning out.
Now isn't the time to argue.

Caleb felt the tingle run through his body as Ishek forced him to produce more adrenaline, adding his own mix of sense-enhancing chemicals to the mix. Breathing in deeply, Caleb made his plan and set himself, preparing to spring into action.

The two soldiers circling around to the other side of the tent paused at the front next to where it was lodged against the barrel-belly.

"The flap's open," he heard, picking up the speaker's voice, tinged with a bit of a British accent, through the leader's internal helmet speaker. These soldiers had to be from Pathfinder. But if so, why would they be so intent on killing him? He was on their side. Hell, he had come to *help* them.

"The creature survived?" one of the other soldiers commented.

Creature? Do they mean me?

Ishek sounded offended.

What if they mean me? Caleb replied.

One of the two at the flap, a woman, leaned forward, pushing it open with the muzzle of her rifle while activating a spotlight on her armor. Knowing they would be more alert as soon as they realized he was missing, Caleb made his move.

He continued around the tent, finding the leader about to follow the others around the other side of the tent. With the man facing away from him, he had surprise and his knowledge of his opponent's armor as an advantage. He rushed forward, a quick flick of his wrist slicing the claws of one club through the connector linking the leader's helmet to his armor. With the other, he pulled the magnetic attachment to the man's power pack free of his armor.

Just as he attempted to turn around, Caleb kicked him

in the back of his right knee, bringing him down on the other one. He dropped both clubs and ripped the man's helmet off. A kick to his temple laid him out, unconscious.

The two on the other side of the tent whirled around and leveled their rifles at him. Caleb ducked to snatch up his clubs as they fired their rounds passing over his head.

He whirled, ruining their aim again as he swung both clubs, not only knocking their rifles out of their hands but managing to damage the encasements and the delicate rails inside. He could see the female's wide eyes behind her faceplate as she froze, knowing her gun would likely blow up in her face.

Yesssss.

The other soldier fired. His gun sparked and smoked an instant before it exploded. He cried out when it blew his hand off and sent a jagged piece of the casing through his faceplate and straight into an eye to penetrate his brain. Caleb tossed his clubs down. Before the dead man hit the ground and the woman could move out of his way, he had her wrapped up in his arms, his left around her throat, the other one across her torso, bringing her back tight to his chest. He held her there, knowing her last two comrades, one now on each side of them, couldn't get a clean shot at him. One of them tried anyway, the slug whizzing past his head.

That was a little too close for comfort.

Caleb reached up and removed her helmet. Her eyes were on fire as she glared back over her shoulder at him, confirming once and for all that he was fighting other humans. His people.

"I'm not your enemy," he ground out, his face near her ear. "Why are you people fighting me?" he asked, looking back and forth between the two men, their rifles still aimed at him.

"Demon bastard," she assailed, struggling to free

herself. When that didn't work to her advantage, she tried dropping through his hold. With his superior size and grip, Caleb held onto her. She finally gave up the fight, turned her head toward each of the two shooters and gave one distinct jerk of her head.

Cal—

Ishek's warning came too late. The shooters did what Caleb considered the unthinkable. They opened fire, their rounds passing through the woman's armor and into her body. He dropped her dead weight, bullets chasing him from both sides as he dove for the man closest to him, the one between him and the tree line. All but one of their bullets missed him, the round punching through his armor's overlay. His underlay stopped it short of biting into his shoulder. The rest of the slugs dug into the ground around him as he rolled onto his feet and went for his target. The other man stopped firing at Caleb then, either out of ammo or afraid he'd hit his own man.

Cal grabbed the rifle from the hands of the man in front of him and twisted it out of his hands, bashing his faceplate in with the stock. Blood splattered inside his helmet, his nose breaking as he dropped to the ground, clutching his shattered faceplate.

Hearing the man behind him run toward him, Caleb ducked low, the man's rifle swinging by his head in a near miss. Turning, Caleb swung his captured rifle into the man's knee, right at the soft spot between the armor plates,hoping to break the man's kneecap. He figured he'd done just that when the soldier screamed and dropped to the clearing floor. Caleb dropped the rifle and pounced on his back, quickly wrapping an arm around his throat in a tight chokehold. He didn't let go until the man stopped struggling, unconscious from oxygen deprivation.

Three down, two to go. The fear is so tasty.

Ishek was giddy on the terror. Breathing heavily, Caleb

was anything but. He couldn't make sense as to why these people were willing to kill one another just to kill him, while he didn't want to hurt them at all.

At this point, he wasn't sure he had a choice. They'd taken Ham, hopefully to protect him. But what would they do when he told them that his captain was a comrade, not a slave to a khoron? Would they kill him too? Had they killed him already?

Caleb rose to his feet.

"Die, demon."

The voice came from behind him. He went absolutely still and then slowly raised his hands, slowly turning around to face the two men standing there, rifles trained on him. One was the rear guard, the other the last man that had gone around to the open tent flap.

"You really don't want to kill me. Believe it or not, I am your only hope."

The soldier laughed. "Not likely. You're about to die, demon."

"You killed your fellow soldier to get to me. Why won't you listen to me?"

These soldiers are from Pathfinder, it's been over a hundred years since they passed through the wormhole. Who knows what might have happened to change them?

When the man who'd spoken to him seemed to hesitate, the other spoke. "Quit palavering with the asshole, Larkin! Kill him!"

Still, he hesitated.

"Oh, for Pete's sake!" The other soldier stepped around the one he'd called Larkin and once again raised his rifle.

There are only two options remaining.

Ishek was right. And he didn't like either option. Run away, or be prepared to kill. He chose the only option he could accept. He dove behind the tent, bullets whizzing past the side of the tent. If he'd continued to stand there, they would have dug into his armor instead of blazing past into the jungle.

The gunfire stopped, offering a welcome lull in the action. However, Caleb was aware he was running out of time. Ishek's boost was fading, and neither soldier he'd knocked out would stay that way forever. There was also a strong possibility the two still standing had called for backup.

He made up his mind, his final decision only possible because of his bond to Ishek. Circling the tent, he locked eyes on the leader's discarded rifle. There was no guarantee he would survive the next ten seconds. But if anything happened to Ham and he didn't fight like hell to help him, he wouldn't be able to live with himself anyway.

He threw himself out from cover, diving toward the downed soldier and his rifle. The two soldiers immediately spotted him, turning to open fire. Obviously trying not to hit their commander, their carefully placed slugs chewed up the dirt around him. He scooped up the gun and dove onto his stomach, rolling the leader on his side for cover in front of him. Rounds whistled over his head, and he shot back, knowing exactly where to aim. He needed only a dozen rounds to silence the two remaining soldiers for good.

With the area clear, he lowered his rifle, more saddened than satisfied by the outcome. He had no problem killing Relyeh. This was different. Only their eagerness to kill him, their willingness to kill one another to do it, had freed his conscience to do the otherwise unconscionable.

He kept the rifle, maglocking it to his back before returning to the squad leader, picking up his helmet and seizing him by a plate on his armored shoulder. He dragged him to the tree and left him, returning to the other surviving soldier to bring him over, too. When he arrived, the man's eyes were open, looking up at Caleb.

"Demon bastard," he said. "You'll get nothing from me."

Before Caleb could respond, the man bit down on something in his mouth. He began choking, foam bubbling from his mouth as he toppled over and died.

Well, that was unexpected.

Caleb stared down at the man, realizing he needed to get back to the leader to stop him from committing suicide, too. Rushing the short distance back to the tree, he froze when he reached the man.

He was already too late.

CHAPTER 24

Caleb stared at the dead soldier, shocked and confused. Shooting the woman soldier to get to him had been one thing. Killing themselves to prevent him from questioning them reached a whole other level. The soldiers had made it painfully clear they considered him an enemy. A demon bastard, as one of them put it. Because of Ishek? Or for another reason?

He had no way to know, because none of them had been willing to listen to reason. They had refused to see him as anything other than an evil being, with such intensity that it almost left him feeling like he really was evil. If the squad's actions had told him anything else, it was likely reinforcements were already on the way, called in the moment they had realized he wasn't in the shelter. He didn't know how long it might take for them to arrive. A few minutes at least. He didn't want to waste a second lingering around here.

First, he claimed the dead commander's sidearm—a conventional firearm with a fifteen round magazine and a rounded, futuristic frame. He stuck it to his hip before returning to the commander's battery pack, discarded on the jungle floor. He quickly turned it over and laid down with his back to it, trying to lock it into place on his armor. The connectors weren't the same style, their location a hair different, making the pack unusable with his armor. As much as he wanted power for his SCACS, he wanted the overlay's protection even more. It had saved him from severe injury or death a couple of times already.

Moving on from the commander to the two shooters, a quick search uncovered a replacement battery and two extra magazines for the railgun he had picked up. One of the soldiers also carried a knife, which he was happy to snap to his left thigh, opposite the sidearm. Re-armed, he began searching for the mule.

Caught in the initial blast, it had been thrown into the vines nearly twenty meters away, all four legs either twisted out of alignment or completely sheared off. Its featureless face was melted, but at least the hardened pack was still sealed and intact. He opened it to retrieve only the greatest necessities—a full water pouch and a handful of MREs. He would miss having the comfortable shelter at night, but having discovered there were humans on the planet, he held out hope he wouldn't spend the rest of his life living in the jungle.

Finishing up at the site within a couple of minutes, he headed in the direction from which it seemed the soldiers had approached, picking carefully through the thicket, the fire having died out enough for the darkness to creep back in. Arriving so quickly, there was no way the soldiers could have been on foot. They had to have a ride around her somewhere, but it might be camouflage. Difficult to locate.

He had to try.

It was clear from the attack that the enemy wouldn't allow him anytime to rest, especially now that he'd inadvertently killed an entire squad of their soldiers. It was going to be difficult for him to convince them he wasn't a demon, even if he did carry a khoron in his armpit. Even so, he had to know what happened to Ham. He had to find him, no matter what. Once he found them, he would try again to talk to the people who had him. But if they still wouldn't listen...

All bets are off.

"Exactly," Caleb agreed. He paused, a thought slipping into his mind. "It's a good thing the soldiers didn't hit us with that disruption attack a second time."

Yes. It is...fortunate.

Ishek's hesitation and tense mental tone didn't sit well with Caleb. "They did hit us with it, didn't they?"

Before I respond, consider that we would be dead right now otherwise.

Caleb winced in response to the admission. "Who did you sync with?"

I'm uncertain. A powerful Relyeh, for sure. But not an ancient. She asked me who I was because she didn't know me. I didn't reply. I only needed a few seconds. And I proved my theory correct.

"Great. I feel so much better about it now. At least your theory is correct, and will remain correct when the enemy horde comes looking for us."

I did what I had to do to save our lives. You could at least show a modicum of appreciation.

"You're right," Caleb agreed. "For now, you kept us standing. We can worry about the consequences later."

He continued backtracking through the jungle, his eyes steadily adjusting to the lack of ambient light. Ishek helped him out, too, somehow altering his chemical composition to slightly improve his night vision, which in turn enabled him to move faster through the jungle. Ten minutes and nearly a full kilometer later, he came upon a corridor cleared of the jungle's vegetation. Nearly twice as wide as the path he had chased Ham's abductor along, it stretched in both directions, running perpendicular to the nearby mountains. Jogging along it, it didn't take him long to spot the soldiers' transportation.

The hovercraft rested with its undercarriage on the ground. A simple armored rectangular shape from the rear, a sealed hatch occupied most of the vehicle's backside, while a weapon's turret that was either remote controlled or automated was visible on top. Though Caleb didn't believe anyone had remained on board, he carefully approached the vehicle by leaving the road and sneaking up on it from the flank. The roundabout approach through the jungle took him longer than coming at the vehicle head on, but it allowed him to locate the forward boarding hatch, hidden from the front by the gun turret and to get a better look at the viewports along the vehicle's side.

Anti-gravity technology had just been invented at the time of the Relyeh invasion of Earth. The first models of hoverbikes were being released, and the military had started placing orders for combat vehicles that could essentially ignore minefields and IEDs planted in the dirt. It might have been a pretty exciting time for the planet, technology-wise, if things hadn't gone completely sideways. As it was, in the years of war that followed, only a small number of hovercraft had ever been produced. He was certain this one had to be from that era.

The head of a bulldog had been freshly painted on the front quarter panel of the APC, above a faded Union Jack. An identifier that confirmed it had come from Pathfinder was nearly scratched off beneath the flag. The iconography left Caleb excited, confused, and saddened. He was so close to finding the missing generation ship that he was looking at one of the vehicles loaded onto the ship back on Earth over two centuries earlier. At the same time, he feared the condition he would find the colony in.

Returning the railgun to his back, he drew the sidearm he had lifted from the squad leader. He didn't think anyone was still on board the APC, but he wasn't taking any chances. Avoiding the viewports, he boarded the vehicle at the stern, advancing between the blowers to the forward hatch, where he opened a small panel beside the hatch to reveal the manual entry pad. Since the APC had come from Pathfinder, it was most likely running the same operating system as the military gear built for the other generation ships.

Which meant he knew the passcode.

He typed it in, positioning himself to swing his pistol into the hatch as soon as it began to move aside. Rushing into the vehicle, he quickly swung around to check and confirm that the back storage area was clear before heading forward through the empty seating in the main bay to the driver's compartment. He found it empty as well. Returning the pistol to his side, he pulled the railgun from his back and set it down on the floor before sitting in the driver's seat and flipping the power on. The display in front of him and the screen to the right of the yoke immediately came to life. Night vision cameras feeding the display allowed him to see much further along the road, both forward and aft, leaving him only mildly surprised when he spotted a second APC approaching from the rear.

He knew the group that took Ham would send reinforcements.

He'd just hoped to have more time.

CHAPTER 25

Caleb's attention briefly remained on the angled front of the oncoming APC before his eyes shifted to the control display on his right. While the turret on top of the vehicle had been designed for manual operation, or at least gunner-assisted operation, it did have an automated setting that could be enabled by the driver. He would need to mark the targets on a radar grid, but that wouldn't be much of a problem at all. And since the other APC likely believed the one he was sitting in had to be empty, he could turn them into a fireball before they knew what hit them.

Yesss. A fine plan.

Caleb ignored Ishek. The people in that APC were descendants of the colonists who had fled Earth on Pathfinder. The people he was supposed to protect. He'd only shot the two soldiers because they'd left him no choice. It had been kill or be killed. One hundred percent self-defense.

He'd tried to talk to them. To defuse the situation. He didn't understand why they were so hell-bent on killing him, but he had to assume they had a good reason. The only other option was that they'd all gone insane.

They have to be insane. They shot one of their own to get to you. You didn't have a choice then, and you don't have a choice now. They're too close. If you try to run, they'll see you.

"I do have a choice," Caleb replied. "And a plan."

A terrible plan.

"We'll see."

"Alpha, do you copy?" a voice said over the APC's comms. "Alpha, are you there? This is Delta. We've got eyes on your ride. We're two klicks out and closing fast. Do you copy? Over."

"They sound like perfectly normal, sane soldiers to me," Caleb said, countering Ishek's argument that they were crazy.

We'll see.

He reached for the radio, activating his end of the channel. He could fake a decent accent.

He hoped.

"Delta, this is Alpha. I copy. Damn, I'm glad you're here. This routine cleanup has turned into a real mess. Sarge and the rest of the bulldogs are unresponsive, their vitals in the gray. They're all dead." He did his best to sound panicked while smirking in response to his quick thinking to throw in the unit's nickname, which he'd guessed from the stencil on the chassis.

"Alpha APC, this is Delta. Who is this?"

"Me?" Caleb said, glancing around the front of the APC. He spotted a tablet resting on the seat opposite him and scooped it up. "I...uh...I..."

"I need you to calm down, soldier," a gruff voice said through the comms. Caleb assumed it was Delta's commander.

"Y...yes, sergeant." The tablet interface requested his biometrics or a passcode to enter. He tapped the passcode option. While he didn't know the password the squad leader had set for the device, he didn't need it. Every piece of software used by the various Space Forces for the generation ship program had a backdoor accessible via a master root password. As one of General Haeri's most trusted assets, he knew that password. "I…I'm trying. I just…I didn't expect…"

He quickly entered the password, unlocking the tablet and navigating to the active duty roster, which at first only showed him the team he'd encountered outside. The commander was Sergeant Larone Tyson. Not the most British name he had ever heard. Corporal Emily Campbell. Private Ho'chin Sun. Private Samuel Jones, and Private Kelsey Nelson. Looking at the picture of Private Nelson, he couldn't have been more than a hair over eighteen. And he had killed himself rather than talk to Caleb. He flipped to the rest of the roster, quickly noting it was only twelve pages long. This group didn't have all that many soldiers.

"I need a name and rank, soldier," the sergeant growled through the comms. "Now."

I told you this was a terrible plan.

Caleb navigated the list until he found someone who sort of looked like him, or at least someone he could pass as through night vision filters. "Corporal Darren Hicks, Sergeant!"

"I'm going to need your identifier, too, Corporal. You have ten seconds to comply, or we'll have no choice but to consider you compromised."

Compromised? Caleb wondered silently.

It seems they might have dealt with a khoron infestation in the past. That explains a lot.

How do they know I'm carrying a khoron?

Maybe because you aren't from this planet.

Neither is Ham.

I don't know. Perhaps they have sensors that can use to identify us.

My plan is shot if that's the case.

How many times do I have to tell you it's not a good plan?

Can't you shut down or something?

I'm a khoron, not a computer.

Then find some way to make yourself not a khoron.

They seem to have an understanding of how a collux works. Perhaps they have a means to detect its presence.

So shut your collux down.

If I could do that, why have I been singing non-stop for the last five years?

Give me something, Ish!

We're screwed.

Let's hope not.

"HMSF one-one-three-six-niner-niner-four-seven," he read from the Corporal's profile on the roster.

There was no immediate response from the second APC, leaving Caleb ready to bolt for the exit. Did the man in the other hovercraft know Hicks well enough to know he wasn't him? He'd placed a risky bet to avoid having to fight his way out of this.

Would it pay off?

"Identifier verified," the sergeant finally replied. "This is Sergeant Nadel. We've almost reached you. What's your situation? Are you hurt?"

Caleb exhaled his pent up tension, nearly forgetting to continue to sound disturbed. "Negative, Sergeant. I'm not injured. I...I'm not even supposed to be here. Sergeant Tyson pulled me from my bunk at the last second to drive the bus and manage the sync. He didn't have a spare a-tac, so I've been holed up in here the entire time. Sarge said the detail would be a cakewalk, but it went sideways, fast. That demon bastard isn't like the others."

"They're all tricky and slippery little SOBs," Nadel said. "Do you have a weapon, Corporal?"

"Yes, Sergeant."

"Good. We're approaching your position, meet us outside."

We're screwed.

"Outside?" Caleb asked. He had been hoping they'd let him loiter in the APC while they surveyed the scene and hunted for the escaped demon. Once they had gotten far enough away, said demon could have made a run for it, in the direction of the soldiers' base.

"Do you have primordial fungus in your ears, Corporal? Yes, outside."

"Sergeant, I don't have a-tac."

"I heard you the first time. You won't be out there alone."

"Copy that, Sergeant." *Plan B, Ish.*

It's still almost as bad as Plan A.

Almost? That means I'm improving.

Caleb stood and scooped up the railgun. He carried it to the back of the APC and rested it against the hatch while he removed his SCACS overlay and stuffed it in a foot locker. There was no way he could play the part of one of them wearing the more advanced armor. He was still taking a risk that Delta could spot the minor differences between the newer and older second-skin and call him out on it.

He waited until he heard the hum of the anti-gravity plates before opening the hatch and stepping back out into the jungle. Keeping his rifle cradled in his arms, he circled to the front of the vehicle and came to attention. He heard the second APC's rear hatch opening, and then Delta unit was coming his way, headed up by Sergeant Nadel.

"Hicks," Nadel said. "Why the hell aren't you at least wearing cammies over your second skin?"

"Sergeant, I told you. Sergeant Tyson pulled me into this detail straight from my rack. He didn't even give me a chance to piss, nevermind grab my cammies."

Nadel had a hearty laugh at his expense. "Well, isn't

that just like Larone. No matter. Take us to the site, Corporal."

"Sergeant, aren't you going after the demon?"

"Do you know which way he went, Corporal?" Nadel asked.

"No, Sergeant."

"Then we need to get a look at the scene to pick up his scent."

"He's clean, Sergeant," the soldier standing behind Nadel's right shoulder said.

"Clean?" Caleb asked before he could stifle himself.

"We can't be too careful, can we Corporal? You haven't got a slimy in your neck, do you?"

That's a base khoron. I'm an Advocate. He should show some respect.

How did you avoid the scan? Caleb asked.

I turned off my collux.

You said you couldn't—

For more than a few seconds. I'm glad I timed it so well.

If you hadn't—

We would not be having this conversation.

"No way, Sergeant," Caleb said out loud.

Nadel pointed into the thicket. "Ladies first." The other members of Delta laughed.

"Sergeant, are you sure? I don't have a helmet. I can barely see."

"You can thank Sergeant Tyson for that when we see him," Nadel said. "Let's go."

That was a cold thing to say, even for me.

Caleb couldn't argue with Ishek or Nadel. He guided Delta squad back through the jungle, pretending to see even worse than he did, occasionally tripping and stumbling as he led them slowly back toward the scene.

"Pick up the pace, Corporal. I don't want to be out here all night," Nadel complained.

"You have a hot date tonight, Boss?" one of the other soldiers asked.

"Yeah, with a demon. I aim to succeed where Tyson and his squad failed."

"That shouldn't be too hard, judging by Hicksie, here."

Delta squad started laughing behind Caleb.

Are you sure you don't want to kill them and move on?

They'll just send another unit out here if I do. We're sticking to Plan B.

B as in bad.

Caleb returned to the scene of the ambush, pausing when he reached Privates Ho and Jones, the two soldiers he had shot. "I didn't see all the action," he said. "It looks like the bastard shot them."

"With one of our guns," Nadel added, crouching between the pair. He turned his head toward the shelter. "SOP would be to hit the target with a Ramrod. That tent should have been incinerated." Straightening up, he looked to the hole where the explosive had hit the jungle floor. "The strike was good. It tossed the tent nearly ten meters."

"It looks that way, Sergeant," Caleb agreed.

"What the hell kind of material survives a blast like that?" He made his way to the shelter. Without power from the mule, it had lost its rigidity, making it seem a lot weaker than it really was. "I've never seen anything like it. Have you, Corporal?"

"No, Sergeant." He pointed to the open flap. "It appears to me the bastard got out of the tent."

"Sure does," Nadel agreed. He pushed through the thicket until he came across Campbell. "Ooh. Campbell was pretty. That outcome sure isn't. She must have gotten tied up with the demon to end up cheesed like that." He turned his head, scanning the area nearby and locating Private Nelson. Moving to him, he shook his head. "Killed himself before the demon could infect him. Smart kid."

That's dumb. Khorons do not infect people. We can only control one host at a time.

You and I know that, Caleb replied. *It appears this group doesn't.*

I'm more confused than before.

Me, too.

Nadel needed a couple of minutes to locate Sergeant Tyson. "There you are, Larone. Same fate as the kid. But it looks like our demon removed your power pack. Why?" He turned to Caleb. "It looks to me like Alpha did everything by the book, and it still got them killed."

"I don't understand, Sergeant," Caleb said. "Where did the demon even come from?"

"Dunno. Perimeter scouts came across him earlier today, along with a prisoner who turned out to be clean. They managed to nab the prisoner, but needed backup to engage him. Standard procedure. Like Larone said, it should have been a cakewalk to sneak up on him and blow him to smithereens. He's got gear I haven't seen before. It seems Crux is improving his tech while we're hiding scared in the jungle. If you ask me, we need to go on the offensive. Make a move now, before we're discovered."

So they're in hiding. Interesting.

Caleb recalled the duty roster. Less than two hundred soldiers. *They seem to be the remains of a defeated military.*

That doesn't seem to realize it's been defeated.

"Sarge," Caleb heard one of the other Delta members say through his helmet's comms. "We just got a call back from base. They said they found Hicks asleep in his rack, like you suspected."

Uh-oh.

CHAPTER 26

Sergeant Nadel's eyes shifted toward Caleb, unaware that his hearing was good enough to pick up the chatter through the soldier's helmet comms. Before any of Delta team could react, he lunged at the man, punching him square in the helmet. His fist cracked the faceplate and sent the sergeant sprawling to the jungle floor. Caleb sprinted by him, taking cover behind a big tree as the rest of Delta opened fire. Bullets tore at the trunk of the barrel-belly. He shifted direction, using it as cover as he scrambled away into the darkness.

Time for Plan C?

"Shut up," Caleb hissed, tripping over a tree root and tumbling into some vines. The thorns tore at his hands and face, and he cursed under his breath as he sprang back up, ducking behind another barrel-belly, bullets ripping through the surrounding vegetation. "How was I supposed to know they would check on Hicks?"

You didn't sell the panicked soldier very well. It left Nadel suspicious.

"Because I don't know anything about being a panicked soldier."

I've tasted your fear.

"I said I've never panicked, not that I've never been afraid. There's a big difference."

He burst from behind the trunk, moving perpendicular to Delta squad. Even with night vision, the density of the jungle made it harder for them to track him, and he managed to evade detection on his way to another tree. Pausing to listen, he could hear the unit spreading out, hoping to smother him before he could get away.

He couldn't afford to let that happen.

Again breaking from behind cover, he kept his eyes on the ground ahead, watching out for roots and vines as he scrambled through the jungle. Doing his best to stay ahead of them, he expected the gunfire to resume at any second. When it didn't, he still maintained his breakneck pace relying purely on spatial memory to remain aware of his relative position. A few minutes passed before he again came to a stop, but not because he was being shot at.

Instead, he looked up as a light in the sky managed to push through the canopy like headlights through curtains. It reduced the level of pitch beneath the treetops as it passed overhead, the illumination fading almost as quickly as it appeared, leaving him shrouded in darkness once more. He still didn't move, picking up a new sound he didn't like.

The crackling swish of movement through the brush about ten meters away.

Caleb pressed himself against the tree trunk, waiting impatiently as the sound slowly approached. A quick glance revealed one of Delta squad cautiously moving in his general direction, rifle leveled.

You can take him out before he knows what hit him.
I'm not taking anyone out, Caleb countered.
Even if it costs us our lives?
We're not there yet.

The soldier continued toward the tree. As he moved in beside it, Caleb slowly circled around to the opposite side, remaining quiet and out of sight.

"Delta, eyes in the sky reported a scout ship incoming," he heard Nadel say through the soldier's helmet comms. "We're going dark."

"Sarge, what about the demon?" one of the others asked.

"I think he's long gone. Maintain your positions until I give the all clear. Radio silence starts now."

The soldier slumped back against the trunk of the barrel-belly, ordered to stand down and wait while the scout ship that had apparently passed over them scanned the jungle.

An interesting turn of events.

That's one way to put it.

Caleb stood on the opposite side of the thick trunk from the soldier. He could try to disable the man, but any change in his health would be synced back to Delta's ATCS and reported to the others, which would now doubt bring them running. He didn't want that. He needed to get away from the man. To keep moving.

The overhead light appeared again, and even though he couldn't see the craft itself this time, Caleb heard the hum of the scout ship's engines. Obviously, it belonged to whoever these soldiers were at war with, no doubt searching for them. But why had it come here, now? Was it a normal occurrence? A strange coincidence?

Because of the link to Pathfinder, he wanted to find out. But these people would never talk to him as long as they were convinced he was a demon, or at least infected by one.

I resent that.

Don't worry, I have a plan.

Of course you do.

Caleb slowly dropped to all fours and began crawling

along the jungle floor, careful to keep his hands and feet positioned on the spongy moss, which soaked up the sound of his movement. As long as the Delta soldier on the other side of the tree stayed there, he was sure he could escape.

Slowly covering the ground, he had gone nearly five meters when he heard the soldier moving behind him. He paused, shifting his weight and tensing, ready to pounce if the man came into view. The muzzle of his rifle did, along with his shoulder. He froze when the overhead light again pushed against the canopy, this time pausing directly above the trees.

That can't be good.

Caleb remained still, his eyes on the soldier. The light struggled to penetrate the heavy canopy, but it was enough for him to tell the soldier was trembling.

Perhaps this is good. I hunnnnggerrrr.

Caleb felt the tingling sensation that occurred whenever Ishek tasted fear. *This definitely isn't good*, he countered, just before a beam of light tore through the treetops. He squinted tightly in response to the sudden burst of energy. The beam hit the Delta soldier, practically splitting him in half. He stumbled forward a step and collapsed.

Every instinct told Caleb he should run, so he remained dead still, staring back and up at the fresh hole the beam had cut in the canopy. All he could see through it was the diffusion of light from bright spotlights and the hint of a dark armored hull that he was pretty sure wasn't of Relyeh design. The ship remained in place for a few more seconds before turning and slowly moving through the jungle.

Caleb finally moved, rising to his feet and sprinting away, no longer concerned about the thorny vines or tripping over tree roots. He suddenly felt like a rabbit whose coyote predators had been replaced by a cougar.

I thought you never panicked.

This isn't panic, this is retreat, he replied.

What's the difference?

I still have a plan.

He looked over his shoulder, searching for the light through the trees. He saw a hint of it in the distance, followed a moment later by another flash of bright light, probably resulting in another dead soldier. The ship could obviously pick up movement, though it apparently couldn't otherwise discern a human from a barrel-belly.

He raced back through the jungle, his attention split between his path ahead and the ship overhead. Thankfully, the ship didn't swing back in his direction, moving far enough away for the light to vanish altogether. That wasn't enough to convince him to slow down or to be more cautious. He stormed through the thicket, his hands slick with blood from the dozens of cuts the thorns inflicted. In the back of his mind, he wondered if the blood might attract another croco-chameleon, or even something worse. He almost laughed at the idea of his luck turning that shitty.

Finally stepping into the cleared road, he was relieved to see the Pathfinder APC still intact and where he'd left it. Still undiscovered by the ship searching the area. He didn't slow until he reached cover against the side of it, slowing to approach the hatch.

Deja vu.

Caleb ignored Ishek as he opened the manual override and typed in the access code. As soon as the hatch opened far enough for him to fit through it, he launched into the APC, ready to fight. He found himself alone, the APC empty.

Turning to close the hatch, a figure in dark combat armor intercepted him, shoving the muzzle of his rifle into the gap before the door could fully close. Caleb ducked aside as the new combatant opened fire, the roar of the chemical firearm in the enclosed space deafening. At least, it would have been deafening if Ishek hadn't astutely disabled his hearing, leaving only bright, silent muzzle flashes and the sparks of slugs ricocheting off inside of the armored vehicle. A few of the spent bullets bounced off Caleb's underlay with enough impact to hurt.

The jammed door gave up its effort to shut, sliding open instead. Caleb didn't give his attacker a chance to move. He leaped up through the hatch, shoving the man backwards. They fell onto the cleared ground, with Caleb on top. He looked down through the man's faceplate, unsurprised to see another human looking back at him. He couldn't say the same for the other guy, whose eyes widened in shock.

"Brother, wait!" the man grunted, his body relaxing in surrender beneath Caleb.

He had been about to pummel the downed soldier. He hesitated now, unsure what to make of the reaction.

He's bonded to a khoron. It's in control. It believes I am controlling you.

Caleb didn't relax, but he also continued to hold the man down. "Who do you serve?" he asked.

"I serve the House of Crux, as do we all." The man's face wrinkled in confusion beneath his faceplate. "But you do not. You are from the ship that crashed here. Where did it come from? Who do you serve?"

As a Relyeh, anything Caleb told the man was likely to go back through the Collective, courtesy of the man's khoron, to the creature's master. The one he called Crux. Caleb had no intention of telling Crux anything. Not until he knew what the hell this was all about.

I have never heard of Crux. This is very interesting.

"I serve no master," Caleb replied. "What do you want with the humans here?"

"Crux is lord and master. They are his subjects. They will bend a knee or they will die. Such is his decree. We have been searching. You are found, brother, and in such a fine host. Perhaps you served no master before, but you will serve Crux now. You will bend your knee, or you too will die."

Caleb considered the ultimatum. While he still had a huge gap in his understanding of the situation, one thing was abundantly clear. It didn't matter that the people on this planet wanted to kill him. They were fighting the Relyeh, just like him. And the enemy of his enemy was his friend.

"I won't serve your master," Caleb spit out.

The man tensed, his face twisting in anger. "Then you will—" His eyes rolled back in his head, and he went limp beneath Caleb.

What a weak, pathetic excuse for a khoron. He didn't even put up a fight.

"Ish, will you please stay off the Collective?" Caleb replied.

We need to know what we're up against.

"It's not worth the risk. I could have taken him."

I will be more considerate next time.

"Thanks." It was as close to an apology as he would ever get from the symbiote. Movement to his right drew his attention. One of Delta's soldiers rounded the back of the APC, rifle leveled at his head.

"Don't move."

CHAPTER 27

Caleb stared at the soldier, whose head shifted slightly as she noticed the dead Legionnaire, under him.

"I've never seen one of Crux's Legion attack their own before. You truly have no soul, do you, demon?"

"If one of you would give me half a second to speak, I could tell you that I'm not part of Crux's Legion, whatever the hell that is. My name is Captain Caleb Card of the Centurion Space Force Marines. I came here in response to a distress signal we received from Pathfinder." He thrust his arm out toward the APC, pointing at the designation on the vehicle. "The same Pathfinder this APC floated off."

He could see the soldier stiffen in response to his sharp reply. "I...I don't understand. You're infected. You're a demon." She thrust her rifle toward him. "I should have killed you already."

"But you haven't because your eyes can see that I killed your enemy, even if your mind can't quite comprehend it." He made a move to stand until he noticed her finger tense on the trigger. "It's not safe for us out here."

She didn't reply. He could almost feel her senses struggling to shake off a lifetime of certainty regarding who and what the enemy was. "I should shoot you." It was the only thing her neurons could come up with.

"You should take me prisoner," Caleb said. "And get us out of here."

That wasn't part of the plan.

New plan, he replied.

I've lost track of which letter we were up to.

The soldier hesitated. Caleb figured she wanted to radio Nadel and ask for permission, but if he had to guess, Nadel was already dead.

"There's no time for this," he hissed. "I'm getting into that APC, and I'm getting out of here. You can either shoot me or come along." He took a step toward the hatch. The Delta soldier followed him with her rifle but didn't shoot. As she started lowering it, Caleb caught a glimpse of a shadow moving out of the jungle behind her. "Get down!"

He didn't wait for her to respond before diving back to the dead Legionnaire, snatching the rifle from his hand and swinging it up in her general direction. Her rifle moved in accordance, trying to get a bead on him before he fired. Too late. He squeezed off a burst of rounds that zipped past her shoulder and into the surprised attacker's faceplate, cracking it open to allow the last bullet through.

When the bullets didn't hit her, the Delta soldier's head whipped around to see the real target, frozen in shock as he fell. "You…you…" she stammered.

"Saved your life," Caleb finished. "And I'll do it again if I have to." He looked up, noticing the light increasing through the canopy overhead. "Come on." He kept the rifle as he jumped inside the APC, the soldier right behind him. "Do you have a name?" he asked while moving forward and dropping into the driver's seat.

"Private Marley," she replied. "I should drive."

"I want you on the turret. I'll drive."

"But you've never—" She fell silent when he powered

up the APC, tapping on the control screen to enable the HUD and sensor projection. Only one of the sensors penetrated the trees, offering a likely but not-very-accurate position for the scout ship above.

"Get to the turret!" Caleb barked, his tone of voice sending her scrambling before she could think to question his right to give her an order.

"We can't hit a Nightmare from the ground," she complained, even as she fell into the gunner's seat over his right shoulder. "They're too nimble."

"That doesn't mean we don't try," Caleb replied, putting the APC in gear. He hit the throttle and the anti-gravity controls at the same time, lifting the vehicle off the ground as it lumbered forward, nearly colliding with the second APC as he maneuvered the big machine around it. A flash of light in the steering display burned a hole in the ground where they had been seconds earlier. "Do you have air support? Nadel mentioned eyes in the sky."

"Spotters on the mountainside with long-range optics," she replied. "We only have the ship we escaped Atlas in, and it's in no shape to fight."

"Atlas?" Caleb asked, swerving the APC left and right, speeding up and slowing down in an effort to keep the Nightmare's fire control system from getting a lock. A beam hit the ground beside them, churning up the dirt.

"Our capital planet. First settled around four hundred years ago."

Did she just say four hundred years?

"Did you just say four hundred years?" Caleb parroted with the same disbelief Ishek had expressed. "Pathfinder left Earth a little over two hundred years ago. You're claiming you were in this galaxy *before* Pathfinder?"

"You keep using that name, but I've never heard it before. And you claim this APC came from that ship?"

"It's not a claim. It's a fact."

Marley shrugged. "And you're from Earth?"

Caleb threw the APC to the side as another beam hit the ground beside the vehicle. "Originally. Now I'm with the Centurion Space Force. Do you know of Proxima Centauri?"

"No, is that a system in the Spiral?"

"What's the Spiral?"

"This galaxy. It's called the Manticore Spiral."

"Why?"

"I honestly don't know. The founders decided to name it that."

"Who are the founders?"

"They arrived on the ship that crashed on Atlas. They settled the planet, and later built ships and began exploring the Spiral."

"And the ship that crashed on Atlas, was it named Pathfinder?

"I don't know."

Caleb wanted to bang his head against the side of the APC. The conversation was getting him nowhere.

She doesn't know about Pathfinder. I find that strange.

I find that strange, too. But what can we do about it? He glanced at Marley. "Are you even a soldier, with real military training?"

"Yes," she replied matter-of-factly.

"Then why aren't you shooting?" he growled, barely avoiding the next energy beam that flashed down through the treetops. The maneuver sent the APC off the cleared path and into the jungle, where it skimmed the tops of the vines and the barrel-bellies became immovable obstacles.

"I can't get a lock," Marley answered.

"Who cares? Just open fire. You might get lucky."

"We don't have an unlimited supply of ammunition."

"You won't have any ammo if that ship destroys this APC." Caleb cut the throttle and turned the yoke, sending the APC into a hard maneuver that bashed the side against a tree. The impact nearly pulled him from his seat, but he managed to plant his foot and hold on, scraping off the barrel-belly and accelerating through the brush. Two more energy blasts pierced the canopy. One of them hit the front of the APC, burning a hole clean through the armored nose.

Finally listening to reason, Private Marley opened up with the turret, sending a stream of rounds up into and through the canopy. Looking at the sensor projection, Caleb watched the Nightmare slow some and slip aside, suddenly more cautious chasing their prey. Below the treetops, shredded branches tumbled to the jungle floor behind them.

"You've got them taking evasive maneuvers," Caleb remarked, turning the APC again to bring it back toward the trail. "That buys us some time."

"Time for what?" Marley asked.

"To get back to your base. To get help."

"Are you crazy? We can't go back to the base with a Nightmare on our tail."

Caleb nearly slammed on the brakes in a sudden burst of frustrated anger. "Are *you* crazy? We need backup."

"Maybe you don't get it yet, Captain Caleb Card of the Centurion Space Force whatever! Right now, False Emperor Crux has no idea where to find the Empress Lo'ane. If we return to base with that ship still hounding us, the only thing keeping him from cementing his rule across the Spiral will quickly be eliminated."

This sounds like the plot of one of those awful movies you like to watch.

They're not awful, they're entertaining. And yeah, it kind of does. Caleb swerved again, barely avoiding a large branch shaved off its tree by another of the Nightmare's energy beams. "If we can't go to your base, where can we go? We need to lose that ship or shoot it down."

"We have almost no chance of either."

"Then why did you get into the APC?"

"They already killed my entire unit. What chance did you think I had back there?"

Caleb did cut the throttle, jerking forward as the hovercraft slowed in a hurry. An energy beam blinded the forward camera, striking the ground just ahead. Turning the yoke, he made a right angle from a standstill and accelerated again, hoping the quick turn would buy them a little more time.

"Switch places with me," Caleb said.

"What?"

"If you can't shoot it down, I will."

"Do you think because you're infected that makes you a crack shot? The sensors are off by at least three meters in any given direction, and the canopy's too thick to see past."

Ish, new plan, Caleb said.

Ooh, I actually like this one.

"Just switch with me," he replied, standing and shifting aside while holding the yoke. Marley scrambled to take the controls. "Just keep us as straight as you can."

You should have started with her driving.

We would be dead already if I had.

You have a rather high opinion of yourself.

Caleb didn't argue. He shifted to the gunner's seat, taking hold of the joystick that controlled the turret and looking into the display from the camera mounted on the gun. The projection beside the driver seat was represented here as a blotch on the screen. Like Marley had mentioned, lining up the two wouldn't produce a kill. The Nightmare was somewhere in the vicinity of the report, though the direction was impossible to guess. By the time he swept the entire possible area with fire, the ship would have moved.

The hovercraft jerked sideways as an energy beam scraped its side, close enough to Caleb that he felt the heat of the blast through the vehicle's armor. He glanced at Marley's stone face, her eyes focused as she steered them around a tree and through the brush. He knew she was doing her best to match his sighting with evading the enemy fire.

Are you ready? Caleb asked.

You're sure about this?

Not at all.

He closed his eyes, Ishek's laughter echoing in his mind as he ceded control of his body to the khoron. He could still see, hear, and think, but that was the extent of it.

Ishek didn't open his eyes. That didn't stop the symbiote from using the joystick to turn the turret and open fire. Slugs ripped through the trees and into the hull of the Nightmare, peppering the bottom of the craft from stem to stern. Almost immediately, the trees behind the APC began shaking violently, their limbs shattering as the scout ship came down through the canopy.

"How?" Marley asked, seeing it crashing behind them.

"Drive straight!" Ishek reminded her with Caleb's voice.

The Nightmare slammed into the thicker trunks, throwing it sideways through the brush to where it finally came to rest against a pair of barrel-bellies.

"Stop!" Ishek snapped through Caleb. Marley brought the APC to a quick stop.

Ish, it's my turn, Caleb said.

"Why are we stopping?" she asked.

"We need to make sure there were no survivors." *I don't need to let go.*

Yes, you do.

You can't make me.

Yes, I can. Now, Ish.

He thought Ishek might put up more of a fight. Instead, the khoron gave up control of his body before he had to subject him to mental imagery of the times he had gone fishing with his father. The symbiote hated watching him put worms on a hook and cast them out into the water.

No fun. There are no khoron alive on the ship.

"Marley, we're clear," he said. "Take us back to your base."

"But you just said—"

"I know. We're clear. Let's go."

"How did you do that?" she asked once she had gotten the APC moving again. "You hit it like you knew exactly where it was."

"I did know. Or rather, Ishek knew where the pilot was."

"Ishek?"

"My khoron."

Mention that I'm an Advocate.

"He's an Advocate. Not a basic khoron." The statement sounded as awkward as it felt.

"What do you mean, *your* khoron? Humans don't control the Hunger. The Hunger controls them."

"Not always," Caleb replied. "You and your people have a lot to learn. Maybe now that I helped you escape from a Nightmare, you'll listen."

CHAPTER 28

"Why are we stopping?" Caleb asked as Marley pulled the APC to a halt. He could see the driver's display from his seat. The cleared corridor in the jungle continued into the visible distance.

"Obviously, you can't just follow the road right to the doorstep of our secret hideout," she replied. She had become much more comfortable with him after he destroyed the enemy scout ship, showing herself to be both intelligent and cheeky. And more of a soldier than he had initially given her credit for. She had lost her entire squad out there, not to mention Alpha Squad as well, and so far, she had managed to contain all of the sadness, frustration, and rage he knew she had to be feeling. "This is the part where I cover your eyes."

"Seriously? I shot down a Nightmare for you."

"And I appreciate that. Believe me. But I'm risking execution just by bringing you in. I'm sure you know your khoron—"

Advocate.

"Advocate," Caleb corrected.

"Your Advocate can silently communicate with any

other member of his race, anywhere in the entire universe. He could give up our secrets in totality, and no one would be the wiser."

"He wouldn't do that. I wouldn't let him."

"I believe you. Even if I shouldn't. But the Empress Lo'ane can't afford to take any chances. We've lost too much already, especially tonight."

Caleb nodded. "Understood. Do you have a blindfold?"

She shook her head. "We've never brought anyone in like this before. We'll need to improvise. If you look in the storage locker under the benches in the back, there should be a toolbox with a rag in it. You can wrap that over your eyes."

"You trust me to do it?"

"I'll check your work."

Caleb left the gunner's seat for the rear of the APC. He crouched to open the storage bins under the bench on the left side of the APC. They were mostly empty, though he found a handful of MREs, water bottles, and a personal tablet inside. Crossing to the right side, he located the toolkit, unlatching the top and opening it. The rag was filthy with grease and oil, and smelled twice as bad as it looked.

"You want me to put this on my eyes?"

"I could poke them out instead," Marley replied with a grin.

Caleb smiled back. "You might like that a little too much." He paused, turning serious. "You saw the other squad. Two of them killed themselves. The third took friendly fire intended for me. The shooters didn't hesitate to put bullets through one of their own."

"What happened to the other two?"

Caleb hesitated before answering. "I had to shoot them," he admitted. "I wish there had been another way to stop them from killing me."

"You said you came to help us. That's not my definition of helping."

"Neither is letting them kill me. Besides, I didn't know who you were at the time. And I've never seen any military shoot one of their own on purpose, and with such little hesitation."

"You don't know the horrors we've been subjected to under Crux's rule."

"Pathfinder came from an Earth ravaged by the Relyeh. I was there when the invasion started, and I left on a different generation ship before it was over. I believe I know what Hell is."

"If a Legionnaire captures you, your life is worse than over. They'll infect you with a khoron, and you'll spend the rest of your days as both a prisoner and a slave. Did that also happen on Earth?"

Caleb shook his head. "No. Not that I know of."

"Then you may think you understand what Hell is, but you don't."

"I have a khoron—"

Advocate.

"I have an Advocate bonded to me. I do know what *that's* like."

"But now you and your Advocate are allies. Or so you claim."

"We need one another. It's that simple."

"It isn't that simple for us, Caleb."

He responded by tying the rag around his face, making sure to bind it tight against his eyes. He heard Marley get up out of the driver's seat and approach him, but he didn't expect it when she pressed her lips against his. He flinched and stiffened in response. "What the hell?"

"You're clearly a trained warrior," she replied. "A simple touch wouldn't be enough to startle you. I'm satisfied you can't see." She took his hand next, leading him back to the gunner's seat.

Not the worst test you've ever been given.

Shut up, Caleb silently replied as Marley got them moving again.

"Control, this is Private Andrea Marley of Delta Squad," she said over the comms. "Do you copy? Control, come in."

"We read you, Private Marley," a soft voice replied after a brief pause. "What's your status?"

"Control, I need to speak with General Haas immediately."

"The general is currently unavailable. I'll forward your report, Private."

"Negative, Control. My report is for General Haas' ears only. I'll wait out here all night if I have to, but I'm not talking to anyone else but the Empress herself."

"Standby," Control answered.

She's feisty. We like that.

Caleb didn't respond. He enjoyed the entertainment, but romance was the last thing on his mind.

"Private Marley, this is Colonel Chambers," another woman said after nearly half a minute of silence. "General Haas can't speak to you right now. I suppose congratulations are in order, however. The spotters report you and your team downed a Nightmare. I don't believe that's ever been done before."

"Colonel Chambers, sir," Marley said. "With all due respect, I appreciate your kudos, but I really need to speak to General Haas. I guarantee he'll want to hear what I have to say."

"I see," Chambers answered. "Tell me, Private, what happened to Sergeant Nadel?"

"He's dead, Colonel. Along with the rest of Delta Squad and all of Alpha Squad." Caleb could hear her voice quiver, but she managed to hold herself together.

"What?" she hissed, surprised by the response. "Are you suggesting you destroyed a Nightmare *on your own*?"

"Colonel, please. I need to speak to General Haas."

"You'll answer my questions, or you'll find yourself spending the night in the brig, *Private*."

Caleb figured Marley must have muted the comms, considering what came next. "Stupid, idiotic, stubborn, blowhard bitch!" she growled. Her tone sweetened when she responded to the colonel. "Colonel Chambers, at a minimum, I respectfully request a private channel. Things are happening out here that should be disseminated from the top down."

"Perhaps you're right," Chambers agreed after a short pause. "Standby."

"Finally," Marley exhaled, suggesting she had muted the comms again. "Are COs this much of a pain in the ass where you're from, Caleb?"

"It depends on the CO," he replied. "But I've had my share." She laughed softly in response. "I'm impressed with how well you're holding together, all things considered."

"I've had my fair share of loss," she answered. "Nearly ten thousand supporters of the Empress were killed, including my husband, on the day we were forced to abandon Atlas."

Caleb's jaw clenched. "I'm sorry, I—"

"You didn't know. How could you? This galaxy was on fire once, Caleb. But the flame has nearly been extinguished. We're all that's left. If you want to be on the winning side, you should join Crux. I mean that with all seriousness."

"I didn't come here to be on the winning side. I came to help the right side. And I've beaten the odds before."

"Yes, I can tell you never quit."

"Marley," a gravelly voice said over the comms. "It's General Haas. Do you copy?"

"General, sir," Marley snapped, verbally at attention. "I copy, sir. I…I wasn't expecting you to honor my request."

"You pulled me away from downtime with my wife, Marley. And the only reason I'm on this line is because Colonel Chambers tells me you shot down a Nightmare and won't divulge to her how you managed it. Whatever you have to say, it had better be good."

"Yes, sir. I intend to give you a full debriefing, sir. Before I do, I need to introduce you to someone."

"Introduce me?" Haas replied. "Private, what are you talking about?"

"Caleb, go ahead," Marley said.

"General Haas," Caleb said. "My name is Captain Caleb Card of the Centurion Space Force Marines. I'm the man you sent Alpha and Delta squads out to kill. I shot down the Nightmare, and I'm here to assist in any way I can."

"Is that so?" Hass replied right away. He let out an audible sigh. "Private Marley, I thought we trained you better than this."

"I don't understand, General," Marley said.

"Open your eyes, and use your head, Private. This demon crashes on Galatin from unknown origins, kills Alpha Squad, and then calls for backup knowing we'll send another team out to find him. Then he lets them pick off most of Delta before staging an attack on his own kind, shooting down the Nightmare, and claiming that somehow he's a good guy, despite the fact that he's infected, so that he can convince you to bring him into the only safe place we have left in the galaxy. And you fell for it."

Caleb couldn't see Marley, but he felt the sudden tension in the air, thick as ice. The general had turned all of his good intentions around on him so quickly and completely, it caught him totally off-guard.

"General Haas," he said. "I can assure you—"

"Assure me?" Haas replied bitterly. "Your kind is a stain

on the universe. Cold. Cruel. Cunning. I was there when Avalon fell. I was there when you bombarded Tamat and killed two of my children. I prayed that I would die in battle that day, avenging my boys. But here I am, still weeping for their loss, still wishing I could see them again. I know what you are, demon. I know how your face can change to get what you want, and how you leave nothing but suffering and anguish in your wake. The only thing that I can be assured of is that as long as I survive, you will never, ever harm the Empress. Neither will your companion. He's refused to renounce you, demon. His execution is at dawn. Do not return to us, Private Marley. By intent or stupidity, you've thrown your lot in with this one. Consider yourself an outcast."

The comm channel fell silent, leaving both Caleb and Marley stunned.

CHAPTER 29

Well, that was both an unexpected and completely logical outcome. I wouldn't trust us either, if I were him.

You could have warned me to expect this ahead of time, Caleb replied to Ishek.

What would be the fun in that?

"Caleb," Marley said, her voice trembling. "Take off your blindfold." He did as she said, reaching up to untie it and letting it fall into his lap. She stood in front of him, her rifle inches from his chest. "I didn't want to kill you in cold blood, without you seeing it coming. Just in case you weren't lying to me. General Haas is right. I'm a fool to have fallen for your deception. I may have signed my own death warrant, but at least I can protect the Empress from you."

"Andrea," Caleb said softly. "It's no deception. I am what I say I am. I've done everything I can to prove that to you. I understand why Haas doesn't believe me. I understand why he's so angry and afraid. But I didn't do those things. I just arrived here a few days ago, through a wormhole that not only carried me across space, but apparently also through time."

"I wish I could believe that. But Haas is right. Crux and his minions are cruel and cunning. This is exactly something they would arrange to get close to the Empress."

Don't forget the data chip.

"I can prove it," Caleb said, grateful to Ishek for the reminder. "I have a data chip from one of the engineers on board Pathfinder. She describes the wormhole. The APC has a reader. Please. Tie me to the chair if you need to, but just look at it before you compound the mistakes of both Alpha and Delta squads."

Marley stared at him. He could see the battle raging in her mind, her loyalty and duty in conflict with her compassion and instinct. Finally, she nodded. "Where's the chip?"

"In the pocket of my overlay. I hid it in one of the compartments in the back."

"Combat armor doesn't fold."

"Mine does. I saw wire back there, too. You can bind my hands if you want."

She nodded. "You'll have to get it so I can keep—"

Caleb lunged forward, grabbing the end of the rifle and pushing it aside before Marley could fire. He ripped the weapon out of her hands and shoved her back into the instrument panel. Throwing the weapon aside, he absorbed a few offered punches before subduing her in an armlock. "I know you'll probably think I'm still trying to trick you, but try to realize how quickly I could have killed you at any given moment. I've been a Marine far longer than you've been alive." He let go of her and backed up, picking up her rifle and handing it back to her.

Marley glared at him, still stuck between a rock and a hard place. Finally, she submitted. "Forget it. You're right. So is Haas, as far as his thinking goes, but I threw my lot in with you. I don't have any good choices, but the best choice is to see this through. You say you you didn't come from Crux? Then prove it."

Caleb retreated to the rear of the APC, well aware that Marley could shoot him once he was a few meters away. She didn't, sticking to her decision and waiting patiently while he retrieved his armor and the data chip. "Do you want the wire?" he asked, looking back at her.

Her laughter was a good sign. "Do you mean for myself?" She sighed. "I didn't start the day planning to become a traitor."

"First, I convince you that I'm not your enemy. Then we convince Empress Lo'ane."

"That's your plan?"

That's your plan?

She and Ishek asked that simultaneously, though Ish sounded more incredulous.

"Haas has too much personal history to be logical here. It'll take a mountain to move him, and I don't blame him for it. The rest of your people don't have the power to do much more without ending up an outcast like you. I have to see the Empress."

"You think she doesn't have personal history? Crux killed her parents and her three elder brothers. She was fourth in line to the throne, and crowned only a week before he assaulted Atlas and sent her into exile."

"Then it seems like she could use a friend like me."

"Because you're so special?" Marley quipped, forcing a smirk from Caleb.

"I'm stronger than you because I'm a man. I'm faster than you because I have more experience and know what to expect. I shot down that Nightmare because I have something the rest of you don't."

"A khoron."

An Advocate. And I shot down the Nightmare.

"An Advocate," Caleb corrected. "I didn't kill the Legionnaire you found me standing over. Ishek overloaded his khoron's mind through the Collective. He killed it remotely. Can you hold this for me?" He passed Marley his overlay. "I'm going to step back into it."

"What is this made from?" she asked, running her fingers along the material. Caleb backed into it, pulling it on and clasping it shut.

"Composite fibers and synthetic alloys derived from Axon metal."

"Axon?"

"Another intelligent alien race. You don't know about them?"

She shook her head. "No. I guess they haven't reached this part of the universe. What are they like?"

"We don't have time to go into that right now. Just be glad you haven't encountered them. They aren't friendly to humans."

Her face blanched and she nodded. "Figures." She continued studying his overlay. "This armor's so much lighter and more flexible than ours. But I guess we wouldn't be able to make it, since we have no Axon metal to derive it from."

"True. I was going to ask you why your tech seems more primitive, despite the time gap. But considering you don't know that Pathfinder came here from Earth through the same wormhole I used, it seems somebody wanted you to forget some things."

Marley's face wrinkled. "Why would anyone do that?"

"Control. Why else? I don't know the reasons for it. What I can tell you is that the woman who created the data chip determined the existence of the wormhole, and then discovered the military on board Pathfinder already knew about it, except their math was wrong. She brought them the corrections, and they tried to kill her for the effort. She died alone on a hostile planet, doing her best to warn others away from the area. It's almost like she knew this was going to happen." He paused in response to the statement, mind working.

You don't think Pathfinder already had khoron on board, do you?

You just read my mind. That's my thought.

Basic khoron can't think for themselves. If there was a scheme, an Ancient put them up to it. But which one?

I'm pretty sure I don't want to know.

"Caleb?" Marley asked in response to his silence.

"Sorry, I was talking to Ish. Are there other Relyeh in the Spiral, beyond the khoron?"

"What do you mean, other Relyeh? The khoron, the Relyeh, the Hunger, they're all one and the same."

"I wish that were true." He dug the data chip out of his pocket. He didn't have time to go into detail about either the Axon or the Relyeh. "You should take a look at this."

Marley put out her hand. He dropped the chip into it, and she returned to the front of the APC, picking up Sergeant Tyson's tablet. "It's already unlocked?" she said as she turned on the screen.

"I unlocked it."

"How? It should have had a passcode gate, and you only get three tries before it locks and wipes."

"I only needed one try." He smiled. "I guess that's two things that make me special. I know the passcode." He pointed to the tablet. "Navigate to the summary video file."

She inserted the data chip into the tablet, tapping on the screen until she found the file. He had heard Benning's explanation before, so he watched Marley's face, enjoying the contortions it went through as Benning brought her up to speed. Her entire visage was pale by the time the video ended.

"Earth is real," she said softly.

"Yes."

"And the founder's ship is Pathfinder?"

"I believe so."

"But you said it left Earth two hundred years ago. But it crashed on Atlas four hundred years ago."

"Benning said the wormhole moves through spacetime. It must have sent you back that far."

Her expression became heavy with sadness. "What happened to us?"

"You were supposed to escape from the Relyeh on Earth. But I think some other people had different ideas. Though I'm not sure if they were still people, even back then. One of the worst things about the Hunger is that their leaders are immortal and have been around for millions of years. They're experts at using time as a weapon."

"The Empress needs to know about this," she decided, her sadness shifting to resolve.

"She does and before morning. Haas said they plan to execute Ham. I can't let that happen."

"Ham? You mean your companion?"

Caleb nodded. "You'll take me to the base?"

"I will, but not in the APC. The outer perimeter guards will destroy it before we get close, and we still need every piece of equipment we have."

"You haven't thought far enough ahead," Caleb said. "The Legion sent a scout ship. We destroyed it, which means it won't be reporting back. They have to know that it at least found resistance here. What do you think will happen next?"

"They can search all they want. They won't find our base."

"Do you remember what I just said about the Relyeh? They don't need to kill the Empress. Locking her down here is good enough. She won't live forever. But they will."

Marley stared at him in shock as she realized the truth of his words. "This is worse than I ever thought, isn't it?"

"It doesn't look good right now. Knuckle up, Private.

It'll probably take at least a day or two for Crux to send a larger force this way, to either launch an assault or barricade an escape. Can you get me to the base before morning?"

"Yes. I think so."

"Then gather whatever you think we need. We don't have any time to waste."

CHAPTER 30

Marley wasn't able to gather much from the APC's gear lockers for extended jaunts through the jungle, but they weren't too far from the Empress' secret base to need much of anything. She assured me it was only a few hours walk to the front of the hill where a boring machine had created an alternate entrance to their underground home. With its grinding teeth and special compacting equipment, it had chewed up the dirt and turned it into a solid encasement which held up the tunnels without threat of collapse.

As she explained while they trekked through the jungle, the settlement had gained entrance from the other side of the hill where a fast-flowing river had carved out a deep ravine hidden beneath the dense canopy. The depths of the river had provided the perfect hiding spot for the large transport barge on which nearly two thousand of the Empress' remaining retinue had escaped Atlas.

Carrying as much equipment as they could stow in its hold, they'd launched in the guise of a fleeing merchant ship on the eve of the Legion's last major assault on the planet. As a civilian vessel, the barge had minimal shields and offensive capabilities. Just enough to hopefully ward off pirates in the event of an attempted boarding.

"Space pirates?" Caleb questioned, not quite ready to believe it. Neither Proxima nor Earth had enough starships for piracy to be a problem, at least in space. "How do they even get on board at those speeds?"

"It's all relative, right?" Marley replied. "The transport wasn't built for velocity, and once they sync up, we might as well not be moving at all."

"True," Caleb agreed. "I don't have a ton of experience in space."

"Obviously." They grinned at one another, already like old comrades despite having only met a few hours ago, and not under the best of circumstances.

"How far are we from the entrance?" Caleb asked.

"Three hours that way," she replied, pointing to their right. "We're skirting the edge of the outer perimeter right now. We have to go around the long way and enter through one of the bolt holes."

"I imagine guards will be stationed there, even if they aren't normally."

"There are always guards at every tunnel entrance. We don't take any chances."

"I'd prefer to subdue them without violence."

"So would I, but that isn't going to happen. The best you can do is not injure them too badly."

"The best I can do? Aren't you going to help?"

"No. Haas already thinks I'm a traitor. I'm not about to attack my own people. They're my comrades and friends. I'll lead you to the base. I'll show you a way in. You're responsible for the breach."

"It's your tail on the line, too," he pressed.

She shook her head. "I won't do it. End of discussion."

Caleb nodded. She wasn't one of his subordinates he

could order around. Despite Haas' reaction, she didn't need to help him at all.

She's helping us to the base because you rightfully pointed out that her Empress is in trouble. She wants to warn her, but knows she isn't skilled enough to get back inside without our help. She's using us.

And we're using her. I guess that makes us even.

"How long will it take us to navigate the tunnel you have in mind?" he asked.

"It'll take all night. If your friend's to be killed before sunrise, we won't make it."

"How likely is it that they would kill him before the sun comes up?"

Marley considered the question. "I would say there's an eighty percent chance we'll make it in time."

"You seemed more confident before."

"I'm confident we can get to the base by morning. I'm not as confident Ham will still be alive at that point. I'm sorry, Caleb. I'm doing the best I can."

"I know," he agreed. "And I appreciate all of this. I couldn't do it without you."

"I'd be dead three times over already without you."

"Isn't that what your leadership wants? For you to die rather than fall into enemy hands?"

"Yes. We all know it's a possibility that we may need to give our lives to prevent ourselves from becoming hosts. And we're trained to shoot through one another if it means taking down a Legionnaire. Because if we don't take them down, more of us are at risk. Do you have a problem with that?"

"I don't have enough experience with this conflict to have earned an opinion on how you handle it. All I can tell you is that khorons can't take more than one host."

"You killed a Legionnaire. You didn't notice the cylinder on his waist?"

Caleb shook his head. "I must have missed it."

I noticed it. I bet she's going to say—

"It holds additional khoron. Sometimes one. Sometimes as many as five. They release them to take a host once they capture an opponent."

The question is, how are they producing so many? We don't grow on trees.

I'm sure she doesn't know, Caleb replied. "I don't have a khoron-carrier, though."

"Which would only further your ruse," Marley countered.

"Fair enough." Caleb looked up at the canopy as a rumble of thunder sounded beyond the trees, a flash of lightning momentarily offering a quick view of their surroundings. A raindrop found its way through the leaves and landed on his forehead. More thunder, lightning, and rain followed, and within a few minutes a steady stream of water spilled down from the leaves above.

Fortunately, the underlays were waterproof, and Marley, being helmeted, remained completely dry. Caleb's short hair became soaked, water running down his face into his eyes and under his overlay as he followed her through the jungle. He didn't mind the rain, only the reduced visibility it caused.

A deeper, sharper crack of thunder sounded, and the next flash of lightning cracked into the top of a nearby tree. Caleb heard it shatter, but none of the effects of the hit made it through the web of branches overhead.

"I've never liked these storms," Marley admitted, stepping through a stream of water running down a barrel-belly. "They can get so loud, you wouldn't believe it."

"We have thunderstorms like this on Earth," he replied. "To be honest, I've missed them."

She shook her head. "You're insane."

He laughed. "Maybe so."

The storm continued for nearly thirty minutes, dumping buckets on the jungle, ensuring the endless greenery had enough fuel to survive. The rate of rainfall had dropped somewhat by the time Marley grabbed his shoulder and pulled him down behind a large green and orange plant he hadn't encountered with Ham, and as such hadn't named.

"Guards," she whispered, pointing forward and to the right. A trio of soldiers moved together through the trees. Their camouflaged armor allowed them to blend in well enough with the background that he might not have seen them without Marley's warning. They swept through the area with their rifles leveled, possibly searching for him, but just as likely on their way to the APC.

Lying prone beneath the unnamed plant's gigantic leaf, Caleb brought a finger to his lips to ensure Marley remained silent. With his other hand, he reached for his sidearm, slowly wrapping his fingers around the grip. He didn't want to use the weapon. It wouldn't help his or Marley's cause to kill any more of the Empress' soldiers. He also had no intention of letting them kill him.

The guards fanned out as they neared, two to the right of Caleb and Marley's position, the other moving to the left. As the nearest guard changed direction, approaching the plant and pausing, Caleb's hand tightened on his pistol.

"Do you see this, Sarge?" the man said, the front of his boot nearly touching Caleb's face.

"I don't think Gertie has this one cataloged yet."

"Are you serious, Private?" the squad leader snapped back, pausing a short distance away. "Gertie can hump her scientific rear out here herself if she wants a picture."

"Aww, c'mon, Sarge. You know I've been trying to get a date with her for weeks. This could get me in the door."

"We don't have time for your crap. Besides, from what I hear, there's nothing but death out here tonight."

"A damn shame about the recon squads," the third

soldier said, closing in on the other two, bunching them all around the plant. Caleb glanced at Marley, unable to see her face past her helmet from his position. Considering the proximity of the guards, he couldn't believe they hadn't already spotted him and Marley. "It's a pain in the ass for the rest of us, stuck out here searching for strays," the soldier continued, "but the Legion has swept the planet before. It'll pass like it always does."

"I don't think it will," the sergeant said. "Not this time. Forget the plant. Let's go."

The soldier was about to move on when a sharp crack of thunder and a particularly bright flash of lighting illuminated the plant, Caleb, and Marley before returning the jungle to darkness.

"Damn it," Caleb heard Marley hiss at the same time he grabbed the soldier by the ankle and pulled him to the ground. He scrambled up the soldier before the man could react. Firearm forgotten, he slid one hand behind the helmet to release it from the rest of the armor and its power supply, while using the other to rip it off. The man stared up at Caleb, already terrified. Ignoring Ishek's pleased cooing, Caleb clamped a hand on the soldier's mouth before returning to his sidearm, grabbing it and smacking the grip against the man's temple, knocking him out.

The other two soldiers recovered from their initial shock around that time. Too close to use their rifles, the sergeant pulled a long knife from his hip while the other man came at Caleb, hoping to hold him for the sergeant. Caleb grabbed the first guard's helmet from the ground and swung it upward, tossing it into the second guard's chin with a crack that knocked him off balance. Right behind the blow, Caleb wrapped his arms against the guard's waist and lifted him off the ground before dropping him back onto it. He swung his gun hand back, firing four rounds into the sergeant's armor, forcing the man to evade the attack and preventing him from shooting back. Rolling off the guard over the top of his head, he grabbed the man's helmet on the way past, holding him down with it as he looked to Marley. True to her word, she remained tucked beneath the plant, doing her best to avoid the fight.

At least she warned us.

Caleb batted the soldier's helmet with the gun, the barrage of blows leaving him stunned. The sergeant swung his rifle toward Caleb, only to curse when Caleb shot the weapon multiple times, destroying the inner rails. He put a few more rounds into the sergeant's armor before putting his attention back on the guard, pouncing on him and turning him over to get him in a choke hold.

The sergeant gave up trying to shoot him, instead returning to the knife and lunging at Caleb. Marley decided to pitch in, jutting her leg out to trip the man before he arrived, sending him sprawling. Caleb threw the other soldier into the sergeant, sending them both to the floor again.

"Help me, before they use their pills," Caleb growled at Marley. She sprang into action, wrapping her legs around the sergeant's neck and squeezing. He tried stabbing at her legs, unable to get an angle that would penetrate her armor. His flailing lessened as he lost consciousness, until he stopped struggling altogether.

Caleb's guard stopped fighting too, leaving them with three unconscious soldiers.

"Where's the poison?" he asked.

"Behind the back molar," she replied, removing the sergeant's helmet and forcing open his mouth. She retrieved his pill and tossed it into the jungle. Caleb did the same with his guard, followed by the first he had dropped.

"You know," Marley said. "The sergeant's about the same size as you."

Caleb looked over at the man. "You want me to trade my more advanced protection for his?"

"It would certainly help you blend in better."

He couldn't argue with that. "Thanks for helping me out."

"You're welcome. Don't expect me to do it again."

"Give me a minute to swap armor, and then we're out of here."

"Yes, sir."

CHAPTER 31

"Comms check," Caleb said, reaching up to shift the sergeant's helmet on his head. The man's melon was a little larger than his, leaving the fit a bit loose on him. His biceps were also smaller, leaving that part of the fit a bit tight on him. Even so, it was nice to have the tactical combat system online, comms with Marley, and night vision. And since he had used the master passcode to switch them to a separate encrypted and password-protected channel, they didn't need to worry about the rest of the Empress' military listening in. "Marley, do you copy?"

"I copy," she replied. "Loud and clear. How's the new, old suit working out for you?"

"A little cozy in all the wrong places, but I'll live," he replied. "How's your fit?"

"Same," she replied, adjusting the armor she had claimed from the first soldier. It was a little big on her overall, except around the chest.

Caleb glanced at the three unconscious soldiers. He'd already collected their rifles, helmets, and power supplies, which he'd scattered in a thicket a short distance away, a needle in a haystack to find in the darkness without night vision. Unable to call back to base, they'd need to beat him and Marley back there to raise an alarm, which was unlikely.

The sergeant groaned and began to stir, the first to start recovering. He lifted his head, face twisting in a sneer when he saw Caleb in his armor. His eyes shifted to Marley. "You'll pay for this, traitor."

"I strongly suggest making your way back to the base as soon as possible," she replied. "This whole planet will be crawling with Legionnaires soon enough."

He pointed at Caleb. "Like him? You've already thrown in with the demons. I hope you burn in hell."

Caleb scowled at him. "Keep in mind, if I were your enemy, I could have used you as a host while you were out. But since I don't have a carrier full of Khorons, I could have killed you. Except I didn't. I don't want you dead. Believe it or not, I want you to live. *We're on the same side.*"

"That's the biggest load of crap I've ever heard. Demons can be cunning, but they don't change sides."

"I haven't changed sides. My khoron works with me; it doesn't control me."

Advocate.

Not now, Caleb answered silently.

"That's impossible," the sergeant insisted.

"And yet here I am." He turned to Marley. "Let's move."

They hurried away from the position, Marley moving at a faster clip now that Caleb could see the jungle ahead of them. He noticed so much more wildlife along the way, simply because he had night vision. Nevermind the octo-monkeys and cuttle-shuttles, he spotted creatures that more closely resembled the croco-chameleons, fairly large and reptilian, lurking in the branches of the trees, waiting for something to get too close. He thought he saw one of the large floating squids as well, its long tentacles draped over the branches near the top of the canopy. He saw smaller appendages of the same creature here and there, their tiny bodies hidden among the leaves, suggesting a nest somewhere above.

It was all fascinating, and kept his mind occupied while they made the trek through the dense vegetation. He didn't share the names he created for the creatures with Marley. He figured Gertie, whoever she was, had already given more official names to the animals and insects. Counterintuitively, they didn't converse much at all, both of them remaining in their own thoughts, each with their individual concerns about the hours ahead. Even Ishek remained relatively quiet, probably because he was gorged on pheromones from the recon squads.

All the while, the rain continued falling, though the thunderstorms moved on. An hour passed. The rain finally stopped. Another hour went by. The darkness began lifting, the planet's sun rising, the new day approaching.

"How much further?" Caleb asked.

"We're almost there," she replied. "We lost a little time because I had to circumvent some of the automated guard posts to get us to the inner perimeter. If you climbed a tree here, you'd be able to pick out the ridges in the mountains where the spotters camp out. They're a good fifty klicks from the base, meant to throw off the enemy if they're discovered."

"Are we going to make it?"

"I honestly don't know. I hope so."

"Hope isn't a strategy, Private," Caleb rasped. "We need to pick up the pace."

"Caleb, we've been walking all night. I haven't slept in over twenty-four hours. I can barely stand up."

"General Haas plans to execute my friend, and I can pretty much guarantee the Legion is on its way here right now. If that isn't enough to keep you going, just point me in the right direction and I'll leave you here. I'm not giving up on Ham, or on your Empress, and I don't even know her."

Marley sighed and nodded. "You're right. I'm just beat."

"We can rest when we're dead," Caleb replied. "We've got work to do."

She responded to the last statement by breaking from double time into a jog and then into a run. Caleb easily matched her speed as they nimbly jumped tree roots and trampled down vines. He knew they were getting close, because the flat jungle was gradually giving way to an increasing incline, the density of vegetation shrinking.

Finally, Marley pulled to a stop, gesturing for him to crouch low behind some thick brush. "There's an entrance just on the other side of that rise," she said, pointing it out. "The approaches are all monitored, but we shouldn't have a problem making it inside. Just pass the sergeant's security identifier when requested, and we'll be granted access."

"Won't it look suspicious to enter through an emergency bolt-hole?"

"Not really. The perimeter guards use it all the time when they're sent out for whatever reason. Otherwise, they'd need to trudge out of their way getting from the main entrance to get here, which doesn't make sense. It's just not efficient."

"Copy that."

"There are two guards stationed inside each entrance and exit. Since we have credentials, they might not ask questions. But coming back as a pair instead of a trio may set off alarm bells in their minds."

"So it's better to play it safe and take them out."

"That's on you to decide. There's a chance we could get into the base and disappear before they think too much about it." She paused, turning to face him. "I'm taking a huge risk here, Caleb. Please don't take advantage of my trust. I really don't want to die as the idiot who destroyed the empire."

"I won't betray you," he replied as sincerely as possible. "I promise."

Marley looked back toward the top of the hill. "Are you ready?"

"I'm ready. You?"

"Switch your comms to channel nine. Let's do this."

CHAPTER 32

Caleb and Marley crested the rise just ahead. Pausing momentarily at the top, Caleb quickly scanned the jungle ahead. A slight depression led to an even steeper rise, covered in the same moss that seemed to blanket the entire planet. There was no visible sign of an entrance, though he was pretty sure he figured out where it was hidden based on the arrangement of vegetation against the slope.

He and Marley descended toward the spot he had picked out, confirming his hunch and leaving him wondering if any of Crux's Legionnaires would also identify the potential entry point.

They would need to approach this area first. And you benefited from knowing the tunnel is here beforehand.

He couldn't argue with Ishek's observation. He glanced over at Marley, planning to follow her lead to get into the base. She didn't stop moving until she stood less than a meter from the rise. He stopped, too.

"Identifier," a cold, synthetic voice requested through his comms. Caleb read off the sergeant's identification code for the system. "Accepted," it answered after a short delay.

A round patch of moss sunk inward before shifting aside. Cooler air escaped from the tunnel behind it, revealed as a long, gray and brown corridor with narrow strips of LEDs and exposed wiring running along the top. As Marley had promised, a pair of guards in combat armor waited a short distance back from the entrance, rifles cradled across their chests.

I'm linked through the Collective until we disable them.

Caleb winced slightly in response. He hadn't told Marley about Ishek's method for evading their scanning technology, or how it could potentially lead the Relyeh directly to him, and by extension their secret base. He didn't enjoy the omission, but she would never have brought him here otherwise, and he couldn't just let Ham die. Besides, it wasn't guaranteed the enemy would track them here.

You promised you wouldn't betray her. If they find us like this, that's because of me. I made no such promises.

Nice try, he replied. *I'm responsible.*

Then why did you promise?

Because I intend to convince the Empress to get the hell out of here before the bad guys ever arrive. No harm done.

What if you can't convince her?

Then it won't matter. We'll all die here.

Marley said they have a ship. We can grab Ham and steal it.

Even our bond can't convince me that would be an acceptable thing to do.

Well, you can't blame an Advocate for trying.

Don't you mean khoron?

You aren't funny.

The corner of Caleb's mouth lifted slightly in amusement as he and Marley approached the two guards. They hadn't leveled their weapons at them yet, which was a good sign.

"Sergeant, how is it out there?" one of them asked when he neared. "Rumor is we lost two squads tonight."

He sounds nervous.

Ishek's observation put Caleb on higher alert. *Because of the rumors, or because of us?*

Unclear.

"Same as always," he replied, doing his best to mimic the sergeant's deeper voice. "Hot, wet, and uneventful."

"Really? Rumor is the spotters reported a Nightmare went down about thirty klicks from here," the other guard said.

"I also heard there were casualties," the first said. "Judging by the activity around the place, I think it might be true."

Caleb shrugged. "Well, we didn't encounter anything unusual except a new plant. I got a picture of it for Gertie."

They're both very nervous. I can taste their fear. Take them out.

"She'll like that," the second guard said. Caleb noticed his hands shifting on his rifle, preparing to change its position. A sidelong glance at the other guard revealed the same. It seemed like they were just waiting for him and Marley to start down the long corridor so they could shoot them in the back.

"Are you okay, soldier?" Caleb asked. "You sound tense."

"Tense? Uh. No. I'm fine."

He's a terrible liar. Take him out.

"You?" Caleb asked, turning to the other guard.

What are you waiting for?

"I...uh..." The rifle shook in the guard's hands. "I'm fine."

"Don't you need to report in for debriefing, sergeant?" the first guard asked.

"We do," Caleb agreed. "Come on, Private."

He waved Marley ahead before passing between the two guards. He had just come parallel with them when he reached out in both directions, wrapping his hands around their rifles and pulling. The second guard didn't keep a strong enough grip on his weapon, losing it. The first held fast, but was dragged off-balance by the unexpected move.

Caleb swung the first guard into the second, knocking them both into the wall. He was on them in an instant. Using the captured rifle as a club, he cracked the stock into the helmet of one guard with enough force to leave him dizzy before slamming it into the other man's chest with enough force to break both the end of the rifle and crack the plate on his armor, taking the wind out of him.

Still on the attack, he dropped the rifle, needing both hands to unlatch and twist the helmet off one guard. Hitting him across the temple with it, he knocked the man unconscious. The other one stumbled back. Caleb tackled him and put him in a chokehold, but it took more time than Caleb wanted for him to finally stop moving and settle face down on the floor.

"Come on," Caleb said, jumping back to his feet. "They know we're here. We need to get clear before the reinforcements arrive." He didn't wait for her to respond, sprinting down the corridor. A second door waited there, currently closed. With every step, he expected it to open, a wall of guards behind it, ready to gun them both down. *Ish, if you're still linked through the Collective, drop it. There's no point now.*

Already done. Why did you wait so long to attack them?

I needed to be sure they were on to us for one. For another, I needed a better position to disable them both on my own. My challenge left them on their back foot, unsure what I would do.

Caleb approached the second door, outpacing Marley by nearly a dozen strides. It didn't open until he neared, triggered by a signal from his armor. The corridor beyond was clear, at least for the moment. A short passage with a t-junction directly ahead.

Caleb raised his hand, signaling Marley to switch the comms back to their private encrypted channel. "Which way?" he asked.

"Left," she replied.

"Then we go right."

"What?"

He reached the junction, barely slowing as he offered a fleeting glance to the left. The adjacent passageway was longer than he expected, and he spotted a squad of soldiers entering it at the other end at a full run, obviously desperate to get to the tunnel before he and Marley made it out.

"Pick up the pace, Private," he growled into the comms. "We've got incoming."

She didn't answer him, appearing at the junction a moment later. She froze when she looked in the direction of the oncoming soldiers. "We're dead."

"Knuckle up, Private!" he barked. "Follow me!"

The sharpness of his tone broke her out of her daze. She accelerated in his direction, just as he swung his rifle up and opened fire at the incoming guards. His volley of gunfire stitched into the floor ahead of them. It was enough to slow them down, though it didn't prevent them from shooting back. Rounds filled the passageway, most zipping past, a few hitting the plates on his armor, and the front of Marley's suit. She cried out and stumbled when a round grazed her leg, managing to find a weak spot. Reaching back for her, he caught her before she could hit the floor, hoisting her over his shoulder and carrying her back the other way, rounding the corner. Stopping there, he offloaded Marley, and she scooted out of Caleb's way as he laid down cover fire, her back against the wall.

"Are you okay?" he asked.

"Physically? Just a flesh wound. Emotionally? I don't know."

"With friends like these, who needs enemies," Caleb remarked, drawing a sardonic laugh from her. "Which way from here?"

"Back around this corner and past the guards chasing us," she replied.

"Smart ass. Where does this way lead?"

"It doesn't matter. It's over, Caleb."

"We don't quit—"

"Until we're dead. I get it. But we'll be dead soon enough. We're two people. We can't knock everyone on the base unconscious, especially with you carrying me."

"We just need to get to the Empress. We need to show her the data chip. That's all."

"Well, the Empress is back that way! Through the guards!" She pointed back the way they'd come, sounding, on the verge of hysterics.

Caleb fired a few more rounds down the corridor before dropping the rifle. He stood and took her hand, pulling her to her feet and into a bride's carry. Shoving his faceplate against hers, he could see the defeat etched in her face. The fear, doubt, and resignation. "I can leave you here to die if you want, but is this really how you want to go out? The Relyeh know we're here, Andrea. I don't mean the planet. I mean right here. Inside this base."

Her expression hardened instantly. "How?"

"Ishek told them."

"What?" Confusion turned to anger. "You son of a bitch, you promised—"

"But Ish didn't. We only have one option left, and that's to live long enough to reach the Empress."

Her anger shifted to resolve. "You tricked me."

"I had no choice. I still don't. We're running out of time."

"Then put me down; I can run. Maybe not as fast as you, but don't wait for me."

Caleb set her on her feet and bent to scoop up his rifle. As he did, a canister hit the side of the wall and bounced off, rolling to a stop between his legs.

CHAPTER 33

"Down!" Caleb shouted, kicking the canister away as he turned and lunged at Marley, taking her down and covering her with his body. The explosive detonated, spewing heat and shrapnel. A sharp pain jabbed Caleb's shoulder, a fragment of hot metal finding a less-protected spot in his armor. He gritted his teeth against the pain, planting his hands on the floor to push himself off her. "Are you okay?"

"Still alive," she replied.

He grabbed her arm, helping her to her feet. "We have to move."

She didn't argue, joining him in a sprint down the passageway, away from the guards. While she had initially refused to engage her own side, the explosive and his warning had triggered her change of heart. She fired back down the corridor at their pursuers, sending bullets off their armor and forcing them back behind cover.

You don't know for certain my connection to the Collective allowed the Relyeh to pinpoint us.

No. But it served as strong motivation. Can you do something about my back?

Not until you remove the shrapnel.
No time for that right now.

"We can lose them in the service tunnels," Marley said as they neared the next junction. "Right up ahead, halfway down, then left. The heavy equipment is there. Recycling, cooling, water, and sewage treatment. The place is a maze."

"And you know how to navigate it?"

"Not completely, but neither do they."

"Are you sure about that?"

"It's not much, but it's our best chance. You can trust me, even if I can't say the same."

That was unnecessary.

We deserve it, Caleb countered, wincing in response to the statement. "Lead the way."

They made a right at the end of the passageway, following another long corridor that branched out into new tunnels, all on the left side. Despite all the running, they were still moving along the perimeter, perpendicular to the base. While they had made it inside the compound, they had yet to truly enter the main part of it. That changed when they made the left at the centerpoint of the corridor, just barely staying ahead of the pursuing units.

Rounds bit into the wall just behind them as they cut into the next passageway, where it sloped downward beneath the rest of the base. Almost immediately, the simple light strips were joined on the top of the tunnels by different types of tubing and pipes that split off at various intervals, climbing through small holes bored through the earth.

At first, the service tunnels didn't seem to offer anything that would help them evade the guards, but the further they ran, the more frequently the tunnels began branching off. The passageways had all been dug out to bring essential services to the rest of the facility in as efficient a footprint as possible. This led the corridors to intersect in a pattern understandable only to the AI that designed it, creating the maze Marley had promised.

Caleb quickly lost track of the number of turns they made and tunnels they entered or exited as they worked their way toward a low thrumming sound that rose from the center of the labyrinth. That was where all the heavy machinery had been installed. The noise, the only point of reference they had, could only guide them halfway. Once they reached the middle of the service tunnels, they were on their own to find a way out that wouldn't put them in the hands of their pursuers.

The thrumming steadily grew louder, though a few wrong turns and reversals both slowed their approach and allowed the guards to gain on them. There was no doubt in Caleb's mind they would be confronted from other directions soon enough. More units would be committed to the chase, descending into the service tunnels from every entrance and exit, additional forces left behind to ensure they couldn't escape the lower tunnels.

Marley was right. We can't win this one. Maybe if we could kill—

We're not killing anyone, Caleb replied sharply. *Maybe we can't win, but we have to try. Too much depends on us. Ham is depending on us.*

Ishek knew better than to try to talk him out of something he'd set his mind to, even if the odds *did* seem insurmountable. He had overcome the impossible before, both on Earth and elsewhere. Like any other game, you couldn't win if you didn't play.

A trio of guards happened upon them near the passageway's midpoint, just as the largest of the underground machines came into view. They turned the corner and nearly collided, neither Caleb and Marley, nor the three guards walking abreast expecting the others to be there.

Caleb was first to react, grabbing the guard in front of

him and shoving him into the woman in the middle, making her stumble into the bulkhead. The other one lunged at an unprepared Marley. She backpedaled to escape him, remaining clear as Caleb grabbed his power pack, using it to pull him away from Marley. He kept hold of the man, shoving him into the woman, the two of them falling to the deck. He came down on top of the woman, her head cracking into the deck hard enough to stun her.

The guard Caleb had shoved pulled his sidearm and swung it toward him. Slipping inside the man's reach, Caleb elbowed his arm aside, the weapon discharging wildly. Caleb broke the man's wrist, forcing him to drop the gun before tugging his head down into his knee, cracking the man's faceplate and dazing him. Spinning on his heel, he brought his forearm up just in time to block a knife slash from the guard who'd fallen on the woman and was back to his feet. The knife glanced off his armor, the force knocking it from the guard's hand. Caleb pressed him back against the bulkhead, his arm tight against the man's throat, but he didn't get a chance to choke him all the way out.

Pain seared across Caleb's shoulders. The woman, back on her feet, had picked up the fallen knife and stabbed him in the seam between his helmet and armor, missing his spine by millimeters. He gritted his teeth as he whirled around so fast the guard didn't have time to pull the knife back out. His left arm momentarily numb and useless, he threw a roundhouse right into her helmet, knocking her back long enough for him to jerk the knife out of his back and throw it down the passageway.

The man with the cracked faceplate, a scowl stretched across his ugly face, came at Caleb again.

Can't we at least kill this one?

Caleb answered Ishek by meeting the guard head on, shoving his shoulder into him and lifting him to slam him hard into the bulkhead. He had to admit, this would all be so much easier if he didn't have to hold back to make sure he didn't injure the guards too badly. Turning, he body-slammed him to the deck, knocking the air out of him. He barely had time to gather himself before the woman, knife back in hand, thrust it toward the vulnerable spot in his armor where his right arm met his chest. The knife slid off a thicker chestplate, leaving her open to Caleb's gut punch. She doubled over, and he shoved her aside.

Winded and bleeding, Caleb looked up to see the guard with the broken wrist, the man he'd bounced off his knee, facing him with his gun in his good hand. He put three rounds into Caleb's armored chest. Even though they didn't fully penetrate his overlay, the force behind them knocked him back into the bulkhead. Before he could get off any more shots, Marley intervened. She jumped on his back, wrapping her arm around his throat and squeezing as he struggled to toss her off.

Looking past them, Caleb saw more guards coming their way. Even with Ishek bolstering his adrenaline, his blood loss had left him without enough fight to handle them all. And that was if he and Marley survived their rifle fire.

"Marley, we need to go!" he gasped into the comms as he pushed off the bulkhead. She looked up at him and then back over her shoulder at the approaching guards, immediately scrambling off the guard before she could finish choking him out. Caleb took her hand, pulling her around the corner. "We need a way up," he growled as he let go of her hand. "Where's the nearest exit?"

"I... I don't know," she replied.

"C'mon, Private. This is life or death. Which way?"

"You...you're bleeding."

"It's nothing," Caleb replied, ignoring the wet feel of blood soaking the back of his underlay. Both the shrapnel and knife wounds had cut him deep. They weren't exactly nothing, but he'd had worse. Still… "This was a bad idea. We need an exit."

"No, this was the best idea out of a series of terrible ideas," she countered, looking over his shoulder. His ATCS registered the approaching targets coming now from both ends of the passageway they had just left. "I was right the first time. This isn't going to work. It's over, Caleb."

"I don't accept that!" he snapped. He grabbed her hand again, towing her behind him to the next intersection. He paused there when he saw more guards coming from both directions of that passageway as well, leaving no way to escape.

"We're boxed in," Marley said, her voice taking on a strange tone of resolved resignation. "At least we won't be alive to see Crux slaughter the Empress."

Caleb turned to face her, an idea spawning in his mind.

You've had bad ones before. This one is the absolute worst. Hands down.

You don't have hands, he replied. "Marley, I need you to shoot me."

"What?" she replied, her wide eyes framed in her faceplate.

Don't do this, Caleb.

"Do you trust me?" he asked her.

"Not really."

"Then you should want to shoot me for betraying you." He looked past her to the incoming soldiers, their rifles trained on the two of them. "There's no more time. If they see you kill me, they might let you off the hook."

"And what do you get out of that?"

"I get to die knowing I wasn't responsible for your death, too. Do it, Private."

She stared at him, hesitant.

Caleb, I don't like this. At all.

Too bad. It's the only way.

He didn't give Marley any more time. He lunged at her, wrapping his hands around her throat and squeezing, his faceplate pressed against hers. She looked shocked, frightened, and angry by his attack, her eyes bulging as he choked her air off.

He felt the muzzle of her pistol dig between two of his armor plates, followed by the muffled pops of her sidearm as she fired twice. Having been shot before, he knew what to expect. The point-blank rounds penetrated both his overlay and underlay, but he barely felt the bullets slam into his gut. The strikes still sent him stumbling backward to collapse on the floor as the guards reached them.

Two of them grabbed Marley, ripping the gun from her hand before pinning her arms behind her back. She didn't struggle, her eyes locked on him as he lay there, bleeding out. He was only vaguely aware of the muzzle pressed against the side of his helmet. The railgun it belonged to could easily put a round through both the headgear and his skull.

"Good night, demon bastard," the soldier holding the weapon uttered, finger shifting to the trigger.

I think you may have miscalculated.

Caleb laughed out loud at the comment, growing delirious from the loss of blood. The outburst confused the soldier enough that he held his fire. Not that it mattered. Pain finally blossomed in Caleb's chest as his heart suddenly seized. His laughter ceased with a gasp and then nothing as he lay there.

Dead.

CHAPTER 34

Caleb was only assured he would wake up when he did just that, greeted by waves of pain from the untreated wounds to his abdomen and back. But what else should he have expected? Dead men didn't need treatment. And as far as anyone else was concerned, he had died.

You're welcome.

Ishek's voice was weak in his mind, signaling his symbiote's exhaustion.

Where are we? Caleb asked. His eyes were open, but he still couldn't see. He was naked and cold. *Morgue?*

The medical staff wants to perform an autopsy on us. Once they determined we were dead, they brought us here, stripped you and shoved us in the cooler. I give them credit for recognizing that I am not a basic khoron. They lose points for not correctly identifying my hibernation state.

I had a feeling they wouldn't, since they don't seem to know about Advocates. How long since Marley shot me?

Thirty-six minutes. They rushed us here to preserve us as much as possible.

I'm glad they didn't try to remove you.
As am I.

How's my physical state?

You are healed enough that you won't pass out again. I can provide you with endorphins to dull the pain, if you wish.

No, let's save the chemicals for when we really need them. Besides, you need to recoup your energy. I can handle the pain.

What do we do now?

Dying got us out of that mess. Now we try to reach the Empress without getting into another one.

Caleb heard muffled voices, beginning at a murmur and growing louder as they approached. *Perfect timing.*

Yes. I hunnggeerrr.

Again?

Keeping you alive is hungry work.

Despite his own stomach cramping from hunger, Caleb remained still and silent, listening intently as the voices drew nearer. Two people, a man and a woman. Obviously, the medical staff charged with cutting them open to see what made them tick. They shared a somewhat nervous laugh before quieting. Caleb heard drawers opening and closing, light metal objects clanking on a metal surface, and the hum of a machine.

"Are we ready?" the woman asked.

"Yes, Doctor," the man replied. "We're all set."

"Not quite. You forgot your hazmask."

The man laughed. "Of course. It's been a while since we kept a Legionnaire. The last one I assisted with was almost two years ago now, back on Atlas."

"I was in the room when Doctor Yu performed the autopsy on the assassin that killed His Highness La'ki," the doctor replied. "I'll never forget the sight of that disgusting thing crawling out of the murderer's neck while he was on the operating table, so desperate to escape. Or watching Doc Yu stab it with a scalpel. I was still in residency at the time. It was such a shock to everyone."

"I'm sure it wasn't as shocking as what came after," the

assistant replied, his voice more muted. No doubt from the hazmask. The door to the cooler vibrated as he turned the handle to open it.

"In a way, it was more shocking. The attack seemed inevitable after the discovery, though of course none of us wanted to entertain the idea at the time. We all would have liked to pretend the one that came out of the assassin was unique."

The door to the cooler opened, immediately allowing warmer air into the enclosure, along with enough light for Caleb to see he was zipped up in a body bag thin enough to let a bit of light through. He remained still as the assistant pulled out the drawer, which transferred effortlessly from the cooler to the waiting table. Despite being unable to see through the bag, he was aware of the man moving to stand over him and when the doctor sidled up to him on the other side.

"Let's see what we've got in here," she said.

This is my favorite part.

Shadows drifting over the bag let Caleb know when the doctor's assistant reached for the zipper. He closed his eyes as the zipper rasped open, the sides of the bag falling down over the drawer's edges. Caleb held his breath, keeping his body still as the doctor gently wrapped a hand around his right arm.

"Strange," she said as she moved his arm aside to better expose Ishek. "He's still so warm and relatively pliable."

"Look at the size of that thing," the assistant said.

He means me.

Don't make me laugh, Caleb silently replied.

"I've never seen one that size. It's too big to hide under his skin."

Still me.

"I wonder what benefit it offers?" the doctor responded.

"It's more vulnerable in that position. Unless this is a more primitive sample."

Now she's referring to you.

"Magnifier," she requested. "I want to get a closer look at the connection before I start cutting."

Caleb heard the assistant lift the tool from the table and hold it out over him.

"I wonder who pushed his eyes closed," the assistant said.

"Nobody," Caleb replied, his eyes snapping open.

His left hand shot out, grabbing the assistant by the back of the neck. Simultaneously, he ripped his right one away from the pretty dark-haired doctor, wrapping his hand around her throat. Sitting up, he slammed the assistant's head down into the edge of the metal drawer hard enough force to knock him out.

Yes. Delicious.

Caleb let the man drop to the floor but kept his grip on the doctor's neck as he slid his lower half off her side of the drawer. Her brown eyes were wide with fear, but she still had the presence of mind to slash his forearm with her scalpel, the stinging gash deep enough to drip blood. Growling low in his throat, he grabbed her wrist in his free hand before she could do anymore damage. Pressing his thumb down on the major nerve in her hand, he forced her to drop the blade.

"I'm not going to kill you," he said calmly to her. "But I do need you to go to sleep for a while." He continued holding her throat while he shoved her against the cabinets behind her. Bonded to Ishek, he could taste her fear as well, but while the symbiote enjoyed its meal, he felt badly for causing her such distress. "I'm sorry to have to do this."

Her eyes narrowed in confusion just before they rolled back in her head. Caleb released her throat, catching her before she could fall and injure herself. He laid her out on top of the body bag before quickly looking around.

Stop feeding and heal this cut, he ordered Ishek.

A tasty snack, yet I keep needing to waste it on you.

"Sorry, not sorry," Caleb said out loud as he soaked in his surroundings. The room was a proper morgue, with storage for half a dozen corpses, two autopsy tables, cabinets, a multitude of drawers, and all the necessary equipment a pathologist would need. It hardly felt like a rebel hideout in the middle of a jungle. And there was no way they had the resources to line any part of a cavern floor with metal decking, or install a basic sliding hatch at the front of the room. "We're on their ship."

Obviously.

Of course, it wasn't all that surprising they had brought him here. Why duplicate any functions inside the excavated base that the ship could fulfill? Might that mean Ham was also here, locked up in the brig?

That would be a much greater risk than bringing a corpse on board.

"True," he agreed, circling the table to reach the assistant. The man wore a pair of basic light gray scrubs, baggy enough that Caleb was sure he could fit into them despite being considerably more muscular. He also had a plastic-looking device clasped around his neck and over the front of his face, covering his mouth, nose, and ears. "What the hell is that thing?"

It appears designed to prevent a khoron from entering through an orifice, or tunneling into the back of the neck.

"It looks ridiculous."

And also ineffective. Khoron don't need to enter through the neck. It's the most efficient location, not the only one.

Caleb checked his forearm to ensure it had stopped bleeding. "Maybe they don't know as much about your kind as they think they do," he said, wincing as he bent to remove the autopsy assistant's shirt, the pain in his gut more noticeable now that he was less focused on survival.

Apparently not.

He put on the shirt before removing the man's shoes and pants, putting the pants on. It was a far cry from his underlay, but it was better than wandering around naked. He tried the shoes, but they were too small to get his feet into.

"It figures," he said, frowning. "Nothing says escaped corpse like bare feet." He gritted through it, making his way to the hatch. "Let's hope there's nobody in the passageway, or this is going to be a really short resurrection."

CHAPTER 35

The door to the morgue, operating on a motion sensor, slid open as Caleb carefully approached it from the side. He peered cautiously out into the passageway beyond.

Thankfully, it wasn't occupied.

Even so, Caleb didn't move right away. Instead, he stood there absorbing the look of the starship's interior. It reminded him more of the generation ships than it did anything produced by Proxima in the last one hundred years or so. Probably because the ship was at least that old, if not older. The bulkheads were dull and scuffed, and rusted in places. Only half of the overhead lights were functional, and the water pipes running across the ceiling had three different leaks just in this corridor alone. He could not only hear the ship's reactor, he could feel its vibrations running through the floor, an uneven shiver that suggested something was out of whack. Glancing back into the morgue, he wondered if it was actually the nicest compartment on the ship, the one in the best condition.

The dead certainly aren't going to mess it up.

Ishek was right. The morgue was probably also one of the least visited spaces on the ship. Only members of the medical staff would ever have a need to visit it. That fact worked out in Caleb's favor, allowing him to move out into the passageway and quickly pad along the length of it, toward another hatch at the end. He didn't know which direction he was headed, though the length of the corridor suggested he was moving either forward or aft, rather than from one side to the other. Port to starboard or vice versa.

He slowed when he neared the next sliding door. The morgue didn't have a placard beside its door identifying the room behind it, and neither did this one. Looking down at his bare feet, he thought he might try each door in the hopes of finding some boots, but ultimately decided against it. Instead, he advanced on the door at the end of the passageway. He ducked to the side as it opened in response to his proximity, barely squeezing into the corner beside it before he was in view of anyone who might be in there.

The room was empty, but a large muscular man in dark gray coveralls emerged from another room just down the corridor from him, carrying a toolbag in one hand and a large wrench in the other. He moved away from Caleb, giving no indication he'd seen Caleb or heard the door behind him slide open. He continued toward the junction ahead, turning to the left and moving out of sight.

He has boots. You need boots.

Yes, but I don't need attention, and he's too far away. Caleb moved into the passageway, remaining alert. *It's quiet here.*

Not surprising. The morgue is probably on the lower decks, likely amidships.

Why do you think so?

That brute looks like he's going to fix something important, like an out of whack reactor. Plus, nobody wants the morgue where they have to look at it all the time. Even if it doesn't have a name on it, people know what it is and don't want to walk by it every day. We rode an elevator to get down here, and the morgue wasn't far from it. It's probably around that corner up ahead. Also, I figure the ship's hangar is nearby.

Let me guess, because it's easier to move incoming dead to the morgue?

Precisely. I'd also venture a guess that sickbay is up one or two levels.

Do you think you can guess where the exit is? Or where we might find the Empress? Ham is still in trouble. Marley might be, too. I have no idea how these people would react to her after she killed me.

Either celebrate her as a hero, or schedule her for execution with Abraham, I would imagine.

Talk about two extremes.

Someone's coming.

Hearing the light click of boots a few seconds after Ishek, Caleb hurried to the nearest door. Not equipped with a motion sensor, he had to tap the controls beside it for it to slide open. He ducked into an empty compartment just as a woman in navy coveralls came around the corner ahead, the door whisking shut before she could see him.

"Too close," he whispered, leaning against the bulkhead. He counted to twenty before opening the door and peeking out. The passageway was clear.

I hope she wasn't with the medical staff.

Caleb froze. What were the odds? *I don't think so. I'm wearing light gray scrubs. The doctor's scrubs were off-white.*

He returned to the corridor and hurried to the t-junction in the corridor, his sense of urgency increasing. The same mechanic he had seen headed in the opposite direction two minutes earlier stepped back around the corner, right in front of him. Both men came to an abrupt stop, their eyes meeting.

"Oh, excuse me," the mechanic said with a broad smile. "Sorry for almost running into you." He shook his toolbag.

"I was on my way to check on that stutter in the reactor, and I forgot my torque wrench."

"I hate it when that happens," Caleb replied. "I forget my torque wrench all the time, usually in a cadaver's stomach."

The mechanic's smile faded. "Huh?"

"Sorry, I just got done with an autopsy. Bad corpse humor."

The mechanic shook his head in disgust. "You cadaver cutters all think you're comedians."

Caleb shrugged. "We try."

I think his boots will fit.

I don't want his boots.

You should take his whole uniform. You look more like a mechanic than a cadaver cutter.

"Yeah, well, anyway, I've got to stay on schedule," the mechanic said. "Sorry again."

"It's no problem, really."

The boots, Caleb.

Forget the boots!

The mechanic started to go around Caleb. Luckily, he hadn't noticed his bare feet. "Hey..." Caleb stopped him. "...you know anything about an execution?" he asked. "I heard from my boss that I should expect more work today because of it. Something about an enemy sympathizer?"

The other man stopped again and nodded. "Yeah, I heard about that from my mate in the Guardian Corps. It's not just the guy they brought in. We had related casualties. Almost two full squads."

"You're kidding."

"I wish I was. Do you know about the pod that crashed about a hundred fifty klicks from here?"

Caleb shook his head. "No. I don't usually keep up with that kind of stuff."

"Turns out one of Crux's bastard demons was on it.

Another mate of mine is the scout who scanned him and the man with him. The other guy wasn't infected, so he grabbed him and brought him back, thinking he was doing him a favor. He gets him back, delivers him to Haas, who starts asking him if he's okay, where he came from, that sort of thing. Then the guy insists that the demon isn't a demon and they should go back to help him. Crazy, right?"

Caleb smiled and nodded. "Yeah, that sounds completely insane."

"I'm telling you, if I ever get a shot at that demon, I would shove a wrench so far up his tail he'd crap iron for a month. Tyson was a good friend of mine. We joined the Corps together. I hear he didn't make it back."

"That's rough," Caleb said. "My condolences."

"Not the first friend I've lost to the Legion, and it won't be the last. But thank you. I hope they at least recover his body."

A guilty pang clenched Caleb's stomach, eliciting a wave of pain from his gunshot wounds. He did his best to hide the sudden fire in his gut. "I hope so, too. You said you were in the Guardian Corps?"

"For twelve years. I'd still be in, but nowadays they need me to fix stuff more than they need me to kill stuff." He laughed. "Anyway, I've got to get going. If you want to see them dose the traitor, it's being done publicly in the grand chamber. If you hurry, you can still make it in time. I'd go, but I've got a reactor to fix."

"Where do I find the grand chamber?"

The mechanic raised an eyebrow. "You don't know where the chamber is?"

"I'm an autopsy assistant. I spend most of my time shuttling between sickbay, the morgue, the mess, the head, and my rack."

"I feel you. Take the lift to Deck Six, double back amidships and turn left to reach the port side linkage. That leads directly into the tunnels. The grand chamber is straight ahead from there. Probably eighty percent of the community will be there, the sick bastards. Just follow the crowd, you won't be able to miss it."

"Thanks. I appreciate your help."

"It's funny, we've been hiding out here for months and I've never crossed paths with you before."

"It's a big ship. I don't know everyone, either."

The mechanic dropped his toolbag to put out his palm. "Dwayne."

Caleb took the offered hand. "Jack."

"Good to meet you, Jack," Dwayne said, his grip firm as he shook Caleb's hand.

"I guess I'll—"

Both his and Caleb's heads turned as the hatch at the far end of the passageway opened. The autopsy assistant he had knocked out stumbled through, dressed only in his underwear, the hazmask discarded. He had a huge welt on his forehead, and the beginnings of a black eye. When he saw Caleb, he pointed, his face flushing. "Infected! Demon! Stop him!"

Dwayne's attention turned back to Caleb, tightening his grip so Caleb couldn't pull his hand away. Any hint of cordiality vanished in an instant.

Damn. How did he recover so quickly? Caleb wondered.

Who cares? This guy's boots are as good as ours.

CHAPTER 36

All of Dwayne's earlier friendliness was gone, his expression instantly furious. He held Caleb's hand tightly, trying to restrain him as he swung the wrench at his head.

Caleb pulled back on Dwayne's arm, using the man's grip to tug him off balance, the wrench just missing his head. Caleb cracked his elbow into the mechanic's chin, knocking his head sideways, the blow powerful enough to break Dwayne's hold on his hand. As he slipped away, Caleb glanced toward the nurse, who seemed to be heading straight for a particular hatch.

There were no comms units in the morgue. I bet there's one through that door.

Caleb needed to stop the man before he could raise an alarm. The toolbag Dwayne had dropped on the floor caught his attention.

Dwayne squared off with him. "You son of a bitch. I'm going to kill you."

"I've already been there today," Caleb replied. "It didn't stick."

He faked a couple moves toward the mechanic, convincing Dwayne to attack. Ducking sideways, Caleb scooped up the toolbag before using it to block Dwayne's incoming wrench. The force sent a painful shockwave up Caleb's arms, all the way to his shoulders. He managed to hold onto the bag, turning it to tangle the wrench in the handles. He tugged the bag toward him, again jerking Dwayne off-balance. The mechanic let go of the wrench, turning his fall into a two-handed lunge at Caleb. Stepping aside, Caleb rushed forward, desperate to reach the nurse before he reached the door. Caleb knew that if the man made it into the room, it would be all over for both he and Ham, and possibly Marley, too.

Dwayne crashed into him, catching him around the waist and lifting him off the ground. He slammed him face down on the floor, creating fresh bursts of agony from the still-healing wounds in his stomach and back. The mechanic tried to drop onto him, but Caleb bucked him off, flipping over to wrap his feet around the man's neck. Grunting, he twisted him down to his knees. He pulled back one leg and kicked him in the face. The man's head flew to the side as he stumbled back, blood spewing from his mouth and nose.

Caleb threw himself toward the bag, stretching out just far enough to grab the wrench before Dwayne seized his ankle in an iron grip. Caleb tore the wrench free of the bag and swung it back at Dwayne. The mechanic let out a howl of rage and pain as Caleb nailed him in the wrist. Caleb broke free, picking up the bag as he scrambled to his feet.

Dwayne crouched like a raging bull in front of him. Caleb threw the toolbag at him, more as a distraction than an effort to take him out of the fight. His major concern now was the doctor's assistant, the door to the compartment he was so eager to enter beginning to slide open. He used Dwayne's dodge as an opportunity to scoot past him, getting beyond the mechanic's reach before he could recover.

Too late to waylay him in the corridor—the man was already through the door and into the compartment—Caleb got there when the door was well on its way to sliding shut. He had just enough of an opening left to jam the wrench end-to-end between the door and its frame, stopping the door in its tracks. He had barely enough space to squeeze through.

Just as the nurse reached for an intercom mounted on the wall, Caleb caught hold of his shoulder and spun him around. A right hook to his jaw laid him out cold on the floor, but not before Dwayne was at the door. Too husky to slide through the available opening, Dwayne powered the door open, grabbing the wrench as he rushed in.

Caleb had just enough time to throw his fist into the intercom, smashing the cover and the circuit board behind it. He hit the circuitry a second time to be sure it was toast before whirling back toward the charging Dwayne, wrench raised over his head, his features twisted in a murderous rage.

"Wait!" Caleb cried, putting his hands up. "Please!"

Dwayne obviously didn't expect Caleb's sudden surrender. He held up his attack, staring in confusion at him.

"I could have killed him in the morgue," Caleb said, pointing at the man on the floor. "I didn't. I didn't hurt the doctor either. I only knocked her out. I didn't kill Sergeant Tyson. He swallowed his poison pill when I tried to talk to him. I shot two members of his unit, but I didn't know who they were or whose side they were on. All I knew was that they were trying to kill me, and I regret I had to kill them. I know now that Crux and his Legion are hunting you. I know you think I'm your enemy because I'm bonded to a khoron—"

Advocate.

Caleb rolled his eyes, otherwise ignoring Ish. "So I understand why you want me dead. But all I've been asking for is a chance to be heard. For someone to stop being afraid just long enough to listen to me. Private Marley listened, and she decided to help me. If you'll listen, you might choose to do the same. *Please.*"

Dwayne continued glaring at him. Tense seconds passed as Caleb waited for him to decide what to do.

"I don't believe you," Dwayne said at last, muscles tensing to bring the wrench down in a fatal blow.

"Dwayne, wait!" the man on the floor cried out.

It took more effort for him to hold back his strike this time, but the mechanic paused, only taking his attention off Caleb long enough to glance down at the man. "What? Are you serious, Merrick?"

"Just wait a second," he repeated, bracing a hand on the deck and slowly rising to his feet. Looking pale, he put two fingers to the lump at his temple, his eyebrow flexing before he turned his eyes to Caleb and then looked back at Dwayne. "I'm not saying I trust him, but he's right. He could have killed Doctor Ling and me back in the morgue. He didn't. And it couldn't be because he wants to infect us. He was naked, Dwayne. He didn't...he *doesn't* have any khoron on him, other than the one bonded to him. And it's a different kind of symbiote than I've ever seen before. I think he's different, Dwayne. I don't know what it means yet, but I made a promise to do no harm. What if he's telling the truth and we kill him without listening to him?"

Keeping the wrench raised, Dwayne returned his attention to Caleb. "I don't know. This could all be a trick. The last assassin that went after the Empress got close by infecting a palace servant. Jack here could have some other trick up his sleeve."

Caleb groaned in frustration. "Weren't you listening? I was naked when I got to the morgue. Nowhere to hide anything. Yes, I'm carrying a symbiote. There's no secret in that." He jerked his shirt up and raised his arm, showing

Ish to Dwayne. "You ever seen or heard of a khoron bonded to the outside of someone's body? Ishek is different. He's a more advanced form of khoron, an Advocate. He's more intelligent and free-thinking. He's been with me for five years. If we're separated, we both die. If he dies, I die. If I die, he dies, so he heals my wounds. Makes me stronger than a normal man. Prolongs my life. We operate together toward the same objectives. *My* objectives." He dropped his arm and shirt back down.

I beg to differ.

"He's even able to block his collux from detection to keep me alive."

Maybe I should rethink that.

Shut up, Ish.

"Wait a minute. Are you saying Crux doesn't know you're here?" Merrick asked.

"No, I'm not saying that. Ishek and I shot down a Nightmare. Crux knows something out of the ordinary is happening here, and he's bound to send ships this way to find out what. Look, it's a long story, and I'd prefer to tell it once, directly to the Empress. If you want to bind my hands, then do it. If you want to give me a battalion-sized escort, fine. I need to speak to her before Haas kills my friend."

"I'm not letting you near Her Majesty," Dwayne said, finally wiping some of the blood off his face and swiping it off on the thigh of his coveralls. "Maybe I'll let you talk to the General."

"No. I already tried that. He refused to listen."

"And what makes you think she will?" Merrick asked.

"Because it's obvious how much she cares about her people, that she's still trying to fight, even in the jaws of defeat. She needs an edge, and I might just be that edge. But she'll never know if nobody will let me present my case to her."

"If you aren't lying..."

"I'm not. Even if I were, what's the worst that could happen? Crux is on his way. He'll find her and kill her here on Galatin, or he'll barricade the planet, jam communications, and use it as her prison. Either way, she'll lose contact with the people loyal to her, and in time they'll give up hope. And Crux will win. I don't know him. Never met him. But I'm positive I don't want that to happen."

"I don't know," Dwayne said. "If we help you, Haas might brand us as traitors, too. Next thing you know, we'll be getting dosed along with your friend."

"If you help me, I might be able to help you fight back against Crux. If you don't help me, one way or another, you're definitely going to lose. Isn't it worth a conversation?"

Both men considered it. Dwayne glanced at Merrick. "He's got a point. We never planned to hide here forever, but it does seem like everyone's been getting a little too comfortable lately. I have some wire in engineering we can use to bind his wrists."

Merrick nodded. "I'm going to need my scrubs back if I want to move through the ship without getting undue attention. I can get you a pair of your own from sickbay."

Caleb stripped off the man's scrubs, unashamed to stand naked in front of the two men.

"You're bleeding," Merrick commented, looking curious. "I could have sworn that wound was bigger twenty minutes ago."

Caleb glanced down at his stomach. "It was." The wound had opened just enough for blood to ooze from the damaged skin. "Maybe you can bring me some bandages, too."

"I thought you said your symbiote heals you," Dwayne said.

"He does, but he's a little drained at the moment.

Bringing me back from death's door pretty much sapped him." Caleb said, handing the scrubs back to Merrick.

"You bled all over the inside of the shirt, but at least it didn't go through the material."

"Are you sure you want to put that on?" Dwayne asked. "It may be infected somehow."

It doesn't work like that.

"It doesn't work like that," Merrick echoed Ish as he pulled his scrubs back on and started for the door.

Caleb stopped him with a hand to his arm. "I take it I can trust you not to sound an alarm. Haas won't give me a chance. I don't blame him, but it would be a mistake."

"I'm going to sickbay to get you some clothes. That's all." Caleb nodded to him, releasing his arm, and he left the room, letting the compartment door close behind him.

Dwayne considered Caleb for a moment after Merrick left, finally exhaling sharply. "I assume your name isn't Jack."

"No," Caleb replied. "Captain Caleb Card, Centurion Space Force Marines."

"Not just a Marine, but an officer." He stiffened to attention. "Sir." Smiling, he relaxed his posture. "That explains a lot. I was in the Corps long enough to know you're a better fighter than I ever was. You could have killed both me and Merrick with your hands tied behind your back, if that's what you wanted. You're having trouble managing your objectives because you're holding back. And there's only one reason you would do that."

"I came here to help," Caleb said.

"I believe you," Dwayne responded. "I hope you can convince Her Majesty of that. We could use all the help we can get."

CHAPTER 37

Caleb settled into the chair behind the bare metal desk in the corner, his feet up to help keep the blood closer to his wounds to give Ishek an easier time healing him. Dwayne stood beside the door, just in case they had any unwanted visitors before Merrick returned.

In less than eight minutes, the nurse was back with scrubs for Caleb.

"It's about time," Dwayne said as Merrick stepped through the door. As he'd explained, he still needed to fix the rattle in the power supply or there was a chance the reactor might shut down, never to be restarted. Every minute he delayed increased the odds of catastrophe, and while he didn't believe the situation was dire just yet, he didn't want to take any more risk than was necessary. It was something he needed to do asap.

Merrick wasn't alone. Doctor Ling entered behind him. Caleb dropped his legs from the desk, wondering if she'd already reported him to her superiors.

"We meet again," Ling said, eyes fixed on Caleb. "Perhaps you can keep your hands off me this time." She raised her head, showing him the bruises his chokehold had left.

"I'm sorry," Caleb replied. "I had no choice."

"There's always a choice," she replied. "You could have spoken to me, instead of attacking me."

"I haven't exactly received the warmest reception. How was I to know you might listen to reason? Besides, I don't have a whole lot of time here to waste."

"For one thing, I'm a doctor, not a soldier."

"Here are your scrubs," Merrick said, tossing them to Caleb. "And some bandages." He dropped a stack of medi-patches on the table. "And some footwear." He held up a pair of simple white slip-ons before dropping them on the desk next to the patches. "Doctor Ling was in the passageway when I came back down. I gave her the quick summary of everything that's going on. Don't let her fool you; she's more intrigued than angry."

"It's not every day that I have the chance to observe a human-khoron bond up close, especially one so unique. I never thought a positive bond was even possible before now. The hypothesis has always been that the khoron overwhelms the human host, turning them into what amounts to an organic mecha."

That's a new way of putting it.

"It depends on the mental fortitude of the intended victim," Caleb replied. "If you've ever studied common characteristics of people the khoron infect, you've undoubtedly noticed that certain patterns emerge."

"Yes, I have read literature on that observation, though I haven't participated in any of the studies. Khorons tend to find greater success among the weak-minded."

"Ishek underestimated my strength," Caleb said, pulling on his pants and the shoes while sitting. Merrick had accurately guessed his size. "Bonded, we're stronger together than we would be separately. And I remain in full control of my own faculties." Privates covered, he stood and finished dressing.

"Yes, I've already witnessed the strength of your bond first-hand. You were shot three times in the stomach, and when I reached you in the tunnels you were unquestionably dead. I can see that your body has undergone a week's worth of healing in an hour. I'd love to hear more about your experiences."

"Maybe later," Caleb replied. "If the Empress doesn't have me executed first." He put out his hands, wrists together, palms up. "You did remember the wire, didn't you?"

Merrick produced a box that reminded Caleb of dental floss. "I have it, but we're not going to use it."

"We aren't?" Dwayne and Caleb both asked simultaneously.

"Not after Doctor Ling told me how you apologized to her before choking her unconscious. Maybe I'm a gullible idiot. Maybe I'm going to help you kill the Empress. But nothing you've said or done leads me to that conclusion, and you were right that we need to do *something*."

"In any case," Ling said, lifting a pen-like device from the pocket of her coat. "I'll have this laser scalpel trained on your symbiote. It will take less than a second for me to cut it in half."

I recommend avoiding that outcome.

"Fair enough," Caleb replied. "So I take it you have a plan to get me an audience with the Empress?"

"Anyone in the Corps who isn't on guard duty will be at the dosing," Ling said. "So will the Empress."

Merrick shrugged. "I figured we would just march you up there."

"Won't the Guardians grab me before I can get close? Or use their collux exciter or whatever it is against me?"

"You mean the hypersonic repeller?" Dwayne asked. "It actually works?"

"In certain circumstances. What's a hypersonic repeller?"

"They're standard issue on every starship that berths more than fifty."

"We use them to keep rodents and other pests away," Merrick added. "The version the Corps is testing is more powerful than a standard repeller by an order of magnitude. It's experimental."

I'm so embarrassed right now.

"Well, it knocked me and Ishek for a loop earlier. That's the only reason your scout friend made off with Ham."

"Your friend's name is Ham?" Dwayne asked, laughing.

"Short for Abraham." He glanced at Dwayne. "The question remains. Won't the Guardians prevent me from reaching the Empress?"

"The attention will be on the front of the room, with Haas running the proceedings," Ling said. "It should be fairly simple for Merrick and I to walk you over to her. She and I went to school together. We're good friends, so it isn't unusual for me to greet her and pay my respects."

"You're right. I should have spoken to you, instead of attacking you."

"You can make it up to me later, when you tell me about how you became bonded with your symbiote."

"Deal."

"Well, it seems like you two have things well in hand," Dwayne said. "I'd love to see how all of this turns out, but the reactor doesn't give a damn about the drama of mere mortals." He stepped forward, clapping Caleb on the shoulder. "Good luck, Captain Card. I'll be rooting for you while I'm wrenching the heck out of a stubborn conduit."

"Better the conduit than me," Caleb answered. "Thank you for not bashing my skull in."

"Like I could have." He came to attention and nodded

before picking up his toolbag and wrench from the table and hurrying from the room.

"We need to go," Ling said. "The execution is scheduled for zero seven hundred. We have twelve minutes to reach the grand chamber."

"There's still time," Caleb replied with a grin, his confidence building that he could stop the Empress from killing Ham. "Thank you both for believing in me."

"I'm not doing this for you," Ling said. "I'm doing this for Empress Lo'ane and for the Empire. If there's any chance you can be of service to us, then it's a chance we need to take. She cares too much about us to see that such desperate measures must be taken."

"I understand. And I remain thankful."

"We need to move," Merrick said. "It's fifteen minutes to the grand chamber at a normal pace."

"I'll carry you both there in ten if that's what it takes."

CHAPTER 38

The starship's passageways were sparsely populated, the interest in watching the execution of a traitor, even one who was a stranger, predictably high. The few people that Caleb, Ling, and Merrick passed on their way to the portside linkage with the caverns were still on board because they had tasks they needed to fulfill and didn't have the time or wherewithal to pay much attention to a man in medical scrubs that they didn't recognize. That Caleb accompanied the recognizable doctor and a familiar morgue assistant handled any leftover curiosity passersby might have had about Caleb. That enabled them to reach the linkage without the interruption of a raised alarm and to do it within just a few minutes.

That chance to see more of the ship allowed Caleb to get a better indication of its size. He already knew from Marley that Glory had carried a bit less than two thousand loyalists from the Empress' home world of Atlas to Galatin in a final desperate escape. No doubt, the Empress and her immediate retinue had their own compartments on the barge, but from the ship's mere twelve decks, at least some of the berthing for others would have been double-occupancy.

That many people would put a huge strain on available resources without the expansion into the tunnels.

Glory had a grand name, but that was the only thing grand about it. The barge was rusted and run down, the passageways dimly lit, the bulkheads stained, the decking dented and dull. Considering Dwayne's current effort to shore up the reactor before things went critical, Caleb doubted the vessel could survive another launch if a second escape became necessary. Seeing more of the ship also increased his understanding of why the Empress had yet to offer any solid path forward for her followers who had given up so much in service to their leader.

Caleb also understood the alternatives. Crux knew they were on Galatin. He probably also knew where to find the rebel base. It wasn't only Ham who was running out of time.

They all were.

Ling and Merrick led Caleb toward a pair of guards flanking the ship side of the linkage. Their gaze slipped over the doctor and her assistant, pinpointing Caleb. He made eye contact, almost daring them to challenge him, his heartbeat quickening. He hid the urgency beneath a friendly smile and nod in passing, the gestures working to temper any threat he might have initially presented. He began breathing easily again as they passed through an open hatch and into a short telescoping corridor connected to a round cast iron aperture that led into the tunnels.

"Are we going to make it in time?" he asked as they emerged into a bare rock tunnel where two more guards stood.

"We need to hurry," Ling whispered as one of the guards, looking oddly at Caleb, stepped forward to meet them. "Is there a problem?" she asked him, the forcefulness of her tone shifting his attention away from Caleb to her.

"No, Doctor Ling," one of them said. "There's no problem. I just don't recall ever having seen this man before." His eyes shifted back to Caleb.

"He's new on the medical staff, fresh out of training. He got tired of the heat in the galley, and apparently he wasn't much of a cook either."

Caleb managed to look a bit embarrassed. "What can I say? I can barely boil water without burning it."

The guard chuckled and looked back at Dr. Ling. "I assume you're heading to the big event?"

Caleb's lips thinned in displeasure at hearing Ham's execution referred to in quite that way. He quickly flattened the expression and shrugged when the guard's eyes again flicked his way.

"That's right," she replied, drawing the guard's attention back to her. "I'm typically not in favor of public executions, or executions of any kind, but I heard the prisoner refused to renounce a demon."

"I heard that, too," the guard said. "The last thing we need are more sympathizers to Crux and the Legion."

"I don't understand how someone can be in favor of what's happened to the Spiral," Merrick added. "It's disturbing."

"And disgusting," the guard agreed, again looking at Caleb. "What do you think?"

"I think everything about the situation is horrible."

"What do you mean by that?" the other guard asked.

"Look," Ling interrupted, "we don't have time for a discussion on the morals of public executions. We're going to miss the proceedings if we don't get going and then we have work to get back to."

"Of course." The guard stepped back, gesturing for her to pass. Merrick and Caleb quickly followed behind her.

"Be sure to give the bastard a good heckle for us before they dose him," the guard called out behind them.

Ling waved her hand to acknowledge him before

continuing down the tunnel. "Less than two minutes," she groused. "We need to run."

Caleb was ready to sprint past her as she broke into a jog. He was ready to take on the entire population of the base to save Ham, but thought better of drawing more unwanted attention to himself, remaining behind Ling, with Merrick right behind him. Fortunately, they didn't pass anyone else in the tunnel. Almost everyone interested in the execution was already inside the grand chamber. No doubt, Caleb thought, they were all impatient for the spectacle to begin.

"I haven't asked," Caleb said as they ran. "Why do you call it *dosing*? Is it a lethal injection?"

"Sort of," Merrick replied. "The injection is lethal, but not in the way you think. The chemical causes hallucination and suicidal ideation. An assortment of methods are provided, but the prisoner takes their own life."

Intriguing.

Horrifying, Caleb countered. "And you're okay with that?"

"There's no place for sedition in the best of times, and we're at war. The brig only holds a dozen, so capital offenses are met with fast and harsh punishment."

"Okay, but can't you do something a little more humane? Hanging, firing squad, anything but tricking prisoners into killing themselves?"

"I'm not saying I agree with it. But this is how capital punishment is done. It's one final way for the convicted to connect with the pain and suffering they've caused before they end themselves."

Caleb knew they were close when he began hearing the murmuring spectators in the grand chamber. "Are we going to make it?" he asked again, realizing they had less than a minute to get there, and it had yet to come into view.

"It'll be close," Ling replied, finding another gear.

They reached the grand chamber, a large, excavated spiral dug into the earth, at the thirty second mark. The rings of the spiral provided seating while the nearly twenty meter in diameter center formed a sunken stage. Stopping at the top of the spiral, Caleb's jaw clenched when he spotted Ham in the center of the stage, standing there gagged, with his hands bound behind him. Marley was bound and gagged beside him.

"Son of a bitch," Caleb cursed.

So much for earning forgiveness by killing you.

"Who's the other prisoner?" Merrick asked Ling.

"A Guardian Corps member," she replied.

"Private Andrea Marley," Caleb said. "She helped me get here, right before she shot me in the stomach three times and had me brought to the morgue."

"Did she know you weren't planning to die?" Merrick asked.

"No. She did it to save herself. Obviously, it didn't work. General Haas is—"

"Careful," Ling warned. The spectators closest to them turned their heads when they heard the General's name. She pointed off to the side, near the bottom of the spiral. "There's the Empress. She's talking to the General now."

Caleb followed her finger to where a bald, older man in black utilities stood over a lean, hardened middle-aged woman in the same uniform. The only thing that made her stand out over General Haas was a red cross on each of her lapels and her commanding demeanor. She was no damsel in distress, reliant on the General. She had the look and posture of a military leader.

"We only have twenty seconds to get down there," Merrick said.

Ling started forward, moving between spectators already sitting on the rings of the spiral, using them as stairs to descend. Caleb followed right behind her, stepping agilely around the gathered rebels, ignoring their complaints. The seconds ticked away in his mind, ten of them passing before they had even gotten close. Keeping an eye on the Empress, Caleb's heart pounded harder when Haas turned away from her and headed for the center of the stage.

Caleb noticed that different objects had been placed around the perimeter of the spiral's bottom, including a long serrated hunting knife, a pistol, and what looked like a bottle of pills. The sight of them made him sick.

What kind of society had the descendants of Pathfinder created, and why?

Maybe they're better off with Crux in control.

I doubt that, Caleb replied.

"Everyone, find your seats and be quiet," Haas said, his voice carrying well across the chamber. "Now!" he barked the word, and the entire audience fell silent. Ling came to such a sudden stop that Caleb nearly knocked her over before stopping. "Doctor Ling," Haas added, singling them out. "Sit, please."

The people on either side of them shifted closer together to give them room to sit.

"I'm sorry, Caleb," Ling said, gently touching his wrist. "We didn't make it. We're out of time."

CHAPTER 39

"What do you mean we're out of time? We can still stop this," Caleb growled in a harsh whisper.

She shook her head. "The guards at the linkage slowed us down, and so did the crowd. I did my best to get you here, but—."

"Did you…really?"

She glared at him before reaching over, wrapping her right hand around his bicep as if they were there to watch the execution together. She tucked her left hand under his arm, the end of the laser scalpel pressed against Ishek.

"If you're implying I intentionally set a slower pace—"

Uh, Caleb…?

"That's exactly what I'm saying."

"I would never," she snarled back. "I'm sorry. Don't make things worse than they already are."

"Damn you, Doctor! I trusted you."

You need to calm down. She's got a knife to my head.

Calm down? I didn't come here to watch Ham die.

Dying ourselves won't help him.

Relax. She's a doctor, not a soldier, remember?

"Your Majesty," General Haas said, turning to face Lo'ane and bowing his head. She offered a much more shallow nod back before he turned in a circle, addressing the audience. "Assembled members of the Guardian Corps and trusted allies of the true leader of the Atlassian Empire. You're here today to bear witness to the consequences of grave injustice. To see for yourselves the only outcome for those who renounce their own kind and align themselves with our demonic adversaries, the Relyeh." He turned to look at Marley, whose expression bore the terror of her predicament.

Caleb could taste her fear, the sweetness palpable through Ishek's senses, though his symbiote was too worried about the laser scalpel to react.

"Abraham Cortez was discovered in the company of a confirmed demon," Haas continued. "One of our scouts was able to distract the demon and enact a successful extraction. How were we repaid for this act of kindness? Abraham insists that the demon is not a threat, and in fact came to Galatin searching for us to render aid."

"Ridiculous!" someone called out.

"He's lying!" another shouted.

Caleb's blood boiled, but he remained silent. His left hand shifted ever so slowly behind his back.

"He refuses to renounce the demon," Haas said. "And for that reason, he has been convicted of high treason by the Council."

"Who's on the Council?" Caleb asked Ling while the spectators quietly cheered their consent to the verdict.

"The Empress, General Haas, Colonel Campbell, and my superior, Doctor Fischer," Ling replied.

"How do you break a stalemate?"

"The Empress has final say in the event of a tie."

It wasn't surprising, but it also didn't seem very fair.

"Abraham Cortez, do you have anything to say before your sentence is carried out?" Haas asked, pulling the gag out of Ham's mouth.

"You're making a mistake," Ham said, his voice raspy, throat dry. "A huge mistake. I'm not your enemy. I—"

Haas slid the gag back over his mouth and addressed the audience. "As you can see, he has no remorse."

The assembly booed. The whole thing reminded Caleb more of the ancient Roman Coliseum than any kind of real justice.

Haas stepped past Ham to stand beside Marley. "Private Andrea Marley, a member of the Guardian Corps Delta Squad, all of whom were killed in action last night, except for her. Why not? Because she chose to side with the enemy demon, rather than kill it or herself for the safety of us all. She brought it to this very compound, helped it gain access, and then when cornered finally murdered it. Not out of any sense of duty, but in a feeble effort to avoid dosing. Private Marley is the worst kind of soldier. A traitor and a coward."

The words brought tears to Marley's eyes as the crowd booed and screamed at her much more violently than they had Ham. He was a stranger who had taken the wrong side. She was one of their own.

"Do you have any last words, Marley?" Haas asked, freeing her of her gag.

"The Legion is coming," she said. "They not only know we're on Galatin. They know where the base is. You should all be preparing for escape, not wasting time watching us die."

The people booed even louder. Haas covered Marley's mouth again, shaking his head. "If they do know where we are, that's because of you," he spat.

The worst part for Caleb was that Haas wasn't really wrong. But he had put Marley in that position. It was on him to fix it. His hand continued shifting behind his back, so far escaping Ling's notice.

"The verdict has been announced. Last words permitted. Colonel Campbell, will you assist?" Haas asked.

The Colonel, a wiry man with a head of thick white hair, stood from his seat beside the Empress. Another Guardian approached him with a box, which he opened to reveal two syringes. Campbell lifted the syringes from the box and walked them over to Haas, who took one of them. Each man positioned himself on the outside of each prisoner, putting the needles against Ham's right arm and Marley's left.

"May you find peace in the next life," Haas said, nodding to Campbell.

Caleb's heart pounded, mentally fighting to keep his cool as the two officers sank their syringes into the arms of the prisoners. "Why did they dose them simultaneously," he asked Ling, his voice tense.

"So neither would have an advantage over the other," she replied. "Dosed individuals will see other dosed individuals as part of their hallucinations. They'll try to kill the others before killing themselves."

Caleb had been sickened before. He was even more disgusted now. "You mean they're going to fight?"

"To us, it will appear as a chaotic conflict. But the narrative will make total sense in each of their minds."

"This is barbaric."

"So are the things Crux has done to this galaxy."

Haas and Campell took their time removing Ham and Marley's gags and bindings before returning to their seats near the Empress. Neither prisoner tried to attack them, or even reacted like they knew the two men were there. It appeared the chemical dose had rendered them unable to see anyone except each other.

Ham's expression shifted, eyes narrowing, mouth

forming a tight line, hands balling into fists. He glanced over at the knife on one side of the stage, obviously contemplating picking it up. That was when he noticed Marley, who had already started for the pistol on the other end. Forgetting the knife, he rushed up behind her, slamming into her back and throwing her face down onto the stone floor.

The crowd cheered.

Caleb wanted to puke.

Ham tried to jump on Marley's back, but she quickly rolled over, lashing out with her foot and cracking him in the chin. He fell sideways as she scrambled to her feet, more eager to reach the gun. Also aware of the weapon, Ham sprang up and dove at her, catching her foot and dragging her back to the floor before she reached the weapon. Turning her over, he climbed up her body, his face twisted in fury. Bringing a hand back to pummel her, she rocked hard enough to wreck his balance and roll him off her. She again went for the gun, leaving Caleb to wonder how she would use it without the risk of hitting any spectators. Depending on the angle, the Empress was low enough to end up in the line of fire.

Marley reached the weapon and swung it toward Ham, who was on his feet and charging. He batted her hand just as she squeezed the trigger, sending the round wide. It hit an invisible barrier before reaching any of the rebels. Knocking the gun out of Marley's hand, it skittered halfway across the stage floor. He followed that up with a heavy backhand that sent her reeling, blood spraying from a split lip.

Caleb had seen enough. His left hand had nearly reached Ling's, and he snapped out with it, grabbing her closed fist and yanking it away before she could activate the scalpel. Her head whipped toward him as she gasped in pain, trying to keep him seated as he snatched the scalpel from her grip and jumped to his feet. Everyone was so engrossed in the fight that none of them immediately noticed him.

Intent on putting a stop to this madness before Ham, Marley, or both were dead, he shoved spectators aside as he descended the spiral seating. Glancing at the two fighters, he saw that Marley had somehow gained the upper hand on Ham and had his neck scissored between her legs. Ham reached for a large rock nearby, and if he managed to get it, he would no doubt break Marley's legs before crushing her skull.

Marley saw the rock and disengaged, releasing Ham so she could retreat while he lifted the stone. "Why did you have to die!" Marley cried out, her face curling in distress as she ran from Ham, angling for the knife. "I never wanted you to join the Corps. I never wanted to be in the Corps. And now look at me!"

"Cap, I've got a bead on him," Ham said as if he were speaking into his helmet. "Consider the mission already complete."

Angling toward the Empress, Caleb picked up his pace, sickened by the hallucinations forced on his friends. Did Marley see Ham as her dead husband? What or who did Ham think Marley was?

He was only ten rows from the Empress when Haas finally noticed him, first with a passing glance, followed by his head snapping back to zero in on him with a more accusing glare. He immediately put a hand to his ear and started speaking, no doubt deciding Caleb was a threat and calling for the guards. Unfortunately for Haas, they were all at the top of the chamber.

Campbell rose to his feet, as did Haas. The Empress noticed them and looked toward Caleb, confused by his approach. The people he passed on his way down started trying to grab him. He blocked and shoved their hands away with agile martial art moves intended to avoid, not injure. Haas moved to intercept him, and from the response of the crowd Caleb guessed they had shifted their attention away from Ham and Marley to his rush for the stage.

Haas stepped in front of him two rows from the Empress, his large body like a bulwark blocking his path. Expecting the man to block him based on hand-to-hand techniques he had learned in the Marines, Caleb threw a hard punch at his gut. The General didn't disappoint. He caught Caleb's fist in his palm and tried to shove him back. Turning the energy back around, Caleb twisted the man's arm, his side kick knocking him off the stage and onto the chamber floor. Ham and Marley both ignored him, each intent on killing the other.

Campbell stepped into Caleb's path next. Behind him, the Empress. She was also standing now, concerned but not terrified. She began reaching for something under her pant leg at her ankle. Most likely a weapon.

Just as she stood up, bringing a pistol to bear on Caleb, a spectator grabbed his arm from behind. Caleb didn't hesitate. Moving faster than either Campbell or the Empress could follow, he caught the man's arm in one hand, the other working as a fulcrum to hoist and heave the man at Campbell. Their bodies collided, both men tumbling backwards. In the same fluid motion, Caleb struck Lo'ane's hand hard enough to knock her hand and the gun aside. Her finger inadvertently tightened on the trigger, and the weapon misfired. Behind Caleb, people screamed as the bullet ricocheted wildly off into the rock overhead.

Caleb stepped into the Empress' immediate space. Their eyes met, his blazing murderously, hers widening in alarm. She swung the pistol back toward him. He moved with lightning speed, putting her neck in an armlock before pulling the laser scalpel from his shirt pocket. She gasped and froze as he lodged it against her throat. "Stop the fight. Now," he growled in her ear.

"Th-they're dosed," she replied, her voice trembling with alarm. "I can't s-stop—"

"Do it, or I'll slit your throat. I don't want to, but I have nothing left to lose."

You are bluffing, aren't you?

What do you think? Caleb replied.

You're so angry, I'm not sure.

Aren't you enjoying all of the delicious fear?

Not as much, this time.

"Have Haas and Campbell subdue them, and stop the fight," Caleb repeated in the Empress' ear.

Guards poured down the spiral toward him by the dozens, most of them unarmed because they had come as spectators, but there were so many, they could beat him to death if he let go of Lo'ane.

"General, stop the fight," the Empress said in a commanding tone.

"Yes, Your Majesty," he replied without hesitation. "Campbell, take Private Marley. I've got Cortez."

"How long will it take for the dose to wear off?" Caleb asked.

"Ten minutes," Lo'ane replied. "Do you plan to hold me like this for that long?"

"Not if you promise to spare them."

"They're traitors to the Empire. They need to be made an example of."

"They aren't traitors. Neither one of them," Caleb growled. "Ham is a loyal Centurion Space Force Marine, and Marley is one of the most loyal subjects you have. She risked her life to help you when General Haas did everything he could to stop her. She listened to me, when no one else would."

"You…you're—"

"What? A demon," Caleb said. " I'm Captain Caleb Card of the Centurion Space Force." He turned the Empress in his grip so that she was facing him. Then he held up the laser scalpel before tossing it aside and lowering himself to one knee. "At your service, Your Majesty."

A bit dramatic, don't you think?

Caleb looked up at the Empress gaping down at him in astonished silence. "My team and I were sent to answer a distress signal from the HMS Pathfinder," he said. "We followed it through a wormhole and crash-landed here. My orders were to locate the ship and offer any assistance requested. I haven't seen Pathfinder in person yet, but since you're one of the descendants of the original settlers, and not in league with the Relyeh, I'm offering my loyalty and assistance to you."

By the time he'd uttered his last word, Haas had hold of him from behind, standing him up as the multitude of Guardians reached the scene. Caleb again locked eyes with the Empress, refusing to struggle against the general's grip.

The Empress tipped her head, seemingly in consideration. "General Haas, release him," she finally said.

"Your Majesty?" he replied. "He's—"

"I said release him. If he wanted to kill me, he would have done it already."

I can't believe that actually worked.

The pressure on Caleb's shoulders slowly vanished as Haas let go and took a step back. "He's a demon, Your Majesty. The enemy."

"Are you my enemy, Captain Caleb Card?" Lo'ane asked, meeting his gaze once more.

"No, Your Majesty," he answered. "But I am a demon, at least as your people define them." He looked over his shoulder, to where a pair of Guardians held Ham, another pair gripping Marley. "We have a lot more to talk about, but there isn't much time. Marley wasn't lying. Crux not only knows you're on the planet. He knows precisely where. We need to get you out of—"

"Your Majesty," Haas said, interrupting, his finger pressed to his ear. "Our lookouts report incoming Nightmares and dropships. We're under attack!"

CHAPTER 40

The Empress continued staring at Caleb while she absorbed Haas' bad news. He stared back, ready to do whatever she asked.

"Your Majesty," Haas continued. "The estimated trajectory will bring Crux's forces down within two kilometers of our position. Private Marley was right. They know we're here."

"How?" Colonel Campbell asked breathlessly.

"We know how," Haas said, glaring at Caleb. "This was your plan all along, wasn't it?"

"I'm the only one who's been trying to get the Empress to safety," Caleb snapped back. "If you had listened to me in the first place—"

"Enough!" Lo'ane snapped. "Captain Card, I accept your offer of service. You'll report directly to me."

"Your Majesty!" Haas cried in complaint.

"General, we need to evacuate the civilians to Glory. We also need to slow the enemy's approach."

"Yes, Your Majesty," Haas said, swallowing his arguments.

He offered Caleb one last angry, mistrustful glance

before hurrying to the center of the stage. Everyone in the grand chamber had fallen deathly silent, confused and unnerved by what had played out in front of them over the last few minutes.

"I need everyone to remain seated and calm," Haas bellowed, his tone fierce and confident. "Crux's Legion has found us. Dropships are en route to our position as we speak." The crowd began to stir, murmurs rising among them. "Calm!" he shouted again. "I need all Guardians to report to the barracks immediately and begin equipping by unit number. The first units out are to head for the primary entrance as our first line of defense. Secondary units will remain inside the tunnels to offer second line resistance. Tertiary groups will bring up the rear to protect Glory while we prepare for launch. Once the Guardians are clear of the chamber, all civilians will be evacuated to the ship in an orderly fashion. Do not fear, my friends. We've been through this before. Our story doesn't end here. Not today." He clapped his hands loudly. "Move out."

Half the crowd was immediately set into motion, the military members standing and heading for the exit in a somewhat organized fashion.

"Your Majesty," Haas said, returning to her. "By your leave, Colonel Campbell and I will manage the defense from Glory's command center. Please allow me to escort you there as well."

"No, General," Lo'ane answered. "You and the colonel go on ahead. I'll stay behind. My people need to see that I'm not afraid."

"Empress, you'll be unprotected."

"Nonsense. Nearly the entire Guardian Corps will be between me and the Legion. As will Captain Card."

"Captain Card?" Haas huffed. "You can't trust him, Your Majesty. He's—"

"A demon, I know," she rebuffed. "I'm well aware of

that. Which is why he's perhaps uniquely suited to serve as my personal guard during the evacuation."

"Your Majesty, I appreciate the vote of confidence," Caleb said. "What about Ham and Marley?"

Lo'ane looked to where the two Guardians still held them. Marley was sobbing in their arms while trying to scratch at her face. Ham pushed against them, attempting to reach the large stone he had discarded earlier.

"They're useless until the dosing wears off. I'll have them brought to the ship."

"Ham is a pilot," Caleb said. "One of the best in the CSF. If you need an experienced hand on the stick, he's it."

She nodded. "We lost our best people during the assault. If he recovers well from the dose, he'll be an immediate asset. General Haas, see that both Cortez and Marley make it back to the ship."

"Yes, Your Majesty," he replied, though he didn't look happy about releasing his prisoners. He reached up, removing the comms device from his ear and holding it out to the Empress. She accepted it, putting it in her ear. "Colonel, give your communicator to Captain Card."

"Yes, Your Majesty," Campbell said, taking out his earpiece and offering it to Caleb. He accepted the device, tucking it into his left ear and immediately picking up chatter.

"Control, this is Birdseye. We count six dropships, four nightmares. Dropships have reached the canopy and are deploying Legionnaires less than two klicks from the nest. Nightmares are circling, ready to provide support. It looks like one of them is headed this way. Eagles, fall back! Fall back! We're under—" The transmission vanished.

Caleb knew immediately from the Empress' expression that Birdseye was no more. "General, why are you still standing here?" she growled. "Go!"

Haas didn't reply, instead breaking for the door at the

top of the spiraling chamber, Campbell hot on his heels, along with the guards dragging Ham and Marley along. Caleb watched his friend go. He had saved Ham's life. He hoped he would live to see him again.

"Your Majesty," Caleb said. "I'm going to need a weapon if I'm going to protect you."

Lo'ane smiled and tapped her ear. "Major Angle, do you copy?"

"Yes, Your Majesty," the major replied through the comms.

"Have you left the grand chamber already?"

"Yes, Your Majesty. I'm in the barracks, equipping the Corps."

"Pull someone aside and have them deliver my armor and another from the armory, along with a full loadout for each. Captain Card, what is your head and foot size?"

"Head, fifty-eight centimeters. Foot, twenty-eight centimeters," he replied.

"Your Majesty, if I might ask," Major Angle said. "Who is Captain Card?"

"Hero's armor, Major," Lo'ane replied.

"Yes, Your Majesty. It's on the way."

"Thank you." She tapped her ear again, closing the connection to Major Angle.

"Empress Lo'ane!" Doctor Ling said, finally making her way down the spiral. The other civilians remained seated, the Corps members almost finished filing out.

"Qiao," the Empress said, smiling at the sight of her. "Don't be concerned. We'll get through this."

Ling nodded. "I'm sorry, Empress. I helped Caleb get here. He told me he only wanted to speak to you, and I found both his arguments and evidence compelling." She cast an angry glance at Caleb. "I didn't expect him to steal my scalpel and threaten you with it."

"I've always trusted your rationality and judgment,

Qiao," Lo'ane replied. "And as you can see, I'm unharmed. Since you're here, perhaps you can help evacuate the others in an orderly fashion? They know and trust you."

"Whatever you ask, I'll do," Ling answered. She looked at Caleb again, this time smiling before heading for the door to the chamber to direct traffic. A pair of soldiers passed her on the way, carrying two long crates. They placed them on the ground and dropped to a knee in front of the Empress.

"Your Majesty," one of them said. "Your armor and a spare, with armament, as requested."

"Thank you, Corporal Nils and Private Vashni," she replied. "You're dismissed."

They both stood, bowed their heads, and ran back the way they had come.

"Do you know all your people's names?" Caleb asked, opening the top box. His eyes caught on the custom combat armor. Black, with red crosses on the armored shoulder plates and the sides of the helmet, which was smaller and sleeker than standard. A pair of boots and a rifle rested beside it with four magazines, a handgun and four additional magazines for the weapon next to that.

"Not all," she replied, beginning to remove her utilities, confirming her lean, athletic shape in her fitted underlay. "But I try. Unfortunately, it's much easier now that we're such a small group."

Caleb winced in response. She was an Empress whose Empire was almost no more. He picked up her combat armor, listening as more chatter came over the comms.

"This is Staff Sergeant Miter. We're suited up and headed for the front entrance. ETA, eight minutes."

"Copy that, Miter," Major Angle replied. "First Company is thirty percent equipped."

"Step back, Your Majesty," Caleb said, holding the armor for her. She reversed into it before expertly clasping it closed. Caleb moved the first crate and opened the second, surprised to find the armor inside matched that of the Empress. He lifted it from the crate, turning back to her to ask her to hold it for him.

She stared at the armor, a sad expression crossing her face. "That belonged to my brother, Hiro," she said, reaching out to put her hand on the chest plate. "Crux assassinated him, putting me in charge of a dying civilization."

"I'll do my best to make him proud," Caleb replied.

"I don't need or want you to be like Hiro," Lo'ane snapped. "This is the spare armor we have that fits you. Nothing more."

"Understood."

She took the armor from him, holding it aloft so he could step back into it. Closing the clasps, he was surprised by the fit. Physically, he and Hiro were like twins. He quickly stepped into the boots, removing the earpiece and dropping it back in the crate. The ATCS activated immediately when he pulled on his helmet, syncing with the Empress' network as he picked up the pistol, rifle, and extra rounds.

He paused then, for the first time noticing a sword at the bottom of the crate. A falchion instead of the katana Kwon had wanted to see him with, it was made of the same metal as the plates of his armor, the handle wrapped in leather, the hilt inlaid with a pair of what he assumed were rubies. His initial instinct was to leave the blade behind, but it came with the armor, so he picked it up and attached it to the back of his a-tac.

"Now that you're suitably attired, I want you out on the front line, Captain Card," she said.

"I thought I was your bodyguard, Your Majesty?"

"I'm going out to the front line, too."

"Are you sure that's wise?"

"No. It isn't. But we're down to our last gasp, and I won't stop breathing without a fight. The people need to see that I'm not afraid. Even if I fall, they'll go on, perhaps even stronger than ever before."

Caleb glanced at the Empress through her faceplate, impressed by her words. "I'm with you, Your Majesty."

"We shall see."

She started up the spiral, the civilians moving eagerly aside as she ascended the chamber. They greeted her, cheered her on, and patted her on the shoulders as she passed, their Empress and their hero, who could have been first to board Glory as it prepared to escape, but instead chose to stay and fight.

How much of it is real, and how much for show?

Ishek's question disrupted his admiration of the woman. *What do you mean?*

According to Marley, she bailed on Atlas the night before the invasion. Why didn't she stay to fight then?

We don't know the circumstances of her retreat.

No, we do not.

While Caleb had used the statement to suggest Ishek give the Empress the benefit of the doubt, his response made it clear the Advocate was suspicious of her, which given the situation seemed crazy to him.

"Qiao," Lo'ane said, reaching the top of the chamber. Doctor Ling turned toward her, worry crossing her face. "See that the civilians all make it safely to Glory. If I don't make it back—"

"Your Majesty, you should go to the ship," Ling countered. "The people need you there."

"If I don't make it back, I've left contingencies, as well as instructions for a new line of succession."

"If you die, your daughter would be the rightful heir."

"I am the empress, and I make the decrees on how the

line of succession proceeds. My daughter is dead to me. The instructions are clear."

"Yes, Your Majesty," Ling said, giving up the argument.

For now, Caleb could only wonder what kind of issue the empress had with her daughter. He followed her into the tunnels, hurrying through the fleeing civilians and then breaking into a run. They were quickly joined by the Guardians making their way to the main base entrance.

"Your Majesty, do you copy?" General Haas said through the comms, having finally reached the ship's CIC. "Something isn't right. I'm tracking your beacon down tunnel A. I believe a Guardian may be wearing it."

"No Guardian may wear my armor, General," she replied. "I'm headed for the jungle to lead the defense."

"Your Majesty? I don't understand."

"Of course you don't. That's why you immediately chose to return to the CIC, rather than join the fight."

Caleb smiled in response to the ferocity of the rebuke. He liked the Empress more with every passing minute.

"What? Y...your Majesty, my role as General is to command our forces. I can't do that from the front line."

If she were anyone else, he would be tearing her apart for suggesting he's a coward.

And he'd still be a coward, Caleb agreed. *All bark and no bite.*

"Card!" Haas' voice burned into Caleb's ear over a private channel. "What the hell are you doing? You're supposed to protect the Empress, not lead her into battle."

"For one thing, she's leading me," Caleb replied. "For another, she's showing her people courage, strength, and fortitude. When was the last time you did any of that?" He was tempted to ask the general if his sons had died because of his inaction, but he managed to hold his tongue. "I'll make sure she gets back to Glory before we need to take off."

"How can you be so sure you won't die out there?"

"Because I don't want to give you the satisfaction."

"General," Lo'ane's voice cut through on the General's personal line. "I need an immediate update on the enemy positions."

"Yes, Your Majesty," Haas replied, returning to the main channel. "Unfortunately, our spotters were identified and taken out before I reached the CIC. As of their last report, the Nightmares were burning away parts of the canopy, clearing landing zones for the dropships. That was six minutes ago."

"I don't need to know what happened six minutes ago. I need to know what's happening now."

"Seventy percent of First Company is already outside. No contact so far. The other thirty percent are nearing the front entrance. Second company is also en route to the tunnel positions, ready to firm up our defenses."

"And Glory?"

"Engineering reports the reactor is suffering from desynchronization, which is greatly affecting overall power output. We don't have the energy to lift out of the water until it's repaired."

"Who's working on it?"

"Dwayne Masters, Your Majesty."

"ETA?"

"Between ten minutes and two hours."

Caleb's jaw clenched. They wouldn't survive down here for two hours. The timing of the reactor's power issues couldn't have been worse.

Or Crux's timing couldn't have been better. They arrived too quickly for this to be a result of my link through the Collective.

Caleb hadn't considered the timing before. Ishek was right. Less than twelve hours had passed since the symbiote had unblocked his collux. Crux's forces hadn't just arrived. They were organized and ready for a fight. *What if the*

Korath came through the wormhole, and immediately contacted the Relyeh on this side of the galaxy?

Possible. Or there's a traitor in the Empress' midst.

Haas?

We don't like him, but that doesn't make him a traitor.

Caleb dropped the conversation as the comms chatter increased. "Command, this is Captain Viggio of First Company. Units are in position. The jungle is on fire. The canopy is burning. Smoke is increasing. We're reading movement up ahead, but it's hard to see. Nightmares are passing overhead. Circling. We're—"

Like the spotters earlier, Captain Viggio's comms suddenly cut out. Other voices took over, the members of the other units reporting contact and that they were opening fire. Caleb toggled to the linked network of the company's tactical combat system. It came alive in his HUD, dozens of small blue dots engaging thirty or so red dots. The blue dots went out at a rapid pace, the Legionnaires cutting through the soldiers like they were paper.

Until that moment, he hadn't realized how truly overmatched the rebels were. The Legion didn't just have khorons providing enhanced strength, stamina and constitution to the fighters. Their weapons were better, their armor more protective. And with control of air superiority, there was no way First Company could hold them back for long.

"Your Majesty, First Company needs to pull back," Caleb said. "We can defend the enclosed space of the tunnels better than we can survive in the jungle."

"I'm not prepared to surrender any ground," Lo'ane replied.

"Have you checked their tactical? They're getting slaughtered out there."

"To allow the civilians to reach safety. To buy time for Engineer Masters to repair the ship."

"They can buy more time inside the tunnels."

"Are you the Emperor now, Card?" Lo'ane growled. "We will fall back when it's time. That time isn't now."

They reached the last stretch of tunnel leading to the exit, still at a full run. Second Company was in the process of setting up a defensive line, erecting metal barricades and bolting down heavy plasma cannons behind them. Even though frustrated with the Empress' tactics, the sight of the more powerful weaponry in the enclosed space gave Caleb hope that Dwayne could repair the ship in time.

"A good leader doesn't needlessly throw people's lives away," he commented, unable to stay quiet.

"You pledged to serve me," she replied, not as angered by the statement as he might have expected. "Do you wish to renounce your pledge and again be branded a traitor?"

"No, Your Majesty," Caleb answered bitterly.

I told you bending your knee to her wasn't a good idea.

No, you didn't.

It was implied.

"Open the hatch!" Lo'ane ordered the guards at the front of the tunnel. They did as she asked without hesitation. Gunners took positions as they moved the outer cover to the tunnel aside, smoke immediately drifting in. The jungle was lit up by fires burning in the distance, the red and orange hues overcasting the immediate greenery.

Two First Company units had taken defensive positions nearby, lying prone near the thickets, ready to open fire on the first Legionnaires they saw. Shifting light overhead suggested the passing of a Nightmare. A flash of light pierced the canopy a few hundred meters away, the craft no doubt firing on other defenders positioned there.

Ish, it's time to get to work.

Fear is everywhere. It is glorious. I am ready.

CHAPTER 41

Caleb followed Lo'ane into the jungle. Still monitoring First Company's network on his HUD, he knew the Legion was still a hundred meters away, picking through the fighters who had taken position in the branches or behind the stout trunks of the barrel-bellies. Enemy progress had slowed a little from their initial attack, and a few red dots had gone dark, indicating the rebels weren't being totally routed.

The Empress continued past the line of defenders nearest the underground facilities' entrance. She plunged into the dense foliage, landing on her belly. Caleb took position right beside her, braced on his elbows. He couldn't help noticing how the soldiers took notice of Lo'ane's presence. The moment they saw her, most of them went from nervous to defiant, their confidence and morale rising when they saw her risking her own neck to fight alongside them.

"Second platoon, form up on the Empress," Haas said over the comms. "Third platoon, sweep right, cover the flank."

The red dots were getting closer. Caleb's eyes swept over the jungle ahead, searching for targets the other fighters had yet to make contact with.

Seven meters, twenty-one degrees.

Ishek gave him the positioning, seeking out the nearby khoron through the Collective. The Relyeh already knew he was here. It didn't matter now that he gave himself away.

Caleb adjusted his aim, picking out the Legionnaire crouched within the foliage, taking a bead on the Empress. The enemy's red dot appeared on his HUD just before he squeezed the trigger three times, the rounds punching through the Legionnaire's faceplate. The red dot vanished.

You need to kill his khoron.

No time.

I destroyed it. On your right, three meters.

Ishek's directions came in sharply and quickly. Caleb whirled as the Legionnaire came into view, plasma spewing toward Caleb. He narrowly evaded the fiery stream, returning fire, the enemy fighter collapsing like a marionette with severed strings.

Pathetic excuse for a khoron.

Friendly soldiers began appearing in Caleb's peripheral vision, gathering closer to the Empress and firing at the targets lighting up on Caleb's HUD. Lo'ane got into the action as well, sending rounds through the foliage and into the enemy positions. Return fire burned through the thicket, and she ducked and rolled aside, taking a hit on her shoulder, her armor absorbing it.

More Legionnaires are coming. They held most of their forces in reserve.

Of course they did, Caleb replied. *Now that she's fired a few shots, maybe Her Royal Death Wish will call the retreat.*

Plasma fire lit up the immediate area, quickly intensifying as the rebels around him and the Empress searched desperately for cover. Two of them went down in quick succession, plasma burning through their armor and digging deep into their bodies. Caleb fired on a Legionnaire, dropping him, while Ishek overpowered another khoron, killing a second.

"Captain Card, how do you do that?" Lo'ane asked, noticing the sudden death of the last Legionnaire.

"It's not me, it's my symbiote," he replied.

"I didn't know that was possible."

"I'm sure there are a lot of things about the Relyeh you don't know," Caleb said. "But I do." Another rebel succumbed to enemy fire, just before a Nightmare passed overhead, shooting down at them and killing two more. "We need to retreat. Now!"

Another plasma bolt hit the Empress in the chest and she dropped to the ground, the thick plates smoking. Caleb stood over her, eyes narrowing as a line of red dots appeared on his HUD, the reinforcements closing in fast. The Empress scrambled to her feet, remaining behind Caleb. He stood his ground as Legionnaires, outnumbering the nearby resistance three to one, appeared across the entire line of barrel-bellies ahead of him..

The first Legionnaire in the line fell, his strings snipped by Ishek. Likely aware the Empress was nearby, the rest charged toward Caleb and the remaining soldiers, hoping to reach her.

Caleb continued firing on the Legionnaires while accepting a hail of return fire. Plasma bit into his chest and legs, rounds melting the thick armor plating but failing to penetrate it. Whatever his combat armor was made from, it wasn't the same stuff the rank and file wore. The Empress was risking her life, but not quite as boldly as he had first believed.

"Fall back!" she said at last over the general comms. "Fall back!"

The soldiers around her reorganized, laying down heavy cover fire while working to retreat toward the tunnel entrance. A second wave of Legionnaires approached behind the first as a Nightmare again opened fire on their position. The energy bolt exploded in the jungle right next to the Empress, taking out a member of First Company. The concussion would have knocked Lo'ane down, but Caleb caught her, wrapping his free arm around her waist and sweeping her back behind him. Protecting her body with his, he backpedaled, shooting with the other hand.

Ish, pick up the pace.

I'm trying. There's...interference.

What do you mean, interference? You're using a pocket universe, not a radio signal that can be jammed.

That's what I believed, too.

Caleb and the Empress reached a barrel-belly, and he pulled her behind it, taking a moment to reload before leaning past the trunk and shooting another Legionnaire. Checking his HUD, he quickly counted twenty-seven red dots and sixteen blue ones. By his estimate, they were losing fourteen to three. There was no way they could maintain that rate of attrition for much longer.

Another Legionnaire fell dead without being shot, Ishek finally breaking through. A second fell quickly afterward.

"Let's go," Lo'ane said, pulling away from him, backing up while shooting at the Legion. Caleb stayed with her, doing his best to keep her safe. A few minutes later, down to his last magazine, they reached the open entrance to the tunnels. A pair of dead Legionnaires already lay on the ground in front of the opening, torn apart by one of the plasma cannons. For the first time, Caleb noticed the small nondescript canister on the hip of one of the dead fighters, the metal lid sealed shut. Caleb's plasma bolt blasted it to ash a moment later.

"General, sitrep!" Lo'ane demanded.

Caleb had been vaguely aware of Haas' voice over the comms as they pulled back. The general was directing traffic and ensuring every member of the Guardian Corps was armed, armored, and in position.

"Legionnaires are trying to break through the tertiary passage," Haas replied. "The bulk of their force is still on the front entrance. All Corps members are prepped. First and Second companies have both seen engagement. First Company losses are at seventy percent. Glory's reactor remains unstable. ETA to repair is unchanged."

"Damn it!" Lo'ane cursed, joining Caleb and a dozen members of First Company as they sprinted from the jungle to the tunnel entrance and past the hardened barricades. A pair of blasts from the circling Nightmares killed four of them before they reached safety. "Attention all Guardians," she said, returning to the general comms. "This is your Empress. We stand and fight for the future of the Empire. Do not surrender. Do not give up hope. I am with you."

The morale lift was obvious and immediate. The platoon at the tunnel entrance intensified their fire in a more organized pattern, shooting past the retreating members of First Company and keeping the Legionnaires from overwhelming the entrance. Looking again at his HUD, Caleb saw that eight more blue dots remained outside, rushing toward them in a desperate effort to survive.

Two of them vanished a moment later, hit by the circling Nightmares.

Ish, we need to take out those aircraft.

How do you propose we do that?

Overpower the pilots.

It's challenging enough to locate a khoron on the Collective when they're barely moving.

You did it before. With the APC.

When there were only three khoron within hundreds of thousands of kilometers, and they were all on the ship I shot down. This isn't that.

We have to do something.

Crouched behind the barricades, his gaze shifted to the nearby plasma cannon. It spewed heavy bolts into the jungle, preventing the Legionnaires from advancing toward them.

You have to be kidding.

Ishek had read his thoughts, and didn't like them. Too bad. He switched his comms to the channel used by the platoon with them in the tunnel. "I need someone to unbolt that cannon," he said, moving closer to it.

"Who are you?" one of them, likely the Staff Sergeant, asked.

"Captain Card," he replied. "Do I need to ask the Empress to approve my request, or would you like me to save your comrades lives?"

"That gun weighs close to two hundred pounds with its power pack."

"Just unbolt it," Caleb growled.

His tone prevented the sergeant from giving him any further pushback. "Wilks, Habbib, unbolt the PC-1200, asap."

"Yes, Sergeant," they replied.

Caleb lowered his rifle and moved beside the weapon, taking one side of the dual-handled grip in one hand and grabbing the barrel with his other one. It only took the Guardians a few seconds to unsecure the weapon from its tripod mount, the weight all falling into Caleb's grip.

Ish, don't let me drop this thing.

Adrenaline and other chemicals flowed through him, giving him the strength to hold the gun up. "Cover me," he said, before moving out from the barricades. The heavy cannon was hard to maneuver, but he managed to squeeze one of the trigger buttons to send heavy bolts into the enemy line as he backed toward the tunnel entrance.

You're up, he said to Ishek once he arrived.

I don't know which ship.
Just guess then; you'll hit something.

Like before, Caleb surrendered his body to Ishek. The symbiote kept him pressed against the tunnel entrance, keeping them clear of enemy fire as he reached out through the Collective to locate targets in the most unorthodox way possible. The last six members of First Company came into view.

Hurry, Caleb said. *They'll try to hit the fleeing soldiers.*
Patience is a virtue.

The next four seconds that passed felt like an hour. Ishek moved them out from cover, swinging the heavy cannon up toward the trees. Holding down the trigger, he spewed plasma through the already damaged and burning canopy, through the heavy smoke and into one of the Nightmares. It exploded, the fireball so bright it blinded everyone around it, allowing the members of First Company to reach the safety of the tunnel just before the debris rained down, injuring and killing most of the pursuing Legionnaires. At his back, the rebels cheered.

"One down," Ishek said through Caleb.

"Caleb, the Legionnaires have breached the tertiary entrance," the Empress said over the comms. "We need to stop their advance."

"Copy," Ishek replied. *Just this once, I'll give you back control without making it difficult.*

That's just because you're having fun, Caleb said as he regained control of his body. He backed away from the entrance until he reached the barricade. "Thanks for letting me borrow this," he told the two artillerymen, dropping the cannon back on its mount.

The two men beamed at him in admiration. "Any time, Captain Card," they said, quickly bolting the cannon back in place.

The Empress was already running back down the

tunnel. Caleb retrieved his rifle and raced to catch her. The Legion, facing stiff resistance at the front gate, had gone through the tunnel Caleb had used to enter. The tunnel they only knew about because Ishek had connected through the Collective to avoid the scan that never came. The outcome confirmed that whichever Relyeh that Ishek had linked to was in communication with Crux.

That didn't make it any less of a bitter pill to swallow, knowing he and Ish were responsible for the breach.

"First and Second Company, fall back," the Empress ordered. "Let the Legionnaires in, blow the main entrance and regroup in the linkage tunnel."

"Yes, Your Majesty," the staff sergeant replied.

"Your Majesty, Third Company is moving to shore up the breach," General Haas announced. "Be careful. Some of the Legionnaires may have evaded them."

Focused on sprinting to the area, the Empress didn't reply. Caleb stuck close to her, matching her step for step, both of them slowing as they neared the tunnel and a trio of Guardians blocking their way. Several more were sprawled out on the ground behind them. Those who hadn't swallowed their poison pills, held their throats as they writhed in obvious pain.

The three in front swung their rifles toward the Empress. Caleb didn't need Ishek to tell him they were new khoron hosts and that the soldiers writhing on the ground would soon be fighting for the enemy as well. Both Lo'ane and Caleb opened fire on them. Once they were down, Caleb reluctantly approached them, shooting each in the throat and leaving the surprised khoron in dark splatters on the stone.

No sooner had he completed the gruesome task than fresh plasma began filling the tunnel, a fresh group of Legionnaires charging hard toward them.

"Haas, detonate the charges in the tertiary tunnel. Now!" the Empress ordered.

"Yes, Your Majesty," he replied.

Caleb and the Empress ducked around the corner for cover. He counted to five. Nothing happened. The Legionnaires continued to advance. He reached ten. The tunnel remained intact.

"Your Majesty, there's a problem with either the signal or the charges," Haas cried. "They won't detonate."

Can this really be a coincidence?

Caleb was almost certain it wasn't. Maybe it wasn't Ishek's fault the enemy knew where to locate the emergency tunnel. Maybe someone else in the Empress' retinue had already told them where to find it. And he still thought that someone might be General Haas.

"We need to go," Caleb said, grabbing the Empress by the arm. She didn't resist, letting him lead her away from the Legionnaires. Not sure of which way to go—back the way they'd come or the way Marley had brought him through the auxiliary tunnel—he quickly decided to retrace the steps he had taken with Marley. He headed for the maze of pipes and machinery below the main level, pausing at every corner to lean into the passageway and fire into the oncoming enemy. Between him and Ishek, they each killed at least one every chance they got.

"Empress!" Haas said excitedly over the comms. "Masters did it! The reactor is fixed! We're ready for liftoff upon your arrival, Your Majesty."

"Thank the stars!" Lo'ane cried. "All units, fall back to Glory. We're getting out of here!"

"What about us?" Caleb asked. "We need backup."

"You promised to keep me alive, Captain," she replied. "I expect you to honor your word."

CHAPTER 42

"Your Majesty, with all due respect," Caleb said, taken aback by her comment. "I'm still only one man."

"Not a man," she replied. "A demon, with power over other demons. You've acquitted yourself well in my service in very short order. I expect your good work to continue."

That statement didn't make Caleb feel any better about their situation, but he stopped trying to argue, refocusing instead on getting Lo'ane back to the repaired transport ship. Not that getting Glory out from the river and headed toward space made their escape any more of a certainty, especially with the shape the old rust bucket was in. No doubt, Crux's ships would do their best to take the vessel out before it could reach orbit. But first things first.

Caleb led the Empress past a junction, looking to the right as they ran. A group of Guardians ran toward them, making their way to the starship. He considered pausing, letting them catch up to find safety in numbers, but the sound of the Legionnaires running behind them convinced him it was a bad idea.

You love bad ideas.

Not this time, he replied to Ishek. He grabbed Lo'ane by

the hand when she began to slow, obviously having similar thoughts about linking up with her soldiers. "Keep moving," he growled. "We need to put your Guardians between us and the Legionnaires."

She picked up the pace, and they shot past the approaching Guardians and down the corridor. A few seconds later, Caleb heard the commotion behind them, and checking his HUD, saw the blue dots clash with red ones, slowing down the enemy. Judging by the new hosts they had encountered in the tunnel, the four red dots that vanished would quickly be replaced once they defeated the blues. The upside for him was that the Guardians had thinned the ranks of the Legionnaires chasing them, leaving only eight red dots racing toward them.

Caleb fired back on the Legionnaires as he and Lo'ane reached the end of the cratered corridor where the Guardians had fired on him and Marley only a couple of hours earlier. The smell of gunpowder and other chemicals still hung in the air.

"What happened here?" the Empress asked as they slowed to carefully navigate the damaged portion of the tunnel. It surprised Caleb that she didn't know. What else hadn't Haas bothered to tell her?

He chose not to answer her question as they continued on. "Magazine?" he asked instead, and she slowed to pass her last ammunition magazine to him. It afforded him one last reload of his rifle. He could only hope it would be enough.

"General, have all units reached the linkage tunnel?" she asked over the comms.

"Not quite, Your Majesty," he replied. "I'm tracking four units that have yet to reach the area."

"The Legionnaires have infected some of our people. Every member needs to be scanned before boarding Glory. Stragglers must not be allowed to join the others."

"As you command, Your Majesty."

"Did you just sentence the rear guard to death?" Caleb asked.

"They may be infected."

"They might not be."

"We don't have time to scan everyone, and I can't take that chance."

Caleb opened his mouth to argue, or at least to inform her that the khoron could circumvent the effect of the repeller with relative ease. He hesitated. Would she order all her Guardians to kill themselves on the chance they might be hosts? Once they returned to the ship, he and Ishek could sort out if anyone on board was an enemy spy.

"They shouldn't have to die out here," he said. "Have them held in the brig. You can scan them at your leisure. If they're not infected, I'm sure they'd rather be cramped together in a cell than dead." He added the last part to cut off her argument that the brig was too small.

Lo'ane didn't respond right away. Finally, she acquiesced. "General, have all incoming squads escorted to the brig on arrival. We can scan them later."

"Yes, Your Majesty."

"That boon is yours for saving my life," she said to Caleb.

"I haven't saved it yet."

"You will."

Her confidence was unnerving and at the same time motivating. He wanted to get her back to Glory alive. He would do anything to make it happen.

They reached the hatch to the service tunnels. Caleb didn't slow, pulling her through far enough ahead of the enemy that they couldn't see them. Checking his HUD, he saw the Legionnaires had fallen back out of range of the sensors. Ahead, the service tunnel descended toward a gap in the increasingly dense array of pipes and conduits. He led Lo'ane into hiding among them, their dark armor allowing them to blend in with the shadows.

"We don't have time to stop," she whispered.

"We don't have time not to stop," he countered. Already, he heard the Legionnaires closing in behind them, though from the sound it seemed the group chasing them had split up at the service tunnel entrance. "Stay still and silent."

He shifted away from her, moving closer to the passageway. The Legionnaires rushed past him, five in total. They only knew something was wrong when Ish overpowered one of them, killing the khoron and its host mid-run.

Caleb rushed toward the remaining trio, swapping his rifle for the long blade attached to the back of the armor. Kwon had teased him about carrying a sword, and somehow he had wound up with Hiro's. The thought amused him as he slashed the throat of the first Legionnaire. He stopped and turned, finding the small gap between the helmet and body armor of the next man. The sharp blade sank easily through his neck, cutting all the way back through the khoron tucked against his spine.

As he toppled, Caleb grabbed his rifle and ducked low to avoid an anticipated punch from the female next in line. He brought the blade up and back over his head to thrust it down through her faceplate. Again, he was shocked when the weapon smoothly pierced the transparency, sinking into the woman's eye—all the way into her brain.

Letting go of the blade, he tackled the last Legionnaire, slamming his head back against the rock floor, stunning him long enough to disengage his helmet's locking system and rip his helmet off. Caleb's hands closed around the man's throat, the man's eyes widening in alarm, his hands closing around Caleb's wrists, trying to tear his hands away from his throat. His khoran-assisted strength was great, but Caleb, with Ishek's help, was stronger. He could feel the man's skin moving beneath his fingers, the khoron inside writhing as Caleb choked the life from them both.

Caleb returned to his feet, retrieved the blade from the woman's body and wiped it clean on her arm. He returned to Lo'ane. "I like the sword," he said, returning it to his back.

"It's made from a special alloy, like the armor," she replied. "Developed by Lord Crux himself. Once upon a time, he gave our family the personalized battle gear as a gift, with the sincerest hopes that we would never need to wear it. I think even then his plans were in motion. He knew the lie he sold us and enjoyed its telling."

She's fortunate he didn't gift her painted tin.

"Can we reach Glory by following these service tunnels?" Caleb asked. "Or do we need to double back now that the tunnel's clear?"

"If I recall the planning diagram correctly, this should take us to an area adjacent to the grand chamber, and then it ascends back toward a tunnel connecting to the linkage. I believe remaining in this tunnel is the safest, quickest route."

"Then we need to keep moving."

Lo'ane grabbed his wrist before he could take a step. "Captain Card." He turned to look at her. "Thank you. The stars delivered you to us in our greatest hour of need."

"I'm just doing my job," he replied. "Empress, now isn't the best time, but I believe you have a traitor in your midst. It may be General Haas."

Her face hardened. "This attack reeks of betrayal. But Haas? No, I don't think so."

"Why not?"

"The enemy has taken too much from him. He would not change his allegiance. If there is a traitor, we'll discover the guilty party once we're safe."

Caleb nodded, leading her onward. His HUD remained clear, the area free of Legionnaires.

"Empress, where are you?" Haas said over the comms as they neared the area where Caleb convinced Marley to shoot him. "The Legionnaires have reached the linkage tunnel. Our forces are holding for now, but we can't hold out forever."

"We're on our way," she replied. "We should be there in five minutes. Is Glory ready for launch?"

"Yes, Your Majesty. Ready and waiting."

"Is Captain Card's companion, Abraham, on the bridge?"

"No, Your Majesty. Why would he be?"

"Captain Card speaks highly of his capabilities as a pilot. If the Captain's aptitude is any indication of those abilities, I want the man at the controls."

"Your Majesty? We don't even know if he's ever flown a starship before?"

"He has," Caleb said. "He's as good as it gets. And he has combat experience. He'll stay cool under pressure."

"You heard the Captain," Lo'ane said. "Have Abraham brought to the bridge. If he's capable of piloting Glory, then I want him piloting her."

"Yes, Your Majesty," Haas reluctantly agreed.

The large machines that provided life support to the base were just up ahead, the entire area empty of workers, soldiers, and Legionnaires. From the relative quiet, Caleb might have believed the fighting was over. The threat ended. It was only he and the Empress down here, safe for the moment.

"Is that blood?" Lo'ane asked, eyes on the ground.

Caleb's eyes swept over the stain of his blood that had soaked into the porous rock, larger than he would have guessed. He *had* lost a lot of blood. "Yes. It's mine."

"Yours? I don't understand."

"It's a long story."

You're welcome.

"I'm just surprised General Haas hasn't told you the story already," he continued, about to lead her past the blood stain when he noticed a glint of something beneath the nearby pipes against the wall. Moving over to take a closer look, he was shocked to find Benning's data chip on the floor, nearly invisible in the shadows. How had it gotten there? Had Marley tossed it there after shooting him? Had Haas tried to get rid of the evidence of his origins, perhaps with the intent of returning to retrieve it later? But he would have known there wouldn't be a later.

Unless…

His head snapped up, eyes narrowing as he scanned the area ahead.

"What is it?" Lo'ane asked.

Ish, are there any Relyeh nearby?

Not that I can determine.

Caleb scooped up the data chip, tucking it into his boot. He straightened up, moving in front of the Empress. "Probably nothing," he replied, taking the lead as they continued forward.

The central tanks and multitude of pipes of the water filtration system filled the entire left side of the cavern, its shape suggesting its location adjacent to the sunken spiral of the grand chamber. On the right, the ceiling sloped outward where a simple metal box served as the terminus for dozens of thick wires reaching to the ceiling and spreading away from it like ivy. The reactor delivered energy to the other equipment in the cavern, along with the rest of the underground compound. Other large machinery, additional conduits, and pipes filled in most of the remaining space, leaving an aisle down the center and narrower access passageways between the metalworks. Disparate noises joined forces in the enclosure. The hum of the reactor. The muffled thump of compressors. The sound of running water.

Caleb led Lo'ane cautiously through the chamber. While neither his sensors nor Ishek had registered anything out of the ordinary, his survivor's instincts and warrior's experience left him with a gut feeling that something wasn't right, even if he couldn't put a finger on it. Not wanting to attract attention if they did encounter something, he swapped his rifle for Hiro's sword. Sweeping his eyes across every service alley, he expected his tactical system to report contact on his HUD at any moment.

Nothing. Again and again. They were apparently alone down here.

So why did he feel like they were being watched?

"Captain, every second we spend down here is another second the Guardians are forced to defend the linkage," the Empress said. "We need to hurry. This passage should lead to the connecting corridor, as close as possible to Glory."

"I know," he replied, without changing his approach. "But something's wrong."

"There's nothing here," she insisted.

"Nothing we can see," he agreed. *Ish, I feel like I'm going crazy.*

Ishek didn't answer, leaving him even more unnerved. The unfamiliar feeling left him increasingly tense.

"Captain?" Lo'ane said, her hand falling on his shoulder. "Are you well?"

Caleb froze at her touch. His mind began tingling, his body suddenly moving outside of his volition. *Ish?* he questioned meekly in his thoughts, his grip on autonomy fading. He reached out for his sense of reality, grasping only at air.

No longer in control, he watched himself turn around to face the Empress, unaware of what had happened until he registered the look of surprise on her face. He tried to force himself to lower his gaze so he could see the sword in his hand, but he couldn't. His eyes remained fixed on the Empress' expression through her faceplate. Confused, surprised, frightened. His weight shifted, body pivoting to catch Lo'ane as the loss of blood made her too weak to stand. Lowering her gently to the floor, he managed a brief glimpse of the blade piercing her armor, embedded to the hilt.

Ish! he cried silently. *Ish! What are you doing?*

Ishek didn't answer. He didn't feel his symbiote's presence. Aware of everything, he sensed nothing.

"Caleb, how...how could you?" Lo'ane exhaled, her breathing labored. "I...trusted...you."

Caleb watched his body kneel over her. He heard his voice speak. Softly. Tenderly. "Not Caleb Card, my dear Lo'ane."

Her eyes widened, recognizing the speaker, if not in tone, then in words and inflection. "You? How?"

"I am everywhere."

Dying, Lo'ane shivered beneath him, terrified.

Who are you? Caleb asked, pushing the question out as forcefully as he could. A Relyeh. He had no doubts about that. But which one? And how had it managed to seize control first of Ishek, and then of him without any effort? Without any warning.

The Empress gasped and fell still, her body sinking back in her armor, her eyes glazing over as she died.

At the same time, his control returned. The presence he had felt surrounding them vanished, his question left unanswered.

"Ish?" he said out loud.

He sensed the symbiote's bond, but it was weak. The Relyeh had overpowered Ishek, but rather than kill Caleb as he and Ishek had done to the Legionnaires, the presence had used him to kill the Empress.

And destroy the Empire.

He tensed at the realization of what had just happened by his own hand. Or rather, by some unknown Relyeh who'd somehow taken control of him.

"Your Majesty," Haas shouted over the comms. "You need to come quickly. We're running out of time." He paused to wait for a response. "Your Majesty, do you copy?" Another pause. "Empress Lo'ane, please come in!"

"General," Caleb said, voice stiff. "Lo'ane…the Empress…is…she's dead."

"What?" Haas roared. "You were supposed to protect her. You were—"

"General," Caleb snapped forcefully enough to quiet him. "She's gone. Get your people out of here. Don't wait for me."

It took Haas a few seconds to answer. "As though I would ever wait for you," he seethed back. "This is your fault, Captain Card. All of it."

Caleb remembered what Lo'ane had said about his mention of a traitor. She believed it was possible, but she didn't think it could be Haas. If someone on board Glory was aiding the enemy, they needed to know about it, and Haas was the only contact he had. He had to risk that she had been right. If she wasn't, Haas would swallow the warning as if Caleb hadn't tried to warn them at all.

"General, you need to know. There may be a traitor on board Glory, who sold you out to Crux."

"Traitor?" Haas screamed back. "The only traitor is you! I hope you rot in the fires of the Eternal Sun for this, Card!" He cut the connection. The comms went silent.

Caleb stared at the Empress' face, wrinkled and worn, aged unnaturally by war. She looked peaceful now, one of them finally able to rest. He decided right then that he would never rest. He would find out who had forced him and Ishek to murder Lo'ane. He would not quit until Crux, his Legion, and any other Relyeh in this galaxy were destroyed and Ham was safely back home with his family. Or until he died trying.

The sound of boots on stone registered in the back of his mind. With the rebels all escaping on Glory, there was no question which side the soldiers in the boots were on. Straightening up, Caleb grabbed the grip of Hiro's blade, sliding it out of the Empress' body. With a fingertip, he wiped some blood from the weapon and brought it to his forehead, pressing it against his helmet.

"By your blood, Empress, I will have retribution," he said, the Legionnaires coming into view ahead.

He knew exactly where to start.

CHAPTER 43

Gripping Hiro's sword, Caleb ducked into one of the narrow service alleys, out of sight of the oncoming Legionnaires. He remained in the shadows, turning his attention back to where the Empress lay dead on the floor.

Ish? he prodded silently. *Ish, can you hear me?*

His symbiote still didn't respond. Whatever or whoever had overpowered Ishek and used them to kill Lo'ane had left him dazed and weak. And though it was difficult for Caleb to tell, likely barely alive. Had the Relyeh spared them intentionally, or had it believed Ishek would die, killing Caleb with him.

Was Ishek dying, his own extinction not far behind?

Caleb ran out of time to think about it. He was alive for now, and the Legionnaires had reached the chamber. Checking his HUD, he counted six of the khoron-controlled soldiers in the dark armor as they fanned out in a wedge pattern. The soldier on point spotted the Empress and advanced ahead of the others, who slowed to check each service alley along the way. Reaching the Empress, the Legionnaire knelt down, removing her helmet before looking back at the others. Obviously, the

Legionnaires on the planet and the Relyeh who had killed her weren't in immediate communication, or the Legionnaire wouldn't have been so surprised. In fact, they probably would have already given up the hunt. They had come to finish off the Empire, and their mission was accomplished, even if they had failed to get it done themselves. There was no reason for them to continue the advance.

Caleb was glad they continued forward.

His was the hand of retribution as he shot from his hiding place, sword raised. The Legionnaire turned his head toward him, giving Caleb a better angle to run the weapon through the Legionnaire's neck, decapitating him. Caleb didn't slow as he crossed the corridor to the service alley on the other side. Plasma bolts sizzled just behind him, striking the air filtration system and melting part of its outer shell.

Continuing along the access channel, Caleb paused at a junction, drawing his sidearm with his free hand. Swinging out into the junction, he immediately began walking toward the Legionnaire he spotted there. The man saw him too, and they both opened fire. Caleb's rounds cracked into the soldier's faceplate in rapid succession. The first four cracked the shell, the fifth went through, piercing the man's brain and killing him. The Legionnaire's plasma hissed into Caleb's armor, melting the top layers of protective alloy without breaching the underlay.

The exchange drew the attention of the other Legionnaires, though the sensors in Caleb's a-tac helped him maintain situational awareness, painting the enemy coming down the alley behind him.. Spinning around, he sprinted from his position toward the enemy, firing at the Legionnaire's helmet to distract her as he sliced the barrel of her plasma rifle in half before slamming it into the woman's armor. The sword sank into her chest. The force of the blow drove the woman into the side of the reactor, her expression shifting from furious to blank as she died.

Caleb jerked the blade from her chest, rushing back to the main passageway, where another Legionnaire waited. He took a few plasma hits to his armor as he rushed the man. Using the sword with plenty of anger but no finesse, he swung it at the Legionnaire with all his strength. The man brought his forearm up to block, only to have it slice right through the arm and deep into his chest. Caleb pulled the weapon away, returning it to his back and grabbing the Legionnaire's plasma rifle from his dying grip. Ducking back into a service alley, he checked his HUD. By his count, two more Legionnaires remained, but they had fallen off his sensors.

Where were they?

The chamber suddenly began to vibrate, a sharp rumble echoing through the stone from somewhere in the distance. Caleb knew instinctively that the sound came from Glory, as the anti-gravity coils in the starship's hull powered up. The thrusters would begin pushing the vessel from the bottom of the riverbed soon enough. He could picture the dispersion of water as the large starship began to rise, the water pouring off the top of the vessel as it fought to escape its sunken landing zone and then the planet's surface. How long would it take for the Nightmares to get a bead on the craft once its position was revealed? How long could Glory survive their attack?

At least the Empress had ordered General Haas to bring Ham to the bridge prior to her death. If anyone could get them out of this mess, it was him. Even so, for as good a pilot as his fellow Marine was, Caleb didn't think he could escape without some help.

Advancing to the junction at the backside of the alley, Caleb barreled around the corner, rifle shouldered and ready to fire. Clear of the enemy, he maintained his offensive posture as he crossed along the side of the chamber, heading back in the direction he and the Empress had come. He wasn't sure how he could help the fleeing starship, but he knew he couldn't do anything from inside the rebel base.

He was near the edge of the inner compound's reactor when he noticed a dark shape attached to the metal shell. Moving closer to examine it, he nearly laughed out loud when he realized the reactor was covered in explosives, no doubt tied to a remote detonator or self-destruct mechanism that would go once Glory was safely away. It was another reason to get out of the base as quickly as possible.

Reaching the last alley, he turned the corner ready to break for the chamber exit without confronting the remaining pair of Legionnaires. However, they had other ideas. Possibly having seen him crossing earlier behind the metalworks both of the soldiers were waiting for him at the head of the access. Caleb hit the brakes as they opened fire. He threw himself back around the corner to avoid the plasma bolts, the bulkhead keeping him on his feet. He peeked out despite the ongoing attack, just in time to see one of the Legionnaires break for the next alley, hoping to box him in.

Caleb?

Ishek's tone was weak, but it was there.

Ish. Are you okay?

No.

Caleb remained tucked behind the reactor, which had the potential to explode at any moment. The vibration from the starship continued to intensify, shivering pebbles on the floor and knocking dirt loose from the ceiling and walls. *Me neither. We're pinned down next to a ticking time bomb.*

All in a day's work.

Caleb smiled. *At least you kept your sense of humor.*

We murdered the Empress, didn't we?

We didn't. Someone else did. I don't suppose you know who?

The Relyeh I linked with earlier to avoid the scan. That's all I know.

It's better than nothing.

I hunger.

Of course you do. I don't suppose you're alive enough to overpower a basic khoron.

You can't make it five minutes without me, can you?

Not these five minutes.

I cannot overpower, but I can distract.

I'll take it. Are you ready now?

As ready as I can be.

So do it already.

Caleb swung around the left side of the reactor, coming face-to-face with one of the Legionnaires. He was standing still, shaking slightly, though he still managed to take aim and pull the trigger. So did Caleb, his plasma bolts slamming into the static soldier one after another, and then burning through his armor into his flesh. Caleb spun around before the Legionnaire hit the floor. He returned to the back of the reactor, peppering the second Legionnaire with plasma as he appeared. The man wasn't able to get a return bead, momentum carrying the enemy fighter into the wall.

Looking down at his chest, Caleb noticed the armor over his heart was nearly gone, the last bolt having melted it away to almost nothing.

"You were supposed to keep him still, Ish," he said as he ran along the side of the reactor, heading for the exit.

I'm not as ready as I believed I was. Where are we going?

"I told you, the reactor's wired to blow. We need to get the hell out of here."

You're forgetting something.

"I'm not carrying the dead Empress along with me."

That isn't what I mean. The Legionnaire's helmet. Take it.

"What good will it do me? The system locked as soon as the Legionnaire died."

I doubt the Legion rewrote the software from the ground up. Besides, even if you can't use the electronic functions, you'll look just like one of them with a helmet swap.

"True."

You would be so lost without me.

"I would be dead without you. Which was the only reason I knew you were still alive."

Caleb returned to the downed Legionnaire. Crouching over the soldier, he quickly exchanged helmets, sliding the new one down over his head. As he'd expected, the tactical combat system was offline, the software locked. Ish was right that his master password would probably give him access to the tactical, but he didn't see any current use for it. Instead, his eyes shifted to the small canister on the dead man's hip. Nothing said Legionnaire like a box of khoron. He picked up the canister, magnetically attaching it to the leg of his armor, and hurried from the room.

CHAPTER 44

Caleb sprinted through the tunnels, racing to escape the underground compound before Glory lifted off and General Haas triggered the remote detonators that would bring the entire place down on itself. While the explosives in the tunnels hadn't gone off as planned earlier, he was certain the reactor would blow on schedule. Whoever had tipped Crux off to the base, whoever had betrayed the Empress, no doubt wanted to literally bury any possible evidence.

Returning to the corridor where the last group of Guardians had confronted Legionnaires, Caleb found three dead Corpsmen strewn across the passageway, eyes rolled back, clearly killed by the poison pill they all carried in their mouths. The remainder of the Guardians he had seen were missing, indicating they had either escaped or failed to use the pills, instead falling victim to the khoron the enemy carried.

He hoped for the former, while the latter seemed more likely. As he started down the passageway, heading for the main entrance, a group of Legionnaires moved into the corridor behind him. He offered only a quick glance back, letting them see his helmet, while maintaining his dash to the exit. He was too far from Glory to feel the vibrations of the ship's anti-gravity coils powering up, but he knew from experience the vessel would lift off at any moment.

He wasn't surprised when the entire compound began to shake. The vibration created a roar within the tunnels, rattling loose chunks of rock and kicking up a cloud of dust. Glory was on her way up, pushing through the water to flee the planet, leaving their dead Empress behind.

Almost out of time, Caleb pumped his tiring legs as hard as he could, tearing through the corridors as quickly as possible. He careened into the walls as he cornered, letting them redirect his energy to preserve as much forward momentum as he could. The Legionnaires who had moved in behind him fell out of sight while a new group appeared ahead of him, also at a run, clearly aware of the need to escape.

He caught up to them in no time, drawing quick glances but no outright negative reactions. Wearing a Legionnaire helmet and similar dark armor so scuffed, burned, melted, and dented that it could easily be mistaken for the same model as theirs, he drew alongside them for a few seconds before passing them by.

Caleb had almost reached the main entrance when the reactor finally went. From his position, the detonation came off as a rapid series of low rumbles, followed by a louder crack that shook the entire compound violently enough to take him off his feet. He hit the wall and landed on his knees, looking back to see the Legionnaires he had passed also on the floor. Immediately springing back up, he growled audibly as he pushed himself still harder, forcing his body to perform beyond its normal limits. A hissing roar echoed through the tunnels behind him, lending added motivation to his mad dash to escape.

Reaching the main entrance, he winced beneath his helmet when he spotted Wilks and Habbib, the two gunners who had helped him with the plasma cannon, akimbo on the floor, faces bloody. Offering only a soft Godspeed as he passed, he glanced over his shoulder once more as the roar behind him finally caught up.

A ball of smoke and fire turned the corner behind him, quickly enveloping the Legionnaires he had outpaced and rapidly approaching him. Shouting under his helmet, chest throbbing, legs pumping, he reached the edge of the tunnel and threw himself forward, away from the enclosed space and face down onto muddy ground that had been covered in dense vegetation only thirty minutes earlier. Smoke and fire spewed over him, heat penetrating the back of his armor as it exploded out from the tunnel like dragonbreath, igniting the line of barrel-bellies a dozen meters away.

Caleb remained inert until the heat subsided. Wiping the mud off the faceplate of his helmet, he climbed back to his feet. Looking up through a thinned-out canopy he watched Glory rising under the power of her three large thrusters and anti-gravity coils. As quickly as she could climb, she pushed up toward the atmosphere, a handful of Nightmares were already firing energy blasts into the barge's tenuous shields. Too few cannons fired back at the ships, the only thing keeping the enemy from totally overwhelming the vessel.

Ish, we need to get up there.

How?

Aren't you an Advocate, not a basic khoron?

Yes, but I'm also two-thirds dead.

Which isn't all dead, which we'll be if we don't get up there.

I don't see how—oh, you wouldn't.

I might, Caleb answered after Ishek read his intentions.

You can't always use the threat of self-destruction to manipulate me.

It's worked great for me so far.

I hate you.

Caleb allowed himself a small smile. *Can you do it?*

Working on it.

Caleb glanced over his shoulder, noticing movement behind him. A pair of Legionnaires stepped out of the smoke, barely escaping the fireball. They approached him, their posture hardly threatening.

"Why is your tactical offline?" one of them asked.

"Damaged in the fighting," Caleb replied. "I can't locate the dropship on my HUD."

"It's this way," the other Legionnaire said. "A little over a klick away."

"Did anyone else survive?" He immediately sensed Ishek's dismay over the question.

"Survive? Who cares? We did. What's your unit designation?" Caleb realized he had blundered by showing even a hint of concern for the other Legionnaires. This one had picked up on his unbidden error, immediately becoming suspicious. "Designation?" he asked again, turning to face him.

"It's..." He lunged at both of them, one hand on each of their faceplates. Catching them by surprise, he bashed their heads together, stunning them long enough to bring his plasma rifle up and blast one in the side of his head. The close range allowed the bolt to pierce the Legionnaire's helmet, killing him instantly. Just as his corpse hit the ground, Caleb smashed the other Legionnaire in the faceplate with the stock of his rifle before turning the muzzle on him and quickly finishing him off.

Rookie mistake.

I know. It's been a long day.

A light overhead drew Caleb's attention. Obviously designed to instill fear in its enemy, a Nightmare hung above the clearing. All severe angles and sharp points, it was made from the same dark alloy as his combat armor. Multiple rocket tubes jutted out from each side of the fuselage. Yet its most frightening features were the two large cannons mounted to triangular turrets beneath each angular wings.

This isn't going to be easy.

Caleb watched as it began to shake unsteadily, its pilot in a fight for dominance with Ish. At first, he thought the enemy pilot might win the battle, but it finally stopped shivering and descended smoothly to the muddy ground.

Your chariot…a…waits.

It was obvious that his effort to gain control of the lesser khoron pilot had drained Ishek of a lot of the energy he'd regained, but Caleb knew his renewed exhaustion was worth it.

He ran to the ship, the hatch amidships opening as he approached. A Legionnaire awaited him just inside. "You're lucky we saw you," he said as soon as Caleb leaped onboard.

"And that makes you unlucky," he said, booting the Legionnaire out through the open hatch. Closing it, he quickly moved toward the flight deck. While Centurion ships seated flight crews deeper in the ship with cameras and screens behind armored bulkheads, the Nightmare's flight deck sat in greater peril at the front of the starship, a large transparency allowing for a direct view into space.

The lone pilot was still in his seat, hands shaking on the controls, clearly still fighting Ishek's domination. If Ish hadn't been so weakened by the Relyeh who killed the Empress, the pilot would have already been dead. Caleb stepped up to him, ripping him from the seat and throwing him down on the deck. He pinned him there with his boot and shot him in the head.

"I hope this thing uses manual controls," he said, dropping into the freshly vacated seat and pulling the simple hardened restraint over his head. It snapped audibly into place, not allowing him to adjust the tight fit, making him wonder how he was going to get out of the seat. Getting a closer look at the instrument panel, he quickly realized the Nightmare didn't have external controls at all. "What the hell?" he remarked, staring at the column. There were only a pair of small displays, providing a rear and bottom view outside the craft, proving that it did use cameras, just not anywhere that might better protect the pilot.

I'm discerning a separate collux-compatible network originating from the starship.

"You mean that it's designed for you to fly it?" Caleb asked.

The Legionnaires are khoron with bonded human hosts submissive to their will. Is it a surprise their ships are designed in this way?

"No, but you've never piloted a starship before."

I've watched you do it.

"That's not exactly the same. And like you said, you're two-thirds dead."

Closer to three-quarters after wrangling with the pilot of this ship. I am exhausted.

"And there's no way for me to take over?"

Not directly, but I can tap into your thoughts to help guide my reactions. It is not unlike flying Spirit. Besides, Crux's other ships won't know we've gained control of this one.

"They will once we start attacking them. We have to help Glory escape."

We don't have to.

"Ham is on Glory, along with almost two thousand other humans, including Private Marley. I owe her for getting her into this mess, and I promised myself I would get Ham back to his family."

I didn't make that promise.

"Too bad. That's the plan."

Ishek's mental tone expressed capitulation.

Very well. Here we go.

CHAPTER 45

The Nightmare's anti-gravity plates hummed as the ship rose out of the mud. As soon as they cleared the top of the canopy, the twin thrusters on the back of the ship ignited, shoving Caleb back in the seat as the starship launched powerfully forward. A heads-up display activated on the instrument panel. It provided Caleb and Ishek with a threat-based sensor grid, including information on shield integrity, weapons capabilities, and energy availability. The HUD was only mildly different from the starships he had flown on in the past, reinforcing the fact that despite being designed for a Relyeh, it was partially dependent on humans for operation.

The Nightmare immediately painted its four sister ships chasing Glory as friendlies, while the fleeing transport barge was clearly marked as the target. As Ishek guided the Nightmare onto an intercept course with the barge and the ships harassing it, Caleb got a good look at the outside of Glory.

The size was about what he expected based on the interior layout, the shape comparable to a stick of butter with a pair of massive ion thrusters on each side of the aft section.

Its only offense was the limited number of hastily bolted on guns currently firing ineffectively at the Nightmares trying to rip it from the sky.

As maneuverable as a school bus, Caleb immediately guessed Ham was at the stick by the way it rocked and rolled, shook and jerked, often accelerating and slowing down. The chaotic randomness of the maneuvers was probably the only reason Glory's trajectory still pointed upward.

"Hold on, Ham," he said softly. "We're coming."

He watched as one of the Nightmares launched an energy blast at the barge. Shields captured some of the hit, but not all, and a part of the hull melted beneath the heat, creating a hole into the interior. Debris spilled out of the depressurized area, but thankfully no people were sucked out of the damage, the compartments likely sealed off right away.

"Come on, Ish. Faster."

The Nightmare sped up, racing toward the action as it neared the planet's troposphere.

I'm attempting to target the Nightmares with the ship's fire control system. It will not allow me to do so.

"Not a surprise. Can you override it?"

Do you recall when I suggested the combat armor might still be unlockable through the software root password?

"Yeah."

It appears I may have been incorrect. The Nightmare's system is rejecting the password.

"So you can't override the fire control system?"

I can turn the system off completely and switch over to manual.

"What manual? There are no physical controls."

A figure of speech. There will be no assisted targeting.

"I'll take what I can get. How can I help?"

Concentrate on the targets. It will ease the effort of flying, shooting, and staying conscious.

"I'd appreciate it if you stayed conscious."

Concentrate.

Caleb looked through the flight deck transparency, picking out the nearest Nightmare as Ishek vectored toward it. Coming up on its tail, he opened with the energy cannons, blasting it multiple times in the rear. Not expecting a friendly to attack it, the Nightmare never knew what hit it. It broke apart in a fireball that quickly dissipated, leaving the remains to slow before beginning the long fall back to the surface.

Yeah, one down!

"Don't get cocky. The first one's a freebie with the element of surprise." Even now, one of the remaining Nightmares was peeling away from Glory, while the other two remained on the barge's tail. Climbing higher, Caleb spotted a pair of larger ships squatting in orbit, no doubt the warships that had launched the ground attack. "Ignore the one that's breaking off for us, keep on the Nightmares attacking Glory."

We cannot help Glory if we get dead.

"For once, try not to be like you, and more like me. Glory is more important than we are."

Maybe to you.

"Exactly."

Ishek didn't like the instructions, but he was too weak to continue arguing. He guided the Nightmare toward the Glory's two attacking ships, nearly achieving an angle of attack when the other Nightmare darted in from the port side, energy blasts raking them. Shields flared, absorbing the blows while Caleb maintained the target for Ishek.

"We can't take these hits forever," he said, watching the shield integrity drop.

Neither can they.

The symbiote triggered the cannons, pouring energy into one of the Nightmares chasing Glory. Its shields captured some of the firepower as it peeled away from the target rather than face being destroyed.

Growing more comfortable at the controls, Ishek hit the throttle, picking up speed a little too quickly as they approached the Nightmare still firing on Glory. No alarms went off. The flight deck remained totally silent, but Caleb was sure they were going to hit the ship. The fire control system activated, targeting Glory.

"Ish?" he shouted in question, gut tensing, panic building as he feared he'd again lost control of his symbiote to the unknown Relyeh, and would soon lose control of himself, too. The moment was short-lived as rockets launched from their Nightmare, the distance to Glory too short for the projectiles to hit anything other than the enemy ship directly ahead of them. The warheads slammed into the back of the enemy Nightmare and detonated. Ishek fired retro-rockets and dove away from the scene, shields active, the ship shivering as they blew through the edge of the explosive concussions and its resulting debris field.

I think I'm getting the hang of this.

Ishek swung them wide of Glory, hitting the throttle to overtake the barge. The remaining pair of enemy Nightmares were angling to regain their positions behind the fleeing rebels while the larger orbiting warships slowly changed position, their heavy gun batteries swiveling around to open up on both them and Glory at any moment.

"We're running out of time."

We just need to buy them a little more.

Caleb couldn't disagree. He focused his attention on the HUD, thinking about how he would approach the destruction of the remaining two Nightmares if he were flying their ship. Able to pick up on his thoughts, Ishek integrated some of his own, and their Nightmare flew out ahead of

Glory. Caleb tensed his gut for the sudden change of Gs as the Nightmare flipped over. The throttle maxed out, thrusters slowing their ascent. Glory shot past them, only a couple hundred meters off their port side.

Throwing their Nightmare into a quick turn that tested Caleb's ability to withstand the heavy inertia, Ishek opened fire on the Nightmare closing on their port flank. He sent literally everything they had at the craft. Missiles poured from launch tubes and energy blasts crackled from the cannons, the air between them and the enemy ship suddenly so thick with ordnance it had no chance of passing through it unscathed.

Simultaneously, Ishek reached out through the Collective, grabbing hold of the other Nightmare's pilot and forcing the khoron to change course. The Nightmare's vector changed suddenly, needing only a few seconds before falling into the barrage…and then into the other Nightmare. The violent collision destroyed both ships, the half dozen rockets that found their debris a split second later vaporizing all traces of them.

"Yes!" Caleb shouted, pumping his fist.

Don't get cocky. We still need to get Glory past those warships.

Caleb toned down his jubilation, but he couldn't help smirking at Ishek's response. His symbiote had totally bought into the idea of putting Glory ahead of themselves.

Not really. I just don't want to listen to you preach.

"Whatever it takes," Caleb answered, grinning.

The prior maneuver had left them at a reduced velocity and way behind Glory. Ishek righted the Nightmare and resumed the chase, throttle maxed out as they climbed higher into orbit. The two large warships had nearly closed any gap the barge could slip through, and the HUD flashed a sudden warning that friendly fire was imminent.

"Ham, watch out." Caleb grimaced.

Heavy flashes of energy lanced out from the warship's guns, nearly a dozen in all heading for Glory. One hit the ship near the bow. It went clean through the shields and armor, ripping away a piece of the craft and sending debris exploding away from it. Afraid it had taken catastrophic damage, Caleb's jaw clenched, hands tight on the armrests of his seat, eyes furious.

Glory didn't lose power or change course, other than to take evasive action, rolling slightly and speeding up before vectoring thrusters sent the vessel hard to port. The rest of the bolts flashed past Glory without contact. Their Nightmare's HUD fed them the incoming vectors of the energy blasts, and Ishek adjusted their course to avoid them.

"That's it," Caleb said. "Ish, we need to get ahead of them."

I'm trying.

"Try harder."

The throttle is open one hundred percent. There is no harder.

"How much push can we get if we fire the cannons behind us?"

Negligible.

"More than zero?"

Yes, but—

"Do it, or we can't say we tried everything."

Ishek swung both turrets aft and started firing. The ions from the guns wouldn't provide much extra thrust, but it might get them ahead of Glory a second or two quicker, and right now every second counted. The HUD lit up ahead of the next attack. Caleb watched helplessly while Glory shifted from port to starboard and then dropped its nose to lose altitude before jinking hard to starboard and again gaining altitude. Seeing the maneuvers, he could picture Ham on the stick, his brow likely coated with a sheen of sweat, his face tense and focused.

"Ish, does this thing have running lights, and can you control them?"

Yes. And yes.

"We need to flash them at Glory. Morse code."

And say what?

"Follow."

The Nightmare reached space beneath Glory, their velocity finally outpacing the barge. The warships were closing fast from behind, the next barrage of energy bolts already on their way toward Glory. Ham did his best, but Caleb knew he wouldn't be able to avoid all of them. The first beam ripped through the portside, cutting off a chunk of the barge toward its nose. It left a trail of debris and people pouring out of the wound before emergency hatches could close and seal off the damaged compartments. Caleb gritted his teeth at the sight of the disaster, angry they hadn't made it in time.

"Are you signaling them?" Caleb growled.

Of course.

The next grouping of shots appeared on their HUD. Ishek guided the Nightmare away, making sure to leave room for Glory if Ham followed. He was a little slow, perhaps unsure he could trust them, and a beam skimmed the top of Glory, shaving off some of their sensors and armor but failing to fully penetrate. Meanwhile, the warships were so close that Ham would never be able to react quickly enough if he didn't follow Ishek's lead.

Again the HUD lit up. And again Ishek evaded the projected paths of the beams. This time, Ham maneuvered without hesitation, following the Nightmare's course and just barely avoiding the assault. They did the same a second time, then a third, breaking away from the two warships and shooting toward empty space. Ishek continued to guide them, using the enemy's networked systems against them, helping Glory escape.

The warships' firepower thinned as they moved to give chase, but they were slow and poorly positioned to trail the two ships, though that didn't stop them from trying. Unable any longer to hit Glory with their cannons, they stopped firing, settling for a race they could only lose.

Ishek kept the Nightmare close to Glory's hull as they continued out into deep space, putting increasing distance between them and the pursuing warships.

"Send Ham a new message," Caleb said. "Ask him if there's any way we can link the two ships..." He paused mid-sentence as the stars around Glory suddenly began to bend. "What the hell?"

Ishek instinctively pulled away from the barge as the bend accelerated, within seconds creating an illusion as though there was a dilation of space surrounding the ship.

"Is that a warp bubble?" he questioned, staring at the dilation.

More like a hyperspace dilation field.

"What's the difference?" Caleb stared at the growing field. Glory was abandoning them. "Haas, that son of a bitch! His fist came down hard on his armrest. "He probably ripped Ham out of the pilot's seat the moment they were safe, and he's dragging him to the brig right now."

What should we do?

"Get inside the field," Caleb replied. "I'm not letting them strand us here that easily."

Are you serious?

"Unless you prefer to stay here with the two enemy warships."

They are *khoron.*

"Ish!"

Ishek guided the Nightmare back toward the barge. The ship shook violently when they hit the still expanding shape of spacetime. As Caleb was shaken in his restraints, he momentarily wondered if the ship would stay in one piece.

It did. Space smoothed out as soon as they were inside the field, the much smaller ship tucked within a few hundred meters of Glory's hull.

Looking out through the forward transparency, Caleb watched the front side of the field compress space ahead of it, the separated stars drawn together until it became a wall of nearly pure white. A glance at the rear camera feed showed Crux's warships breaking off the chase, obviously unable to catch them once they had reached faster-than-light speed.

The field completed its formation. The planet, the enemy warships, and the star hiding the wormhole had all blinked out of sight.

Well, I think we're safe.

Caleb's eyes shifted to Glory's rusted and scuffed hull, looming overhead. "We might be." Anger roiled in the pit of his stomach. "I can't say the same for General Haas."

Caleb felt Ishek's uncertainty.

I'm not sure I agree with this plan.

"Knuckle up, Ish," Caleb replied. "I hunnnggggeerrrr."

Thank you so much for reading Galaxy Unknown! For more information on Book Two, please visit mrforbes.com/forgottengalaxy2. Also, please continue to the next page for more information on Caleb and other books by M.R. Forbes. Thank you again!

THANK YOU!

Thank you for reading Galaxy Unknown!

Did you know there are more books that take place in the Forgotten Universe, including Caleb's origin story?

A lot more.

Want to read them, but don't know where to start?

If you're looking for Caleb's first series, go here: mrforbes.com/forgottencolony

Otherwise, head on over to mrforbes.com/forgottenuniverse to see a list of all the books.

Looking for something outside of the Forgotten Universe?

I love writing, and release a new book every 6 weeks or so, give or take. I've been doing it for over ten years now, so I've got a pretty decent-sized catalogue. If you love sci-fi, you're sure to find something you'll enjoy. Flip to the next section in this book or head on over to mrforbes.com/books to see everything on my web site, or hit up mrforbes.com/amazon to look at my stuff there, including most popular titles, reviews, etc.

By the way, you can also sign up for my mailing list at mrforbes.com/notify to be alerted to all of my new releases. No spam, just books. Guaranteed!

OTHER BOOKS BY M.R FORBES

**Want more M.R. Forbes? Of course you do!
View my complete catalog here**
mrforbes.com/books
Or on Amazon:
mrforbes.com/amazon

Forgotten (The Forgotten)
mrforbes.com/theforgotten
Complete series box set:
mrforbes.com/theforgottentrilogy

Some things are better off FORGOTTEN.

Sheriff Hayden Duke was born on the Pilgrim, and he expects to die on the Pilgrim, like his father, and his father before him.

That's the way things are on a generation starship centuries from home. He's never questioned it. Never thought about it. And why bother? Access points to the ship's controls are sealed, the systems that guide her automated and out of reach. It isn't perfect, but he has all he needs to be content.

Until a malfunction forces his wife to the edge of the habitable zone to inspect the damage.

Until she contacts him, breathless and terrified, to tell him she found a body, and it doesn't belong to anyone on board.

Until he arrives at the scene and discovers both his wife and the body are gone.

The only clue? A bloody handprint beneath a hatch that hasn't opened in hundreds of years.

Until now.

Deliverance (Forgotten Colony)
mrforbes.com/deliverance
Complete series box set:

The war is over. Earth is lost. Running is the only option.

It may already be too late.

Caleb is a former Marine Raider and commander of the Vultures, a search and rescue team that's spent the last two years pulling high-value targets out of alien-ravaged cities and shipping them off-world.

When his new orders call for him to join forty-thousand survivors aboard the last starship out, he thinks his days of fighting are over. The Deliverance represents a fresh start and a chance to leave the war behind for good.

Except the war won't be as easy to escape as he thought.

And the colony will need a man like Caleb more than he ever imagined...

Starship For Sale (Starship For Sale)
mrforbes.com/starshipforsale

When Ben Murdock receives a text message offering a fully operational starship for sale, he's certain it has to be a joke.

Already trapped in the worst day of his life and desperate for a way out, he decides to play along. Except there is no joke. The starship is real. And Ben's life is going to change in ways he never dreamed possible.

All he has to do is sign the contract.

Joined by his streetwise best friend and a bizarre tenant with an unseverable lease, he'll soon discover that the universe is more volatile, treacherous, and awesome than he ever imagined.

And the only thing harder than owning a starship is staying alive.

Man of War (Rebellion)
mrforbes.com/manofwar
Complete series box set:
mrforbes.com/rebellion-web

In the year 2280, an alien fleet attacked the Earth.

Their weapons were unstoppable, their defenses unbreakable.

Our technology was inferior, our militaries overwhelmed.

Only one starship escaped before civilization fell.

Earth was lost.

It was never forgotten.

Fifty-two years have passed.

A message from home has been received.

The time to fight for what is ours has come.

Welcome to the rebellion.

Hell's Rejects (Chaos of the Covenant)
mrforbes.com/hellsrejects

The most powerful starships ever constructed are gone. Thousands are dead. A fleet is in ruins. The attackers are unknown. The orders are clear: *Recover the ships. Bury the bastards who stole them.*

Lieutenant Abigail Cage never expected to find herself in Hell. As a Highly Specialized Operational Combatant, she was one of the most respected Marines in the military. Now she's doing hard labor on the most miserable planet in the universe.

Not for long.

The Earth Republic is looking for the most dangerous individuals it can control. The best of the worst, and Abbey happens to be one of them. The deal is simple: *Bring back the starships, earn your freedom. Try to run, you die.* It's a suicide mission, but she has nothing to lose.

The only problem? There's a new threat in the galaxy. One with a power unlike anything anyone has ever seen. One that's been waiting for this moment for a very, very, long time. And they want Abbey, too.

Be careful what you wish for.

They say Hell hath no fury like a woman scorned. They have no idea.

ABOUT THE AUTHOR

M.R. Forbes is the mind behind a growing number of Amazon best-selling science fiction series. He currently resides with his family and friends on the west cost of the United States, including a cat who thinks she's a dog and a dog who thinks she's a cat.

He maintains a true appreciation for his readers and is always happy to hear from them.

To learn more about me or just say hello:

Visit my website:
mrforbes.com

Send me an e-mail:
michael@mrforbes.com

Check out my Facebook page:
facebook.com/mrforbes.author

Join my Facebook fan group:
facebook.com/groups/mrforbes

Follow me on Instagram:
instagram.com/mrforbes_author

Find me on Goodreads:
goodreads.com/mrforbes

Follow me on Bookbub:
bookbub.com/authors/m-r-forbes

Printed in Great Britain
by Amazon